"SPEAK, IN HEAVEN'S NAME"

Mrs. Wizzle demanded. "Who has come?"

"Viscount Wolverton, I expect," Hillary said calmly, and Lady Gardener nodded.

"We are undone!" Mrs. Wizzle exclaimed, looking about as if she would hide in the closet. Even Lady Gardener was flustered.

"But what, I still ask," Hillary continued coolly, "is amiss? So, he is here. Why should that concern me? I have sent him a letter breaking off our arrangement. Did you not assure me that I need not marry him?"

"Certainly," Lady Gardener said, regaining her English aplomb. "You shall simply explain to him that your feelings have undergone a change. You no longer wish to be his wife. He is enough of an English gentleman not to wish to force you, I expect . . . but where are you going?"

"You're not going to . . ." Mrs. Wizzle begged.

"Yes, I am," Hillary said with a determined grin. "I am going to beard the lion. I'm going to see the viscount and face him down."

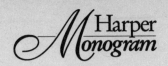

DUEL
OF
HEARTS

HELEN ARCHERY

HarperPaperbacks
A Division of HarperCollins Publishers

This is a work of fiction. The characters, incidents, and dialogues are products of the author's imagination and are not to be construed as real. Any resemblance to actual events or persons, living or dead, is entirely coincidental.

HarperPaperbacks   *A Division of* HarperCollins*Publishers*
10 East 53rd Street, New York, N.Y. 10022

Cover illustration by Bob Barron

First printing: October 1994

Printed in the United States of America

HarperPaperbacks, HarperMonogram, and colophon are trademarks of HarperCollins*Publishers*

❖ 10 9 8 7 6 5 4 3 2 1

To my sister, Astera,
    who urged me to follow my heart.

To my mother, Carol-Calliope, and
    my father, Thomas, who took
    part of my heart with them.

To my heart's love, N. N.

And to all those who believe Love is
    not only the answer but the reason.

❧ DUEL OF HEARTS ❧

1

Hillary looked up when Mr. Massey urged her to do so. "Come, Miss Astaire, his lordship would wish to see your charming countenance."

Next moment Hillary looked quickly down.

One glance at Viscount Wolverton, who was to be her future husband, was all she could bear. Not that he was not pleasing to the eye, but from his reputation as a rake of the first order, she expected immediate advances. The glance had reassured, for he was not even looking at her. Yet she was wary, having heard of his wild ways even as far away from society as she lived in seclusion with her father. Her mother's one-time bosom confidante, Lady Gardener, a well-known hostess of the haut monde had occasionally visited, but mostly kept a long-distance eye out for Hillary—ever since her mother's demise—by writing every fortnight. It was due to those many fascinating letters that Hillary became familiar with England's elite—from all its leading nobles up to the Prince Regent and his princess, who were in essence the king and queen of the realm. Most frequently mentioned was this same Lord Wolverton. Not because he was a friend of Lady Gardener's, quite the contrary, but his escapades apparently were the most entertaining to relate. His giving the slip to a most respected lady, his latest mad-dash curricle race, his bon mot du jour that everyone repeated—all were faithfully recorded, albeit with a coating of disapproval. Indeed, Lady Gardener often commented in passing that she pitied any lady who would ever be in that young lord's charge, for he had, she believed, a cold heart.

Hillary looked toward the vicinity of Lord Wolverton's heart and while the degree of its warmth from this distance could not be determined, her own heart and entire person took on a decided chill when his lordship next spoke.

"I say, Massey, no need to direct Miss Astaire's glance. By Jove, I expect we have both seen all we need or indeed wish to see of each other."

That expectation was hardly flattering. Hillary was shocked, almost to the point of gasping, both by the sentiment and the indifferent tones. But she remained silent, wishing something would occur to disturb Lord Wolverton's polished equilibrium. She had a pleasurable mental image of his tripping and landing at her feet. But the viscount remained upright. Instead he took out a pearl-edged snuffbox and devoted more attention to it than he had to the lady who was to be his wife and whom he was meeting for the first time. Scarcely had he paid her the courtesy of basic civility. A cold bow. A passing glance. A few pro forma remarks, and he was prepared to depart. Now the viscount was one-handedly flicking open the top of his snuffbox while with the other he delicately applied a pinch of his own specially mixed snuff to his nostril. A lace handkerchief wiped away any excess particles of snuff that dared to spot his high cravat. Mr. Massey was impressed with the performance, following each movement with a gape and a gawk. And when his lordship graciously offered some snuff to him, Mr. Massey was properly overcome by such condescension. One sniff of snuff and Mr. Massey violently sneezed. For the first time the viscount smiled and began speaking with enthusiasm. The topic that so engrossed him was not his wife-to-be, but rather the secret mixture of his snuff!

"Stuff his snuff," Hillary thought, almost saying it aloud. Expertise in snuff had never been a first in Hillary's qualifications for a mate. She had often expressed to her father that the essential attribute for her husband must be his being a *gentle*man, with the emphasis on the first part of that word. Wealth or title or even a fine appearance could not compensate for the absence of a kind heart. As for Lord Wolverton, he was anything but kind and gentle. Rather, cold and haughty. Possibly she might have countenanced his insufferable pride if he had not offered such a blow to hers by this blatant disregard. Yet from the beginning, due to Lady Gardener's evaluation, she had every reason to think ill of him. So much so that when her father had like a clap out of the blue announced her engagement to this known rake, she'd merely laughed. Perceiving Sir Rodney not grinning back, she caught her

breath and exclaimed, "Papa! Surely you are gammoning me. This is an ill-timed jest!"

He had quickly assured her he was in earnest.
Only when sharply reminding herself of her father's
lowness of spirits due to his worsening physical
condition could Hillary begin to believe Sir Rodney's
announcement. Previous to his illness—almost all
her life, in faith—he had treated her with the
utmost gentleness, taking her into his confidence
before acting even on such minor matters as buying
a hunter. But upon feeling the breath of death, he'd
become desperate about her future. Nothing she
could say would blunt the fear that some scamp of
a fortune hunter was certain to snatch her up the
moment he was no longer there as protector.
Which explained his turning to a lord known to possess so large a fortune he could not be faulted for
being on the catch. But what of Lord Wolverton's
other faults—of manner, of behavior . . . and most
of all of heart? All inexplicably overlooked in the
dash for security!

This goad was so strong Sir Rodney even risked
his last ounce of health to rise from his sickbed and
travel all the way to London, accompanied only by
his attorney, Mr. Massey. Returning, he'd scarce
had the energy to whisper the success of his efforts
ere taking to his bed in an immediate but relieved
collapse. What was Hillary to do? Naught but push
the pronouncement from her mind and concen-
trate, as she'd done throughout her life, on making
all comfortable for her father.

Her father's health had been the main reason she
had not had a London season upon reaching eigh-
teen, despite Lady Gardener's urging and offering
to take on the full responsibility. Hillary had been

tempted, and her father had been all compliance. But in the end, Sir Rodney had had another setback and she simply could not leave him. Having lost her mother, Hillary doubly cherished every moment she had with her father. But beyond dutifulness, realistically the young lady could not be spared. For Hillary not only ran the estate but kept Sir Rodney in tolerable spirits by reading and playing chess. They were not only father and daughter, but friends, she had thought. How then could she believe he would act in such a callous manner and present the marriage arrangement as a fait accompli?

Yet more astonishing than her father's behavior was that of Viscount Wolverton. Why had he accepted *her* as his mate? For as highly as one generally thought of oneself, Hillary had to admit she was not overly burdened by the qualifications a gentleman such as Lord Wolverton must require. Without even a season to familiarize herself with society's ways, she must be the last lady he would wish. How was it possible such an ill-matched pair had been brought together? And with such speed?

Those questions or indeed any mention of that arrangement, Hillary discovered, led to Sir Rodney's having alarming palpitations. And so she henceforth was silent on that subject until all other extraneous thoughts were wiped from her consciousness in the daze of her father's death. For five months Hillary had been left alone to mourn. Eventually she almost began to believe the pledging of herself to that rakish lord had been a fantasy of Sir Rodney's last illness. Bravely carrying on, Hillary continued to run not only Holly House but the entire estate of farms and cottages, meeting the needs of all her people. What little peace she had achieved was quite cut up by opening a letter from Mr. Massey. One quick glance and her father's last act became a certainty. Mr. Massey was arriving to validate all. Worse, he was to be accompanied by none other than Viscount Wolverton himself.

Hillary's only hope at first was that Lady Gardener had exaggerated Lord Wolverton's faults. For it was true that her ladyship and that lord were on opposite sides of one of the most volatile issues in all England, the split between the Prince Regent and his wife, Princess Caroline.

Viewed from a prejudiced eye, all Lord Wolverton's acts might have been exaggerated. A gentleman could be a flirt without being a libertine. He could be wild yet kind. Possibly misunderstood? Heavens, he must have some decent qualities for her father to have chosen him, she'd continually assured herself while waiting for that lord's arrival.

On actually spotting the viscount, Hillary was a mite hopeful. For as known pink of the ton she'd feared he would be dressed in fashionable excess. In short, she'd been dreading a fop. Yet the tall lord before her had sensible morning dress, with a dark coat, buff skintight pantaloons, a gray waistcoat, and a spotless white cravat. No fobs or seals dangled from his waist, nor was he all aglitter with stickpins. Further, the cravat, while well tied, was not a ballooning monstrosity, as Hillary had seen in *La Belle Assemblée,* a fashion periodical Lady Gardener periodically sent her way. His dark locks were brushed back. His features were classical, Hillary concluded when allowing her glance to rest fully on his face. It was at that point in her perusal that Hillary swiftly looked down in dismay. For she instantly discovered something that not only confirmed her worst fears, but caused her no longer to doubt Lady Gardener. His *expression*. It spoke his thoughts . . . his very nature. Disdain, even downright disappointment, registered there. One could tolerate that, for he was not obliged to find her charming. But his expression went beyond disapproval to lack of interest in her entire existence. A negation of her very self! As if she were of less import to him than a servant one glanced at perfunctorily and then dismissed. Almost immediately that indifference was further proven by his disparaging comment about having seen all he needed of her, and henceforth devoting his full attention rather to his snuffbox! Hillary's spirits sank as low as her gaze. It was with some effort she stopped herself from turning on her heel and leaving the lord's presence. At least she would not give that pompous, arrogant, puffed-up viscount the pleasure of another of her glances.

Mr. Massey had valiantly stepped in and filled the silence between the two pledged lovers. He droned on about the honor of being in his lordship's company and the pleasure both gentlemen must feel at seeing the lovely and much-admired Miss Astaire.

Hillary was somewhat appeased by this obvious fawning. It at least compensated for the viscount's acting as if she were not even in his presence. Admittedly his lordship's disregard nettled her. For everyone, from village boys to the squire's son, had reacted as if she were far from a dose. Her blue eyes were large and before her loss, filled with sparkle. Her long, pale blond hair usually had people comparing her to an angel. Yet that day Hillary's blond glory was completely hidden by a thick, dark hair net, descending from a wide black band covering most of her forehead. Her mourning gown was of black muslin and loosely styled, which undoubtedly made her look more like a lost waif than she was. Actually Hillary was neither angel nor waif. She was a direct lady who had been forced by circumstances to accept an arrangement against her nature. Now somewhat clearer of mind, what she most wished was simply to tell this lord and Mr. Massey both to go to the devil!

The viscount moved a bit, making his boredom obvious. Hillary risked another quick surreptitious glance. He caught it. As if that were a victory, he allowed his bored expression to be temporarily displaced by a swift grin of triumph. She glowered back. Infamous of him to assume he had won points by gaining a glance! Obviously this lord did not need much to reaffirm his own assumption that every women would naturally react favorably to him. He was known for the melting power of his smile, but it had not warmed Hillary a jot.

Determinedly she kept her eyes to the ground. A thought struck. Perhaps if she seemed an empty-headed widgeon he would reconsider his commitment. Yet a second thought canceled the first. As little as she knew about arrangements in polite society, Mr. Massey had made clear no gentleman would ever renege at this point. Nor could she, in all honor. They were both stuck! Heavens, if ever she wished to berate her father, this moment was it, but she instantly chastised herself for such sacrilege, despite the choking rise of anger.

The viscount was deigning to speak. Mr. Massey

was all attention. Hillary kept her head bowed. "I believe we are interfering with Miss Astaire's private moment of meditation. If she wishes to retire and rest, I see no reason for our detaining her any further. She seems to be in a bit of a doze, actually, at this very minute."

That jab earned him not only more than a glance, but a full glare from Hillary. What an insufferable boor, she thought. Every feeling was offended by his careless, grand-seigneur manners. Where were the delightful courtesies and flatteries at which she'd heard the gentry were so adept? Further, how dare he compound his insulting behavior by dismissing her from her own salon! Although actually, concluding this painful visit was just what she'd been wishing all along. But she'd be dashed if she let him in essence dismiss her. That would scarce bode well for her future with this overbearing lord, so overly conscious of his own consequence. Doubtless it was not her comfort he was taking into account, but his own. Along with all the other insults of manner and attitude, now he'd all but said her presence was tedious. Very well, she would delight him by protracting the tedium.

"I am not the slightest bit fatigued," she managed to say softly. She rose. Naturally they both rose with her. She rang for tea. Turning, Hillary had the pleasure of seeing a look of tolerant endurance on his lordship's noble mien. That called forth, for the first time during that taxing interview, a slight smile on Hillary's lips. His lordship missed it as he was giving Mr. Massey a look of displeasure. It had been their understanding that the meeting would be the usual formal ten minutes for a first call. He had an appointment with a rather delectable bit of muslin, and he was anxious to return to London, post haste. Grimly, he sat.

In a very few moments, Hillary was regretting having extended the occasion herself. Mr. Massey talked throughout, his mouth constantly occupied either with chatting or swallowing the two large pieces of cake he was devouring. The viscount nibbled on the corner of a piece of bread and butter and honored the teacup with one small sip. Either that was the elegant social way, or he feared the cooking in such a provincial establishment. Hillary drank two cups of tea to have something to do to cover her silence. When she concluded her last sip, she stood up.

Mr. Massey, still eating, coughed in his hurry to swallow. The lady's signaling that the tea was over had caught him by surprise. But not the viscount. Unhurriedly he put down his cup and rose in one smooth motion. She had not discomposed him in the slightest. His expression was at the best contemptuous, as if letting her know she was foolish beyond permission to attempt to catch him out— certainly not in a social situation. Continuing to act with social correctness, the viscount immediately took his leave, actually with a flicker of relief.

That had Hillary longing to cry out. The meeting could not end like this—going according to *his* plan. She must do something—say something to jar his perfect composure and her inevitable acceptance of her lot. The next moment she did.

"Perhaps, my lord, you would be willing to consider a . . ." The word would not come out. Indeed, there was no word for what she wanted. She wanted her father alive and her life undisturbed. She wanted to go back before the arrangement had been made. The moment she'd begun speaking, she knew there was no way any of that could be brought about.

Both gentlemen were waiting for her next word: Mr. Massey in some concern, the viscount with his usual polite indifference. Hillary had to ask for something, a stay of execution, at least. Catching her breath she concluded, ". . . a delay. I would wish a delay. I am not prepared for the onerous duties that would result from being your wife. I must have a few additional months to myself . . . half a year perhaps?" she attached hopefully.

Immediate to that, Mr. Massey was exclaiming and explaining that his lordship had already been quite patient. He'd waited for the marriage during her father's illness and several months after his demise, surely she could not but see his consideration. . . .

The viscount silenced him with a look. "I shall do my best always to be accommodating to you, Miss Astaire," his lordship said smoothly. "Would a year suffice?"

Hillary was awash in delight. A full year was more than she could have expected and actually from Mr. Massey's shocked expression, more than would be generally given. She said all that was polite on the occasion of his consideration. But all the while her quick sense understood the year offered was for his convenience not hers. Indeed, he shortly revealed that was the case. A year's travel abroad had been on his agenda previous to her request.

Hillary dared to look him fully in the eyes now. Their glances met, and both understood the other was delighted by the length of the reprieve. But what Hillary could not comprehend was if he did not wish this marriage to occur, why had he agreed to it? But regardless of the cause, she was dwelling on the pause and its principal benefit. She would not have to see his cold eyes, now mocking, for a full year! Although disciplining her lips not to smile, in keeping with decorum, still the delight within refused to be squelched and made its way to Hillary's sapphire eyes, which were now looking more jeweled from that inner glow. Her private conjectures infused her with more and more light as she imagined what could happen during that year's interval. Anything was possible. The viscount might meet a European enchantress and be amenable to a dissolution of the agreement. He might ask for it himself, in faith. Or even better, he could die in his travels. His ship might sink and he'd never be heard of again!

The sudden life in her face intrigued the suave viscount. What could she be thinking to bring on such unalloyed joy? As a connoisseur of ladies, the lord was forced to note that the pale, beshrouded maiden was prodigiously improved by a hint of sparkle. But as he began speaking every word quashed Hillary's hopes. In his renowned silken tones, Lord Wolverton expressed himself no end delighted to have so pleased Miss Astaire by his promised absence. He hoped she would continue to be pleased with the rest of his plans for her future.

A sense of dread overcame Hillary at that, but he continued.

Previous to seeing her, from reports of her inexperience, he'd assumed she might not quite be up to snuff in certain areas. That was made evident now. She clearly required some time to be educated in the niceties of society's ways, which were his own. Thus, since he would not be present to train her, he planned to send a relative of his, Mrs. Wizzle, who would serve the function of not only her companion here at Holly House, but subsequently to lend her consequence when she moved to his London town house.

Forgetting her manners, Hillary could not but object to his audacious assumption of control of her life, made to suit his convenience without consideration of hers. "There is scarce need for a stranger to live with me here in a place where I've been in sole control for the last five years! Such an invasion is not only unnecessary but an affront to my father who had permitted this arrangement."

The viscount was taken aback by the surprising willfulness of this delicate lady. His eyebrows arched in disapproval at her questioning not only his authority but the basic rules of decorum. The degree of shock showed in his voice as he responded, "Surely you cannot continue *unchaperoned?* I could not possibly countenance that for my future wife. Nor do I believe your father would have wished you to behave so . . . improperly."

He lifted his eyebrow as he watched her attempt to extricate herself from the trap he had set. To say her father would not agree to it would be to criticize her father, which she could not do. Yet in her heart, Hillary knew she would have been permitted to continue handling things as she'd been doing during his illness.

Allowing her to squirm awhile, at last the viscount smiled. He had won not only the point but control. "Exactly so," he concluded as if she had agreed. "We need, I expect, no longer deal with that issue. Further, Mrs. Wizzle and you shall be remaining here just long enough to become acquainted. Then both shall proceed to London where there can be no possible question of your not needing a lady companion. Yet Mrs. Wizzle has, as do most of the people whom I summon, a dual purpose. Before your presentation, you shall need some time to be made *presentable*."

Hillary felt all the condemnation in that soft pronouncement. Ah, clearly she was not only a disappointment but an embarrassment.

In an ambivalent way, Hillary was pleased and displeased by that verdict. She could not help but feel some satisfaction that he was not overly content with their bargain. For a moment she regretted not having presented herself in such a fashion as to give him a complete disgust. But mourning was mourning—she wore whatever the seamstress in the village had been quickly able to devise. Nor did she wish so to disgrace the name of Astaire by appearing as a positive frump. Admittedly, her own pride was somewhat pricked that he'd found her so wanting.

Meanwhile the viscount continued on the subject of her inadequacy. "You are in mourning now. A year shall be sufficient to remove dark gloves and return to colors. I require my future spouse to have at least a tolerable appearance. As must all good wives, your aim ought to be becoming a credit to your husband."

So indifferent to that goal did Hillary appear, his lordship was forced to give her another incentive. "You would not wish to disgrace your father? Or the name of Astaire? Both shall be judged along with you . . . as well as your mother's exalted family. From my uncle, Lord Sherwood, I've heard much of the prodigious beauty of your mother—a diamond of the first water, in effect. Further, that she and Lady Gardener were the belles of society, not since equaled."

Hillary looked down in defeat. Heavens, he had struck her with so many weapons she could not help but feel bowed.

Unremittingly, his lordship added the coup de grace. "Then too, Miss Astaire, I expect you would wish to honor your father's word? This marriage, I am most eager to make clear to you, was primarily at Sir Rodney's instigation. I merely acquiesced— after much persuasion. He assured me you were a most conformable, gentle lady. Always quick to learn. One would perforce expect you to live up to his expectations and promises, and be, on my return, as well dressed, coiffured, and socially adept as all would wish to see."

Hillary was checked but not mated. He did not scruple to use her grief, her love, her pride. Staggered but not fully surrendering, Hillary made one last effort. "I vastly prefer to remain here whilst you travel. Then on your return, perhaps we can have another delightful meeting such as this and can discuss if there should be the continuation of any future arrangements between us."

Mr. Massey was speaking again, stuttering in his effort to assure them of the impossibility of change at this late date. The viscount silenced him with another glance. With an all-suffering sigh he turned to Hillary and said sadly, "Although one's word is usually sufficient, your father and I, on your behalf, signed an agreement. You cannot have read . . . or rather, it was not sufficiently explained to you. At the moment of the signing, I became not only your husband-to-be, but the full guardian of your property, your future, and in effect, your person."

Hillary's face whitened. That had not been fully explained to her. Nor had she been allowed to read the document in question, although she had requested to do so. Any hope she had of other options was dashed. The viscount was colder, crueler than even Lady Gardener had portrayed. Her heart was leaping in terror at the words, yes, but even more so at the satisfaction he displayed in making that pronouncement. Indeed, he continued inexorably, in a tone of almost pure pleasure, "I wish you now to understand thoroughly that you are in my complete control—body and soul."

The large blue eyes of the young lady were near to filling with tears, although she bravely forced herself to regain her composure. But she no longer had any words left to counter him.

Her stunned appearance caused the viscount condescendingly to soften his statement. "You shall not find obeying me overly onerous. As long as you remember to be a good girl and do exactly as you are told, without *any* alteration."

At that, content that all had been resolved, he bowed and added, "In a year's time in my home at Regent's Park, I expect to see you prepared for your presentation to society, as befits my bride."

Neither expecting nor waiting for her response, the viscount signaled Mr. Massey they were leaving. The door closed after them with a decided click.

Viscount Wolverton was called Wolf by his cronies in the clubs where he beat them all hollow at faro and whist. That nickname was given him as a result of the callous way he pounced on all their winnings. Rich as he was, his lordship still insisted in coming up the winner. It was not the money that attracted but the triumph. That same shameless instinct to conquer served him in good stead with the ladies. It became traditional for him to stalk each season's diamond of the first water. Once winning her heart, Wolf found her of no further interest, allowing the others to take his leavings. That attitude resulted in his reaching nine and twenty without having yet fatally succumbed to any lure sent out by a lady. Actually he'd all but decided he could never be content with just one lady. The moment Wolf was slightly interested in one female, another attracted, and the first was swiftly forgotten.

His uncle, Lord Sherwood, constantly attempted to persuade him it was time to set up his nursery, at least for the succession of the title. Year after year Lord Wolverton dismissed that as gross interference, explaining that he would wed when he was prepared to sacrifice himself to his position. Eventually there came a moment when the viscount attempted to bring himself to the point of proposing. Only to find there was not a single lady of his acquaintance worthy of his name. Worse, when he'd honored a special lady with particular attentions, he found that lady so expected him to propose, he simply could not resist disappointing her by cutting the relationship at the last moment and rescuing himself.

Finally, Lord Sherwood decided to take matters into his own hands. "Not going to find the perfect lady, old boy. Ain't any. Each one has a flaw. One talks. One giggles. One doesn't speak. One never smiles. One eats cabbage. . . ."

The viscount had laughed at that, although he knew it had been a Beau Brummell remark, a gentleman from his uncle's time who'd set the standard not only in dress but in humorous asides. Mr. Brummell had claimed he'd cut his connection with a lady because he discovered her fatal flaw—she ate cabbage. His uncle was still laughing at his appropriated sally, but recovered enough to continue his point. "Devil take 'em all. But we must take 'em. Have to marry, by gad."

"You haven't."

"Ah, but I ain't Viscount Wolverton. Do it for the family name. Besides, I ain't got all the estates you got. Fill 'em with children, old boy."

"Nonsense. Not having had any siblings, I should very likely wish for one son myself. Having set the standard, I see no reason to alter that perfection. Dash it, Uncle Sherry, I would marry if I could find a lady I could stomach for more than a season. But I told you I always find something not quite . . . right."

"Think too much about it. Just pick one and do the thing. Find out later when it's too late."

"That's precisely what I dread. . . ."

A month after that discussion, Lord Sherwood, certain naught would be done by a lord who preferred to roam, made the decision for Wolf. His old friend Sir Rodney Astaire had written him a note. Hadn't seen the blighter for over ten years. But in his day, Sir Rodney had been quite a smart. Married a lady of impeccable birth and legendary beauty. He'd beaten out all her many suitors, one of whom had been Lord Sherwood himself. Still remembered that prime lady. She was Lady Millicent Malvern who with Lady Florence, now Lady Gardener, were the most sought-after belles of the ton. Lady Gardener remained and flourished in society—to the point of being in the thick of the current royal controversy. She had even risked her standing by setting out for Italy to join the exiled Princess Caroline. But Millicent, upon her marriage, had left London and all her flirts and had become a positive provincial. Dashed all Lord Sherwood's hopes of being her cicisbeo. Meanwhile he allowed the friendship he had with Sir Rodney to wither. Not jolly likely he'd want to hear how happy the man was who'd cut him out. It was all he could do to send and receive the occasional note on the holidays. But Lord Sherwood's resentment was shocked into suspension upon receiving notice of the death of the beautiful Millicent in childbirth. He'd sent a letter saying all that was expected. Although, odd's blood, he wished to write the unexpected, such as his own recriminations. "Wouldn't have died if she'd married me. Would have taken care of such a rare lady." Later he received a letter from Sir Rodney that spoke of sufficient suffering to assuage his lordship, proving the fellow was being punished for his poaching. That won enough forgiveness so that a distant and dilatory friendship continued through the subsequent years. Out of curiosity, and finding himself not far from Sir Rodney's out-of-the-way estate, Lord Sherwood had once even visited his old friend only to be taken aback by the introduction of a ten-year-old replica of his dear Millicent— her daughter, Hillary. She'd curtsied with all her mother's charm, but unlike her mother's gentle ways, had asked him directly if he'd dunked his mustache in the tea? At that he'd put down the cup in a hurry! More outrageous, she'd dared to approach and solicitously wipe his wet mustache with a napkin. That had paradoxically pleased, especially when she told him with a great deal of satisfaction that she thought his mustache was smashing and ought to be quite handy as a strainer. Laughing, he agreed it was. After that, Lord Sherwood remembered her with a bachelor's affection and sent her many a gift. Hillary always responded with charming little notes he cherished. There was a disturbance in the relationship during his lordship's many trips to the Continent and the connection had withered. Then came the surprising urgent letter from Sir Rodney. Turned out the fellow had been sickly and Hillary had been caring for him these last years. Sir Rodney did not waste his time hinting—came right out and asked for Sherry's advice on the welfare of his daughter's future. He would be leaving her shortly and realized that, although financially she would be secure since he'd arranged a tidy independence, she would be cast friendless on the world. Who knew who would impose on her good heart? Someone must look out for his treasure!

Moved by Sir Rodney's plight and honored by the confidence, when most people tended to regard him as somewhat of a fribble, Lord Sherwood had roused himself to assist that dear little blond angel he recollected. Could do no less than offer her a gentleman of first consequence—or his own nephew.

Possibly Sir Rodney knew Lord Wolverton was his nephew and that was the purpose behind the appeal. That was the conclusion Lord Wolverton immediately drew, upon receiving Lord Sherwood's letter proffering Miss Hillary Astaire. Not having the smallest inclination that way, Wolf had tossed the letter and recommendation away. A provincial maiden was far from what he'd envisaged as Viscountess Wolverton. He had been particular, searching for the best . . . not, by gad, the least.

But on a visit from Lord Sherwood, Wolf found it not as easy to dismiss the suit. Hard to silence Uncle Sherry on any occasion, but especially not on this topic, as his uncle chatted away. "Stop shilly-shallying, old boy. Screw your courage to the sticky point. Strike! Take Miss Astaire. Just the kind of gel for you. Retiring enough not to get in your way. Kind-hearted enough to devote her youth to caring for her father. Care for you, too."

With his languid air belying the devilry in his

eyes, the viscount had inquired, "Are you indicating or dare I say predicting a serious illness ahead for me?"

Ignoring that sally, Sherry continued with his case. "Best thing for you. Social ladies always want you to socialize, what? You want a lady who could be left without her kicking up a fuss! You go off. Do what you wish. With whom you wish. What?"

That somewhat disjointed and unprincipled argument surprisingly won over the viscount more than any twaddle on duty or conventions. Actually that slant was not unappealing to a gentleman of many interests. It smacked of having his cake and eating it, too, which was exactly the menu the viscount preferred. Somehow then, with Lord Sherwood on one side and Sir Rodney Astaire on the other, the thing had been done. Actually with Sir Rodney having put himself to the life-threatening effort of arriving on his doorstep, the viscount was all obligation. Further, Wolf realized the old gentleman would not have either the will or energy to debate any of his amendments. The result was that every term was written according to the young lord's specification. The viscount was particularly delighted that not even a courtesy visit was requested. Apparently the young lady had not been informed of the arrangements, which spoke well for her malleability. Sir Rodney's description of his daughter as "most obliging" sealed the bargain. "Image of her mother," Sir Rodney concluded. "If it would not be belittling my dear Millicent's memory, I would say, Hilly is even lovelier. Not the flirty lady most are who've had a season. Hilly is honest and direct as the day."

For a gentleman who made flirting an art, it was the height of paradox his preferring a lady with no

arts at all. But that lack appealed to him. Actually
Wolf often resented the thought that his wife would
have engaged in any such dalliances as he had with
most of the eligible young ladies of the ton. Miss
Astaire sounded intriguingly like a blank slate on
which he could write what he would.

Shortly after the papers were signed, it seemed to
Wolf that he had dreamed the whole arrangement.
With no one to remind him, the entire obligation
promptly was forgotten in his absorption in a
delightful affair with a delicious opera singer. Once
more Lord Sherwood it was who brought the engagement to mind when he arrived to console him on the
death of his prospective father-in-law, Sir Rodney.
Lord Wolverton just stopped himself from saying,
"Sir who?" but remembered in time. The viscount
was even adroit enough to say all that was necessary
on the occasion. Lord Sherwood described the
funeral—a small, private affair, local people. He'd
expected to see Wolf there and been disappointed.

"Didn't know about it," the viscount said, defending himself.

"Sent you a note."

Wolf looked at the pile of letters on the salver in
his salon. There was another pile on the mantelpiece. "I've not been available for my correspondence," was all he said. But Lord Sherwood understood.

"Prime piece?" he asked, and Wolf had grinned.

Reminded of his duty, the viscount had sent a
condolence note in a fortnight's time. It was above
a month when, again at the urging of Uncle Sherry,
the viscount had put himself to the trouble of making a personal condolence call. Coming away he'd
been pleased at the outcome. The first view of Miss

Astaire had verified his expectations. With the reputation of her mother, he'd feared another diamond. With her reclusivity, he'd feared a frump. But she was neither. She was truly just what he wished—a lady of much possibilities, but not yet fully developed. He could make an impression on her blankness. She would not only be his wife but his creation. Recollecting Hillary's face, as much as she'd allowed him to see while keeping it generally bowed, he concluded she was most prepossessing, her shyness just what he required in a wife. Her lack of curiosity in his comings and goings was totally unlike any other lady he'd ever met. Indeed, when he mentioned his travel abroad, she'd showed enough animation to assure him she was not a complete ninny, which he could not have accepted. A widgeon would be a poor reflection on his own perceptiveness. But a lady just short of that would not be unusual in society. Most of them fit quite naturally into that goosey category.

Grinning, Wolf reflected on Miss Astaire's only coming out of her stupor at the promise of *his* absence. That had taken him aback. Most ladies could not have enough of his company. They usually hung on his sleeve. Lived in his pocket. He had to brush them off with the firmest of shakings. The thought that his wife would prefer being solitary had pleased when that aspect was first presented to him, but on actually seeing her reluctance, he'd been knocked acock. Probably one could not count on the lady continuing thus. Generally he'd found ladies became impossibly possessive when one simply was known as their beau. As a husband he expected he'd be hard put to win any separation or independence.

Back in London and preparing for his grand tour, Lord Wolverton dismissed his future wife from his thoughts. He made a note to purchase some little something from each country he'd be traveling through. Ladies were always won over by such little attentions.

Mostly Wolf was occupied thinking of the various ladies he would honor with his attentions in the months ahead. Much anticipated, the charms of the Frenchwomen, the sculptured beauty of the Grecian ladies, the passion of the Italian maidens. That last recalled to him his two-fold objective in Italy, the second being in the nature of a secret mission. It was on behalf of the Prince Regent himself. His royal wife, the Princess Caroline, was suspected of indecent carryings-on with an Italian soldier of fortune, Bartolomeo Pergami. For years His Highness had been hoping for proof of her misdeeds. Wishing a royal heir, Parliament had all but forced him into marriage with a German princess. Yet inexplicably, from the first moment of meeting, both had instantly taken the other in disgust. Made it dashed difficult to produce a child. Yet a girl, Princess Charlotte, had ensued and happily ended all future personal contact. Still, the feud between the estranged couple continued and worsened each year until the prince had ordered his wife out of the country. Next in the regent's campaign to rid himself of this marital burden was appointing a Milan commission to collect all evidence of Princess Caroline's indecency. So far all reports were ambiguous, certainly not sufficient to warrant a divorce. His Highness wished for more definitive proof. That was when he turned to a lord known to be able to win anything from a lady—the young Viscount Wolverton.

Nothing loath, Wolf was set to spend a few days with the Princess Caroline. He remembered that she, like all women, had been taken by him. A few compliments would in all probability be the key to uncovering her deepest secrets.

Lord Sherwood escorted his nephew to board ship. It was he again who reminded him of his fiancée by promising to look out for Miss Astaire on her London arrival.

"Ah, yes, do so," Wolf said indifferently, and then added, "I hope to see her somewhat improved." The wind was right for departure and he had no time to dally. About to board, Wolf turned and added as a second thought, "Actually, Uncle Sherry, I do not wish her to be too much altered. She is nigh unto perfect for my purpose just as she is."

3

Within a few moments of Mrs. Wizzle's arrival at Hillary's estate of Holly House, the two discovered they were going to be fast friends.

It was impossible not to like Mrs. Wizzle. She was an ebullient, flighty woman who saw only the good in other people. The viscount, she assured his fiancée, was the kindest of gentlemen. What better proof of his good heart than the dear boy's trusting her with his own fiancée?

Hillary could do naught but stare, keeping her own opinion of his lordship's goodness.

Mrs. Wizzle was a tiny lady with large gushes of warm feelings. Her eruptions included remarks on Hillary's management of Holly House, which was exemplary, on the young lady's beauty, which was angelic, on the flower garden, which was the epitome of the picturesque, and finally on the young lady's reception of her into her private world, which was the height of graciousness. In the torrents of which, Hillary's defenses were swept away, one by one.

To Hillary, the most effective gesture was Mrs. Wizzle's changing to mourning clothes herself. "In respect for your great loss," she said simply, and Hillary could not but respond to that degree of empathy, enough to forgive if not forget who had sent the lady thither.

In a sennight Hillary was as familiar with that lady's history as her own. Relayed with such delight, it sounded more of an accomplished life than the bare facts warranted. She was a nobleman's daughter, Miss Annie Walton, who'd turned down many titled offers to accept a poor clergyman with a living in the coldest region of Yorkshire. To others the place might seem damp and dark, but their love had kept them warm and alight, Mrs. Annie Wizzle said without reservation. That was the happiest period of her life. The saddest came when the Reverend Wizzle died. His ending suited the philanthropic man he was, coming as a result of visiting his parishioners stricken by an epidemic. Mrs. Wizzle was left with just his loving memory to sustain her. Eventually more than that was needed. Practicalities would intrude when she was forced out of the rectory to the shabbiest lodgings. At last, when at the point of no longer having anything substantial to swallow but her pride, Mrs. Wizzle gulped it down and wrote to relations and friends. Having abandoned her social set, they felt free to abandon her in kind. She had given up hope when a lone letter arrived from the least likely of her appeals. It was from the most distant of her distant relatives, in fact the lord at the top of their family tree, Lord Wolverton. Expecting to be fobbed off, she opened it warily and was startled into a gasp of elation. The viscount's reply was brief. "My secretary, Mr. Curtis, shall make suitable arrangements."

Translated that meant a pension and the lady's moving to Bath, a restful watering place no longer in vogue, where genteel people retired. Her daily practice before her constitutional was to pray God to reward the viscount for his goodness. Thus upon receiving a note from his lordship requesting her aid, it was not surprising that the lady was more than tolerably anxious to repay some of her obligation. However, Mrs. Wizzle explained to Hillary, it resulted that her indebtedness was rather increased. For his lordship was granting her the pleasure of living with the loveliest, kindest lady she'd ever met, and further offering the excitement of her re-entering society with that exquisite lady.

Ah, she had such memories of the beau monde! At which point Mrs. Wizzle's tongue went as fast as a fiddlestick describing her own London season. At the description of her gowns, there was a sudden pause, not for breath, but reflection. Frowning, the lady made a small admission just realized. Having been reclusive since her marriage, her knowledge of both society and fashion might be a mite out of date.

That convulsed Hillary with giggles. "Perfect," she said with a groan. "It is clearly a case of the blind leading the blind."

Not understanding the implication, Mrs. Wizzle was quick to express her concern about Hillary's eyesight. Soothingly the young lady assured her that her sight was faultless except for accepting a

husband sight unseen. That must be explained. At
last Hillary concluded it was time for a full, honest
revelation of her present position—how she'd been
forced into this arranged marriage by an anxious
father and indifferent suitor. To her surprise, Mrs.
Wizzle, rather than seeing her situation as tragic,
found the entire circumstance the height of
romance. Obviously the viscount had had a secret
tendre for the beautiful Hillary. It must have been he
who had appealed to her father for the arrangement.

"That would give him extraordinary perception
indeed," Hillary said with a laugh, "for he had not
then met me. Nor was he particularly overcome
when he had that pleasure."

Mrs. Wizzle was disappointed. Nevertheless she
was certain that if the viscount was not immediately struck by her, he would be so, after they'd finished their much discussed and anticipated shopping expedition.

On second thought Mrs. Wizzle concluded that
she was the perfect person to be Hillary's shopping
guide. For despite her years in retirement, she had
kept au courant on the latest fashions, being a great
devotee of *La Belle Assemblée*. Further, another
example of the viscount's goodness—after one
glance at her own gown, he'd immediately suggested she, too, wardrobe herself at his expense.
They were both, in essence, to be refurbished.

"We shall shop! We shall go on outings. Vauxhall
Gardens has grand shows. I recollect one particular
extravaganza. A full battle scene! Rifles were shoot-
ing! I was clapping my hands with each report. Lord
Neville was at my side, booming along with me.
After the show, he continued the charge—with me

as the object. Such laughter. I was much sought
after, in truth. And without half the beauty you possess, dear Hilly. Yet I rejected all proposals, exalted
or not, without a qualm when I found my heart's
love." She sank into a reverie that Hillary was civil
enough not to interrupt, until the lady shook herself
and inquired, "Where was I?"

"Vauxhall," Hillary obligingly inserted, and the
lady was off again, reliving the walks through that
park, the torches, the lamps in the trees, the huge
fountains. "We shall have a jolly time," she vowed.
Eventually, unable to resist this chattering flow, the
dam in Hillary collapsed and she was swimming
along with the lady, actually anticipating their move
to London. Considering the viscount's not being
there, they might have a capital time, after all.

Mrs. Wizzle's chatter was not the only amusement. As had her father, Hillary found Mrs. Wizzle
adored being read to. But unlike Sir Rodney her
choice was restricted to gothic novels of which she
had the foresight to bring several volumes, and ini-
tiated her charge into the thrill of the gothics' chill-
ing prose. Mrs. Wizzle saw the viscount as the hero
and Hillary saw him as the villain. But both enjoyed
shivering and quaking at the heroine's plight and
sighing in joy at her rescue.

Within a week of her coming, Mrs. Wizzle had
persuaded Hillary to order the removal of the black
bunting from the chandeliers and the hatchment
over the door. In two months she encouraged the
young lady to leave off her black and go into the
half mourning of lavender and grays. One month
more, and Mrs. Wizzle, checking the viscount's
written instructions, concluded it was time to pre-
pare themselves for London.

"We have been so comfortable here," Mrs. Wizzle began with a sigh, and Hillary agreed. "We shall be equally so in London!" Mrs. Wizzle added resolutely, and while Hillary would not go so far as to agree to that, she was willing to face her transplanting there with some slight hope of achieving a tolerable bloom.

But neither the shopping trip, nor the joy of London was to be. For Hillary received a letter from Lady Gardener that was two full pages crossed and recrossed with indignant protestations. The news had finally reached her of dear Hillary's engagement to the notorious Viscount Wolverton! She was shocked to the core! Did Hillary know that he was called Wolf by his friends, for good cause!

Every line ended with an exclamation point.

How could her father have allowed such a lovely young lady to fall into the clutches of that man? She must now be direct and say openly what she had merely hinted before—Viscount Wolverton was the worst rake in all society! He was known for the cruelest treatment of ladies! She shuddered to think what would happen if he had a gentle lady such as Hillary in his clutches for life!

But the viscount was not the only one castigated in that burning epistle. Her ladyship faulted herself as well. She had been remiss not to concern herself with Hillary's future. She should have done more than merely offer a season. She should have demanded Sir Rodney agree. Ought, in faith, have come to Holly House and taken Hillary to London herself! However, she'd been enveloped in Princess Caroline's problems and then had sailed to meet Her Highness. Surely Hillary had heard the dastardly schemes afoot against that gracious princess? All the doings of that Machiavellian Prince Regent?

Exile . . . denial of her rights and privileges . . . spies all about! What was worse, the regent's chief aide in that base campaign was none other than Viscount Wolverton!! (Double exclamations after that announcement.)

Before the end of the letter Lady Gardener had found a solution. Hillary must break off her relationship with that monstrous scoundrel, post haste! Apprised of the situation, Princess Caroline was more than willing to send her own courier to direct Hillary to Italy, where under the royal protection and under Lady Gardener's own caring concern, they could resolve the dilemma to everyone's, particularly Hillary's, satisfaction and safety!

Hillary was all agape. Upon finishing the letter, she read it again to understand. Several emotions overcame her at once. First and foremost was relief that she would not have to marry the viscount. If a royal princess agreed to stand buff for her, it must be permissible to break the agreement. Next moment she was assailed by concern that she might still be under obligation to keep her father's word. But relief returned and triumphed as she assured herself that her father would not wish her to keep an agreement if he knew the real nature of the viscount as explicitly as revealed by Lady Gardener. Swinging back and forth, she had finally been able to resolve her problem as she wished. Her engagement to the nefarious viscount was at an end. She would write him a letter and inform him of that. Except she was not certain where the lord was in his travels. Therefore she concluded she would send a letter to that effect to his secretary here in London and count on that estimable gentleman to track him down.

That problem resolved, Hillary sensed a six-foot, scowling weight lifted off her back and future. Now she merely had the pleasure of a trip ahead, made even more delightful by being escorted by a royal courier. All agog in anticipation of the adventure of sailing all the way to Italy, Hillary could scarce pretend all was as usual. Her spirits were jumping so strongly, she could barely keep herself still. For she, who had never traveled beyond the next village, would now become a traveler of the first water—across several seas, in fact! Further, how grand to have the trip culminated by being in the company of the royal Princess Caroline. She had visions of becoming a lady-in-waiting, as was dear Lady Gardener. There might even be a kind, gentle gentleman in that entourage. Lady Gardener would undoubtedly introduce her to several eligible gentlemen. She would have her season after all, but more adventurously in Italy and under royal auspices.

Traitorous to conceal her good fortune from Mrs. Wizzle, yet Hillary did so. For despite being such a dear woman, Mrs. Wizzle was, after all, of the other camp. But how could Hillary permit that lady to continue making preparations for London? One could devise a hundred false explanations for canceling the London trip, but that would be flagrant flummery, which was against Hillary's nature. Nor did Mrs. Wizzle deserve aught but the truth. They'd become too close for gammoning. At last Hillary resolved the problem by simply handing the letter directly to that woman and letting her read it through.

It took a day and a half for that good lady to accept the slightest animadversion against the viscount. What finally influenced was the reminder that his lordship was of the Prince Regent's camp. For years, Mrs. Wizzle had been opposed to the regent. It began when he'd put his own daughter under palace arrest for refusing to marry the doltish Prince of Orange. Nor was Mrs. Wizzle able to countenance the flaunting of the regent's many mistresses. During her own season she could not but recall many instances of his being prodigiously cruel to his royal wife. If the viscount was, as Lady Gardener implied, helping the regent to continue that vileness, she must rethink her evaluation of him.

In a short time, Mrs. Wizzle's desire to confide overrode her instinct to protect her benefactor. Yet her indictments continued mostly of the Prince Regent himself.

"On his very wedding day, His Highness occupied himself in making open advances to his then mistress, Lady Jersey, having appointed her Lady of the Bedchamber to his new wife! What better position for a mistress to assure the lack of tranquility between the couple on their wedding night? The on-dit was that the prince was so far into in his cups, he spent the night in a stupor. How poor dear Princess Charlotte was conceived one hesitates to imagine." Catching herself at that indelicacy of utterance, Mrs. Wizzle blushed and quickly altered the topic to a description of Lady Jersey. "She was not His Highness's usual fare. Most of his women, I will not call them ladies, though they all had that title, were actually similar in form and manner and age to his first common-law wife, Mrs. Fitzherbert. All fair. All fat. All foolish. All forceful."

"Rather stuck on *F*'s, wasn't he?" Hillary inserted with a giggle.

Mrs. Wizzle rarely heard interruptions and never

responded to them when in full flight. Now she was describing his current mistress, Lady Hertford. "Also in that mode. I'm the correct age for His Highness, it seems, but not plump enough a pigeon to please the royal palate." She laughed at that.

Hillary was astounded at the picture drawn. "Are you telling me the prince has all these mistresses *openly?* Yet he dares to consider divorce on the mere whisper of a relationship of his long-estranged and exiled wife?"

"True, most unfair. But that is the way of it in the *bon* ton. The Prince Regent can do no wrong. Happy we were to have him, I recollect. Wore his button, I did—a floweret of his colors to show our support against the mad king. Philandering was acceptable, preferable to lunacy. We had such hopes for their child, our dear Princess Charlotte. After she died, all our hearts were broken. Even the Prince Regent, they say, was somewhat saddened, despite his years of disagreements with that lovely child."

On and on Mrs. Wizzle went until Hillary was as conversant with palace gossip as the most dedicated royal courtier. The result for Mrs. Wizzle was that she'd soon talked herself firmly into the exiled wife's camp. Indeed, if Hillary was to visit Princess Caroline and become part of that royal entourage, she would join her! Certainly she could not allow the young lady to travel all the way to Italy unescorted.

"You must not make that decision so quickly, dear Wizzie," Hillary warned. "Without question the viscount will be more than tolerably displeased. He might feel you have ill paid him for his years of pensions. Although I should be most pleased by your support. Nor, I assure you, shall you ever find yourself financially at a loss."

Mrs. Wizzle dismissed all monetary considerations. "I never worried about money, you know. Why else would I reject the richest lords and choose love and poverty? To be frank I chose love, and poverty came with it unasked. But regardless of where I wound up, I never regretted that choice. Love is all we are granted on earth that bears any connection to our dear God, as my husband was wont to say. I say it as well. Indeed, I say it to you; go for love, Hillary, child, and you shall not fail. As for my own future, I shall merely accompany you. Whither thou goest, I shall go. Thy country shall be my country . . . for you are the daughter I was never blessed to have."

That naturally called for a hug and several tears. The two women then wiped their eyes and instead of the triumphant London season, they set about with maps, planning their exciting travel to the continent.

So diligent were they in their preparations, a sennight saw them up to scratch. Whereupon they merely had to await the royal courier who would bring their tickets and other particulars. But when a gentleman paid a call, he was a prodigious disappointment. For rather than representing the princess, he represented the viscount. He was that lord's secretary.

In some consternation Hillary and Mrs. Wizzle huddled, considering whether to have the butler deny their being present. But Hillary would not have the poor man travel all that distance and be turned away. Further, what was the point of hiding? Whatever he had to tell them would eventually have to be faced. Actually, it might be best to know what the viscount had in mind. Of course, on second thought it was too early for the viscount's reply to the letter she had sent the secretary. Nor did she imagine the secretary, Mr. Curtis, would have dared to open her letter to his lordship. Unless the viscount had left orders for all mail to be opened on arrival.

All this wondering was pointless, Hillary decided. "Tell Mr. Curtis I shall be down directly."

Wizzie looked at her in alarm, but Hillary shrugged. "Best to face things immediately. Besides, as long as I no longer have to meet the viscount himself, his underling should not be too frightening."

Hillary was correct. Mr. Curtis was a small man and very diffident. He had in fact merely come to explain that he was uncertain what to do with the letter she had written to the viscount. Did she want him to mail it to the viscount or hold it for his return.

"When is he returning?" Hillary asked in alarm, hoping she'd at least be at sea before that occurred.

"I am not privileged to be privy to his lordship's exact itinerary. I know merely that he is presently traveling toward Italy. Did you wish the letter sent there . . . Oh, Miss Astaire, what's amiss?"

Hillary had suddenly clutched her hands to her chest as her heart beat at a rapid beat. "You say the viscount is heading to *Italy?* Do you have any idea of his length of stay? Or his purpose there?"

Mr. Curtis had no knowledge of those specifics. To dismiss the gentleman quickly, Hillary expressed her wishes that he mail the letter to Italy. "It should be a delightful welcome for the gentleman, I expect," she concluded.

No longer having to make a decision, Mr. Curtis contentedly took his leave and the ladies reviewed their situation. Previously both had felt such relief

that the viscount would be dealt with through sur-
rogates, or even better, through the post.

"We shall have to face him in Italy, then," Hillary
said with some resolution.

"He shall ruin our happy time there, I predict,"
Mrs. Wizzle said with a groan.

"Yes," Hillary said. "But I shall not let him completely ruin my delight in traveling. Although . . . I
admit he's taken off the edge."

She walked toward the table with the map of Italy
spread wide. Her thoughts were no longer on lovely
landscapes, but on the Italian castles that often were
the sites for the incarceration of the heroines in the
gothic novels. Usually the villains were named Count
Udolpho or Ambrosio or some such. She wondered if
the viscount had a castle there? Next moment, in
dread, she jumped to imagining that haughty lord,
annoyed by her letter of rejection, ordering her
imprisonment. But almost directly after, Hillary
shook her head at that scenario, even grinned. He
was English, after all. Englishmen did not allow their
emotions to rule them. Besides, he had no feelings
for her. His indifference had been clearly evident
enough to assure her he'd accept her decision with
typical English reserve.

But Wizzie either had picked up her previous
thoughts or jumped to the same conclusion, for in a
hushed voice she asked whether Hillary thought
the viscount might have a castle in Italy?

Hillary could not but laugh at the coincidence of
their dreads. Yet as this lady, so close to the viscount,
was giving that possibility credence, she sobered.
Even more so on recollecting Wolverton's cold eyes
and his last words, "You are in my complete control—
body and soul."

Well, she had escaped him. She was free of his control. Besides, Hillary encouraged herself, her body at least would be under royal protection, so he could not control her, even in Italy. Almost in rebuttal, another phrase of his returned to alarm her, "I am the full guardian of your property, your future, and your person."

"Oh, poo!" she answered him, and his lordship's dark gray eyes, fixing her into stultification, disappeared in her giggle.

4

On a warmish July day the chestnut forest was prodigiously cooling to two exceptionally beautiful ladies. Hillary and Victorine were in a cabriolet being driven to their favorite spot by their Italian protectors—Gina and Antonio. The latter two were newlyweds and nothing loath to ignore their duty as guardians to their charming charges. More often they would wave away the young ladies and go off on their own to enjoy the afternoons. So much for one's modesty being protected, Hillary had giggled.

Being at Lake Como above several fortnights, Hillary had learned many things about the Italian people as well as Italy itself. All summed up in one word. Enjoy!

So much had occurred since arriving, she could not keep up in her diary. The trip by ship filled an entire copybook for her observations on the vistas.

Then the journey overland to Princess Caroline's summer resort at Lake Como had kept her too rapt to write. The first view of the princess's marble palace awed Hillary and scandalized Mrs. Wizzle. For the marble was not an expected white or sedate gray but a decided pink. And even more so at sunset.

Lady Gardener had been waiting at the top of the marble staircase, having ordered the staff to notify her the moment Hillary's carriage was in view. She was gently embraced by that lady and told she looked exactly like her beautiful mother. Mrs. Wizzle was welcomed despite her credentials of coming from Lord Wolverton, for Hillary had written of that lady's having changed sides. That last, conveyed to Her Highness, had been enough to persuade her that Mrs. Wizzle was a sign of her victory to come against the Prince Regent and his massive forces. No fewer embraces were offered to the companion than to Hillary herself.

The first view of Princess Caroline had caused Mrs. Wizzle to be somewhat astounded. Actually that royal lady had a way of causing English people to take a second look. There was always something not quite right in her appearance. For instance she was dressed in a young girl's frock of white ruffles that was clearly wrong for a woman in her fifties. *Au contraire,* the décolletage was shockingly low, which immediately took the dress out of the ingenue category. So it was a confusion of styles. Add to it a white turban of satin with feathers, and then long diamond drop earrings, which were not exactly what one wore midafternoon, and the paradox was complete. Yet somehow, as one began to know the laughing, open, generous lady, her appearance of a multitude of delights seemed exactly suited to her.

On the subject of style, Her Highness was quite confident. Enough so that on casting her undiscriminating eye on Hillary, she immediately made an alteration.

"I, too, have losset my deepest love—my daughter. But I know in my heart she is waiting for me in a better place than this. You are to live your life full. Your father, he would cry to see you still in mourning."

Hillary assured the lady her gray traveling dress announced that she was in half mourning, but Her Highness would not quibble. Rather she promptly pulled off the offending black cap, only to gasp at the sight of the long, blond, glowing locks that fell to the young lady's waist.

"But you wear the sun on your head! You must be dressed in sunlight," she decreed with delight. Stroking the long, blond hair, the princess made an official pronouncement. "You shall be my child. I have losset my darling Charlotte. My heart is broken. You must mend it."

What could one say to that but yes? One could not refuse to mend another's broken heart. And so Hillary was all but adopted by the princess.

Having lived so many years without a mother, Hillary found herself in the next week with three mothers all vying with each other to take care of her. Lady Gardener spoke with the authority of knowing Hillary's real mother and used that to coax a total redoing of the young lady's appearance. She recommended the approved muslin gowns with the accompanying de rigueur coiffure of a topknot and ringlets. Mrs. Wizzle, who felt she had become Hillary's mother first, wished to object, but the suggestion was so unexceptional, she grudgingly had to admit Lady Gardener obviously knew the proper outfitting of an English lady. Using her own money, Lady Gardener called in several Italian stylists and ordered them to transform Hillary without delay. Nor did she forget Mrs. Wizzle, ordering gowns for that lady as well, which naturally improved Mrs. Wizzle's opinion of that dignified lady on the spot.

They both reckoned without Princess Caroline. All who did so soon learned their mistake. For the princess had a way of sweeping away all objections and all others' opinions. She herself would design the clothes for the beautiful Hillary and then give a party to introduce her not only to the English society in Italy but to the Italian nobility itself.

Therefore Hillary, after being remade by one mother, was to be unmade by the other and remade again. The result was that she had so many diverse gowns she could pick according to not only which mode but which mood. Actually for a while Hillary submitted to being a different person according to whom she was accompanying that day. The princess saw her as the glorious return of her own Princess Charlotte and ordered gowns that almost duplicated the young princess's wardrobe. Unfortunately the late Princess Charlotte had had her mother's preference for ornate trim and jewels. Her hair had been darker than Hillary's pale yellow locks, so to complete the impersonation, the Princess Caroline had ordered several turbans for Hillary to disguise the difference.

"But, madam, I thought you felt my hair was like the sun and should be shown," Hillary had to object, for she really was adverse in the summer heat of Italy to wearing the heavy satin turbans.

The princess was ambivalent. At last the kind-

ness in the princess's heart won over her mourning, and she agreed the young lady must allow her
sunlight hair freely to shine. Thereupon she canceled the orders for the dozens of turbans and
ordered golden gowns instead.

But having lost with her turbans, Her Highness
felt she was owed a concession on the question of
Hillary's hair. Rather than Lady Gardener's English
topknot, she insisted on having the hair dressed
royally high, depicting the sun's corona. The Italian
hairdresser, attempting to please both exalted
ladies, was pulling and twisting Hillary's hair every
which way hurrying to follow each conflicting suggestion. Hillary was beginning to feel that her hair
was a skein of wool with three cats making it all
atangle. Even dear Wizzie, not to be outdone by the
other ladies, was suggesting changes right and left.
At last Hillary reached her limit and called a halt.

Standing up, she exclaimed, "Thank you. I've
gathered the essence of your suggestions. I shall
combine all and reach a satisfactory conclusion.
However, I must request that no more styling be
done today, for all this pulling and combing has
given me the headache, I own."

Immediately the three women were all concern—
insisting the darling child rest and criticizing each
other for not considering the young lady's feelings.

Promptly Hillary devised her own hairdo combin-
ing the pertinent parts of each of her "mother's"
suggestions. She wore her hair up in a circle of curls
at the crown of her head, but she allowed several
ringlets to fall at the neck and over her ears and
forehead.

"Ah, the sun and its rays shooting out of it," the
princess had approved.

"A somewhat disordered topknot, but in the vicinity thereof," Lady Gardener accepted.

"You look lovely," Mrs. Wizzle said with her warmest smile.

The hairdo hurdle overcome, and with enough dresses from both camps for Hillary daily to choose her own style from each collection, the transformation was deemed complete. Throughout her being perfected, Hillary had spent much private time with the princess and was soon privy to that lady's past, especially the schism between herself and the prince.

She'd begun with hope, she informed Hillary, opening her heart to England, coming to marry its prince.

"The white cliffs wave. The people wave. I am happy. Then I meet the prince. I curtsy to the ground. He come to me . . . and walk past for a drink. He swill down a brandy and walk out. I am still on the floor curtsying. So much for our first meeting. I am disappoint. Not only because he is fat but boorish! Later, more boorishness. He puts his mistress, Lady Jersey, as my personal lady-in-waiting. She lords over me her relations with my husband." The princess bowed her head and whispered, "I do not speak of more personal humiliations. Everything that malice could invent it was done to me by that man and his women. The day after I give birth to my daughter his emissary announces I am never to be in His Highness's presence again. I weep with relief. More tears when he gives my child to strangers, and I am only allowed visits. But Charlotte and I become closer than most mothers and daughters due, I say, to our being tormented by the same man, as well as his many mistresses. How many mistresses through the years. When I left, it was Lady Hertford. They say she still holds on. Yes?"

Hillary could only look confused, not being up to date on such details.

"Most likely. Or she shares with another," the princess answered herself. "*Mein Gott,* with his record, how dare he accuse me of falseness with a mere friend like Bartolomeo—who has given me the greatest gift of his daughter, Victorine? They shall be here soon, and you shall meet her. The two of you shall be sisters. And both my childs."

With that as a preamble, Hillary was prepared to dislike Victorine on sight. For much as she laughed at being the darling of the three women, she had, even in such a short time, become accustomed to it and did not wish to share that affection with another young lady. Moreover, she knew the rumors that Princess Caroline was having an affair with Bartolomeo Pergami and that the daughter, Victorine, was just a cover for that immorality. Having come to care for the flighty, generous, loving princess she was loath to see anything that would have her think less of her.

Yet she met Bartolomeo first. He was not a gentlemen one overlooked. He strode into the garden, all six feet of him, while she was cutting roses for the princess's bed table. That was her official duty, since the princess had decreed only English people knew how to arrange flowers properly. Of a sudden a dark, handsome, broad-shouldered Italian gentleman rushed up and took her hand, causing her to drop several red roses.

"Ah, the beautiful English lady our gracious princess is rescuing from her English monster."

Not having discussed the viscount with even the

princess, Hillary was astounded at this invasion of her privacy. Yet Pergami was almost impossible to repress. Neither moving away nor giving him a cold stare checked his flow.

"You are too beautiful to be the spoils of that dastard. I offer you not only my sword to protect you, but my life if need be. It would be the greatest honor of my existence to fight to keep such a rare beauty in safety and happiness."

"Eh, thank you. However I do not feel I shall need your sword. I do not anticipate being followed here by the viscount. I have written breaking off and do not expect any objections."

Bartolomeo's dark eyes fired up. "But he is not a man, then? For if you were mine, a simple letter would not dismiss me. Only death would part us."

"How fortunate then for us both that I am not . . . eh, yours," Hillary said with a smile.

Bartolomeo objected, insisting that it would be his greatest fortune if she even gave him a rose, let alone the pleasure of being his. And he kissed the several roses still in her hands and somehow she found herself giving them to him, which he took with great delight and assumed something that she certainly had not meant.

In the next instant Hillary attempted to persuade him she was not interested in belonging to any gentleman.

With much bowing and hot glances, he took her basket of flowers and escorted her into the palace, all the time assuring her that when such a beauty existed, it was every gentleman's duty to vie for her. They would not be proper men if they did not. Beauty was the desire of every man with eyes to see it.

Never had this reclusive young English lady been so floridly courted. She began to understand if the princess had fallen for his remarks, especially after years of being treated like a pariah by her husband.

When they entered Princess Caroline's salon, Hillary found herself supplanted. For sitting close to the princess in her own chair was a lovely, dark-haired lady.

"Come," the princess yelled out, signaling Hillary forward. Bartolomeo was coming along unsummoned, as if he did not need the formality of an invitation, which caused Hillary to wonder at the degree of familiarity between the Pergamis and the princess. He bowed before Her Highness, giving her all the flowers Hillary had spent many a hot hour carefully selecting, as if his own tribute. She realized it would be petty to make that point, but suddenly felt herself becoming decidedly petty and jealous. Victorine was talking to the princess in Italian and Bartolomeo changed quickly to that language, leaving Hillary apart from the happy chatting group. Her own cut flowers were placed by the princess's hands into Victorine's dark locks and one in Bartolomeo's buttonhole.

Hillary backed away. She was halfway across the room when Princess Caroline looked up and cried out, "But where is my other daughter going? You must become a good loving family—all of you. Come, we shall all embrace."

Before Hillary knew what was happening, she was in the midst of a joint embrace, the princess holding her to her bosom, Victorine squeezing one side of her and Bartolomeo the other. When Hillary came up for air, she was red with embarrassment, unlike the rest, who were all laughing in delight.

The two young ladies were introduced to each other and ordered to run away into the garden and pick more flowers, for those were crushed. Bartolomeo had trampled all over them.

Hillary assumed this was a ploy for the princess and Bartolomeo to be alone, but when she looked back, she found that Bartolomeo was following them, holding the basket as if they were three young children on their way out for a frolic. The princess was shooing him off and seating herself at her desk to write one of her long letters to her many supporters in England.

Nor were there any longing glances on the part of either man or princess.

Her supposition was correct, Hillary discovered after consultation with Lady Gardener. Bartolomeo was not Princess Caroline's lover but rather part of the princess's growing family. She adopted people right and left. Being deprived of all relations by coming to England and then having her daughter taken away first legally and then permanently by death had given the lady a desperate need to claim people as her own. Young maidens became her daughters. She had, Lady Gardener informed her, about six years ago, even adopted a young English boy named William Austin. The prince had seized on that and claimed she had had an illegitimate child. But the hospital records proved otherwise, and indeed many of his own camp could prove they had seen the princess often enough to know she was not pregnant. She was just seeking children. Subsequently she'd gathered eight foundlings about her. The prince could not accuse her of suddenly giving birth to them all. But the princess insisted on teasing his spies by claiming she had

ten children all told, including Princess Charlotte,
and laughing while they rushed to report that
incriminating fact to their eager master.

There were spies in Italy as well, Victorine had
informed her.

"Her Gracious Highness is always spied upon, by
Italians for pay and by English for spite. We become
accustomed to being observed and questioned,
everywhere we go. But what is one to do? One cannot live to hide from gossip, else we must all go to
convents. And even there I have heard many shocking tales. Best to follow our dear Highness and live
with full heart openly and let all the others bite
their tongues in regret at our joy. We are not familiar, we are familial. As you and I are sisters."

Hillary's good heart and the friendship of Victorine
had succeeded in pushing out all jealousy. The two
were a wonderful contrast. Victorine was quiet and
demure with her dark hair swept back into a bun
that emphasized the long earrings of pure gold in
her delicate pierced ears. Appearing prim in company, Victorine could laugh and romp in private
with Hillary. Day by day Hillary herself was losing
her English reserve and running with Victorine into
the Italian forests.

Having been responsible for her father for so
long, Hillary had never been young, never played
and laughed at will. Now with Victorine she did. It
was grand to have a sister.

One night before dawn Victorine came into
Hillary's room and shook her awake. Hillary was
confused. It was still dark. Was something amiss?

Victorine whispered that they were escaping
from their guardians to fulfill Hillary's desire of
experiencing the dawn.

"Ah," Hillary said, surprised that Victorine had taken her casual remark seriously. Yesterday viewing the sublime beauty of Lake Como from one of the palace's terraces, she had mentioned that the view could not be bested. Victorine claimed a superior view at dawn was to be seen from a boat. Hillary allowed that she would prodigiously care to experience that someday. Being literal, Victorine took that as an appointment and had the boat waiting at the bottom of the marble steps.

Dressing hurriedly in the first white muslin frock handy, Hillary had not taken time to arrange her hair in its approved crown of curls, leaving it long and loose, spilling down her back. In contrast Victorine, as always, was precise to a pin, neatly dressed in a blue muslin with hair coiled at her neck and her golden earrings in place. Stealthily crossing from balcony to balcony, the two ladies reached an unoccupied chamber at the end of the palazzo that had a balcony with steps leading to the outside marble terrace. In a trice they were down, having evaded all their chaperons. One did not count Victorine's twelve-year-old-cousin, Pietro, whose only concern was counting the lire he was to receive for rowing the gondola-shaped boat.

"Now widen your eyes," Victorine instructed as they sat back on the cushioned seat.

Hillary did so. She looked first to the sky where the dawn was just beginning in faint fingers of gold shooting through the dark. A Lake Como morning was sublime indeed. Breaths apart, the light revealed more of the world about them. As the boat drifted, stroke by stroke, through the serenity of the lake, dim outlines of the looming mountains appeared and chestnut forests showed dark green.

From the hidden valleys, the orchards of orange trees threw back their scent. As a climax the lake revealed itself with its long, narrow blueness winding among the mountains. Glancing down, one saw the lake reflecting back the massive Alps, so while drifting, one felt oneself covered in mountains above and below. Every movement of the boat rippled and dissolved the Alps on the lake's surface, only to have them reappear at the next gliding. Hillary stopped looking down into the lake and looked ahead. So much light had come up now, one could see other boats gliding by. From them came the sounds of laughter and strums of a guitar—snatches of Italian songs that faded away across the lake. Hillary could no longer sit quietly as a mere audience. Not when a thousand tints were exuberantly flooding about. Exultantly she rose. The rosy, golden dawn light showered down on her white gown and pale hair. She raised her hands to it as she stood at the boat's prow, mystically outlined in light as if she were the goddess of the lake.

That was how she was seen by an Englishman in a boat a few feet away. He looked up in shock, as if seeing a mirage. Then without saying a word, he signaled his oarsman to follow the boat. Being Italian the man did not need explanation. One look at the beauty of the woman in the other boat and he made quick to follow.

With each ray of dawn light, the vision became clearer. Not a multicolored dream, after all. It was rather a white-gowned lady whose long, pale hair floated like a cape behind her in the morning breeze. The serenity of her stillness reached the onlookers and they were motionless as well. Her sudden movement released them as she returned to her seat.

"*Bellissima!*" the boatman shouted. And the English lord could only nod.

Keeping his eyes on the lady, the boatman was not watching his path and almost sideswiped a sailboat. The exchange of insults in fiery Italian distracted the English lord. When he looked back, the gondola-like boat with the golden girl had slid from sight into the golden mist.

"Blast," he whispered, wondering if he'd ever find her again. But the English lord was philosophical. Probably a closer view would reveal common traits that would wipe out the dream altogether. Very possibly she tittered. Or like all Italian ladies, she would probably have eaten a quantity of garlic. Or worst of all, she might be attainable. In truth, he'd never yet met a lady in reality not his for the asking. Whereupon she immediately lost her appeal.

Yet his lordship could not help but wish to see this one again, close enough to dispel her image. For in truth, until he did, he might have to admit that there was one woman in the world that had all the qualities he'd ever imagined suitable for him—one at last worthy of Viscount Wolverton. But, by Jove, she was probably just a dream and like all dreams would fade away in the reality of the day ahead.

5

Lord Wolverton had come to Lake Como with the express purpose of visiting Princess Caroline and of beguiling her into revealing her guilt. The Prince Regent had given him those specific orders. At first sight of the princess's salmon pink marble palazzo, the viscount was assured of his success. In contrast to all the beautifully aged white marble villas, the royal choice of this marble monstrosity proved instantly that she would be prodigious easy to gull. Wolf waited in the hall with his look of assurance even more pronounced than usual, while his card with a note was sent ahead. To prevent her linking him with her husband, he had added the line, "I hope to remind Your Gracious Highness of our last delightful meeting in London. Certainly to me that moment is unforgettable."

The viscount laughed while writing it, for his last

image of the princess was indeed unforgettable. It had taken place at the opera. Her Highness had signaled he was to sit in her box for the remainder of the performance so that she might look at him rather than the fat, ugly tenor. He had bowed at the compliment and offered several flowery, insincere statements in return. As the evening continued she had unquestionably thrown a lure at him. If he'd not been so discriminating, he might have added a princess to his list of conquests. But he preferred ladies younger, more demure, and decidedly of his own choosing.

Foolishly the viscount had mentioned the episode to the prince, who had frothed and fumed that the viscount had not availed himself of the invitation. "Odd's blood, you might have done me the greatest service since Wellington. Ridding me of me consort would have had me under more obligation than ridding the country of Napoleon."

The viscount merely shrugged. He was quite aware that royalty always forgot its obligations. Nor could he be persuaded to so abase himself in the service of His Highness. This episode had occurred above six years ago, but the Prince Regent not only resembled an elephant but had the memory of one. He called it to mind at the moment he needed an Englishman with impeccable credentials. Over brandies and snuff, the two gentlemen discussed the prince's hope for divorce. "Gave that Italian, Pergy, a title, egad! Chamberlain to her court. Bought 'im an Italian title, too. Baron, egad! Don't do that for an acquaintance, what? She is the canker in my soul," the royal gentleman confided, taking the viscount's offered snuff with such a heavy hand he upset the delicate box. The viscount retrieved it with a smooth bow, apologizing as if his had been the mistake. The regent enjoyed never being called to account for his clumsiness and continued more confidentially. "You are just the man for this delicate task, I see. Got savoir faire. Had it meself when I was young. They called me the first gentleman of Europe. Ladies swooned for a smile from me. Gained some weight since then and lost some of my appeal, but not all."

The viscount smoothly agreed to the addendum, alluding to Lady Hertford as proof of that.

The prince appreciated that reference. Laughing loudly he pocketed the viscount's favorite snuffbox, appropriating it as his own. One could not point out the error to His Highness. Probably it was his way of getting things he assumed should have been offered to him anyway. Royal prerogative. Now he wished himself rid of a wife and could not understand why everyone was not jumping to help him succeed. "A princess from Brunswick, such a small principality—not up to me standards. I said as much to me father. But she was his niece. First view I said, 'Egad, I'll never stomach the lady.' She wore a black beaver hat and she stared at me in shock. As if, blast her, I was a joke!"

"Surely not," the viscount soothed, attempting not to smile.

"True by my hand!" the prince exclaimed. "Odd's blood, heard from Lady Jersey that the German lady accused me of being fat. And drunk. Slander, I say. Just had a drop to fortify myself for the viewing of her, don't you know? Egad, had to be jug bitten to do me duty by the succession. After the birth of our daughter, it was with great relief I sent her the message I would never honor her bed again. Princess ain't much for delicacy. Stab me, she not only accepted that without humiliation but insisted it be put in writing! Wrote it for her, egad. Heard she keeps that letter by her—for what? To show she ain't wanted?" He laughed uproariously.

Since he looked to the viscount for a reply, the lord gave him a logical one. "I expect she wanted her position made legal—in case she was accused of refusing you her bed, which might have been reason for a legal separation."

The prince was dumbstruck. The prominent blue eyes rolled in his red face. "Egad, never thought of that. Might have gotten rid of her then, if I had pushed to stay in her bed rather than rushed out of it. But Lady Jersey was pushing me to break off. And then I had hopes of getting together again with my dearest love, Mrs. Fitzherbert. No, I did what had to be done!"

"Of course," the viscount agreed.

"We've been separate camps since," the prince pronounced with some pleasure. "Not enough! Must be rid of her. She is a canker in my soul!"

"So you said," the viscount agreed, becoming amused by the prince's revealing such intimate details, although they were well known. He lost a great deal of the viscount's sympathy by telling it himself. It was Wolf's belief that once one broke with a lady, one did not tell tales subsequently. He shook his head.

The prince took that as sympathy and continued in the same vein, "She has always made me a laughingstock, by her appearance, by her actions. Vulgar, Lady Hertford calls her, and I cannot but agree. Which explains why the common men and women love her so. She's one of 'em, egad! Made that blasted woman their heroine, don't you know? But we'll show 'em, Wolf, me boy? What say?"

What else could one say to one's prince? Especially since he was travelling to Italy in any event. He agreed at least to take a look at the situation at Princess Caroline's court. Regretted it the moment he was out of the prince's presence. Left that task for as late in his itinerary as possible. Being present, he was determined to do his duty.

As expected, the princess's butler came back with a different demeanor. He bowed and scraped in such a way that indicated to the viscount he was welcome indeed.

The princess was seated in a salon with an open balcony that brought in the view of the mountains. She had a birdcage at her side and a cat in her lap. On her head she had a peacock. But on closer examination it was merely a cap of peacock feathers, some of which went flying as she bobbed up at the sight of him, suggesting she was molting.

"Ah, our sleek Lord Wolf. Yes, I recollect you. You are still looking so fit. You have eaten many a poor lambs since we met?"

The viscount had to laugh at that. The princess never said what she ought, and yet, he had to admit she had some wit. He assured her he was a gentle shepherd to all lambs in his presence.

"Bah, I do not believe that. You have not the look of a shepherd, but of a gentleman on the prowl."

"Looks are often deceiving."

"I am disappointed," she said, and laughed at his astonishment.

He wondered if she were flirting and assumed she was. He was uncertain whether he would be willing to flirt back. While thinking of his course, the princess was jumping up again and exclaiming. A tall, dark, muscular gentleman with positively astoundingly long mustaches had entered.

"Baron, you must meet this viscount. He is from my husband's camp. Come here to prove that you and I are lovers, what think you of that?"

The drawn breath was the viscount's at the openness of the lady. No wonder the prince had been shocked by her ways. Baron Pergami was obviously not shocked or offended by the viscount's aim.

"But everyone is in love with the princess. What is not to love? She is charming . . . all kindness. . . ." He bent over and kissed her hand several times.

"That is enough, Bart, your mustaches tickle. I told you. An Englishman knows how to kiss a lady's hand, he pretends to touch but never does."

She eyed the viscount as if expecting him to demonstrate. He was too dumbstruck.

But in a moment she had forgotten him and talked in Italian to Bartolomeo. Her face was concerned. She looked about. And then as the door opened her face cleared of all concern. "Ah, here is my darling, the baron and I have one true love, and here she is."

A lovely dark-haired young lady entered. She was introduced as Victorine, the baron's daughter and the princess's dearest delight. The young girl allowed herself to be stroked, murmuring a few pleasantries in Italian but basically sitting quietly at the princess's feet, as if she were a royal hound. Occasionally as the conversation continued with the princess asking about his trip, Victorine would get up and bring things to the princess, a fan, or a painting she had been working on, and the princess would drop her conversation with him instantly and devote herself to answering the girl's queries.

Before long he achieved what he wished—an invitation, after broadly hinting he must look for lodgings in the neighborhood.

"*Nein,* you must stay here! You need time to inspect, yes? You must see for yourself what the baron and I do in private? Is not that your task?"

"Your Highness, I do earnestly assure you . . ." he began, but she waved him quiet and even came close and patted his hand.

"I know why you have come. You are not the first that man, that great Mahomet, has sent out. They have either had to leave disappointed or make up their own tales. You I do not fear. For I daresay you are a true gentlemans. So you may stay and look all you wish. That shall only prove me guiltless of all his fantasies. Heavens to Gott, I am tired of being on trial. I went away from England as he wished, leaving my daughter in his care, only to have him let her die."

"She died in childbirth, Your Highness," the viscount reminded her.

"Yes," she said bitterly, "while he was busy visiting Lady Hertford's hunting seat, not returning from his pleasures even when Charlotte's life was at risk. While I, who would have given my life for the chance, was not permitted to be there to hear her last words and drink her last, sweet breath."

Princess Caroline's voice cracked at that point and she dissolved in tears. Instantly both Victorine and her father had surrounded the lady with clicking tongues and embraces.

The viscount took his leave.

That last scene was sufficient for him to report against Her Highness. She had been embraced by her Italian lover. In his very sight. But actually while indiscreet, it was innocent. The daughter had been in that joint embrace. As he looked back, he noted that an English lady he recollected, Lady Gardener, was there embracing the princess as well. No, definitely not incriminating enough. Lady Gardener stepped away from the princess as if struck. Amused, the viscount realized she was eyeing him from across the room with shock. He bowed politely. Too flustered to curtsy in return, Lady Gardener merely stared as if seeing a monster. Indeed, she took out her hanky and clasped it to her mouth, as if to hide a scream.

Leaving the salon, the viscount was curious to the point of confusion. Why would the princess's lady-in-waiting be so flummoxed by his appearance? He had, he admitted, not the most pristine reputation with the ladies, but that woman was old enough to be his mother. He laughed aloud. Dash it, he almost wished he'd thrown her a kiss. Upon looking round on his way up the stairs, Wolf found to his amazement Lady Gardener had come out of the salon and was watching him going up the stairs to his room and her face was whiter than ever before. Her lips mouthed the word "No."

Uncertain what she was objecting to, the viscount could not resist doing what he'd so audaciously planned. He threw her a kiss as he walked across the gallery.

Lady Gardener stepped back as if he'd tossed her a snake, and ran back into the salon, slamming the door after her.

Wolf could not help but laugh aloud at that. This might not be as boring a visit as he assumed. Certainly if Lady Gardener was so overset, it must be

because she or the princess or both together had
something to hide. He would discover what it was
ere he left, and then she would have something to
cry "No" about indeed!

6

After so long having been reclusively situated in her estate of Holly House, Hillary found Lake Como overwhelming. There was always something to be done and scores of people to do it with, including traveling English supporters of the princess who must be entertained by drives or sails on the lake. Victorine was continually present, introducing Hillary to her Italian friends, one of whom, Count Guido, immediately declared himself Hillary's number-one beau.

Daily he brought her flowers and comfits or poems in Italian, which she did not understand, but Victorine, amidst blushes, translated for her. Then there was Bartolomeo himself, sometimes called Baron Bart at the princess's instigation. He followed his young ladies about, he claimed, in order to protect their honor. Yet it seemed to Hillary that she needed someone to protect her from him. For with his snapping black eyes and languid looks, she feared he was developing quite a tendre for her.

Victorine agreed that was the case, but it was not to be helped. "You are so lovely. So blond and angelic, Angelica, dear, what is a gentleman to do but love you on sight? From my father to Count Guido to the embassy man, Mr. Ashton, to Sir Percy and even that Austrian noblemen—they all adore you. If you wished to marry, you have but to point."

Hillary laughed at her friend's exaggeration. "I'm afraid they believe I have quite an independence, but it is not the case, you know. I have a mere competence."

Victorine looked at her in confusion. "These men love you for your face, not your fortune. You are not like a madonna, that is what I am called. I am told I am like that . . . painting by da Vinci." Blushing, she continued rapidly, "But you are in *all* the masterpieces—as the *angel* floating above in the sky. That is why our dear princess calls you Angelica, and the rest of us follow her. Yes?"

Hillary laughed. "I don't know why you have all rechristened me. Actually I'm rather fond of my name Hillary."

Bartolomeo, approaching, heard the last. "Hillary? What is that name? Is it a lady of the hills? A peasant? Or a lady as big as a hill? Bah, in no meaning it is you. Rather you are in truth an *angel!* One worships such beauty—on one's knees!"

And he proceeded to do so. Victorine remained at her side smiling while Hillary awkwardly accepted the homage and asked him please to rise.

It was difficult to adjust to such adulation. But one could not but respond to it. Like a flower, so long in the shade, she bloomed under all this attention.

"Did I not say you were meant to be in society?" Mrs. Wizzle exclaimed in justification. "Every dress brings out another charm in you. There is no color that does not flatter you. Nor any gentleman, in faith. Aren't you pleased that you did not settle for a gentleman who couldn't love you? Since so prodigiously many do?"

Unlike Mrs. Wizzle, who basked in the quantity of Hillary's admirers, Lady Gardener was far from pleased at their quality. "None of them are suitable for you, dear child. This Count Guido's family is simply not our level. As for Mr. Ashton and Sir Percy, their lineage is unexceptionable, but their fortunes are not. Best then if you waited till we returned to England. There we shall more readily find a gentleman of fitting character and suitable lineage."

Without giving Hillary a chance to reply, whether in agreement or not, her ladyship took the rare opportunity of speaking to Hillary privately, away from the princess, to question everybody's suddenly calling her Angelica. Even servants addressed her as Signorina Angelica. Why did she permit it? "It is too familiar! Actually you have a perfectly respectable English name!"

Mrs. Wizzle agreed, but allowed that Hillary looked like an angel, so the pet name was quite fitting. Hillary ended the discussion by blithely saying she would answer to any name as long as it was said with affection, and as for her courtiers, she was not in a hurry to belong to any gentleman. It was vastly more entertaining to have many admirers.

Princess Caroline had a good deal to do with that attitude, often advising Angelica that gentlemen in general tended to disappoint. Even her adopted son, Willikin, who had been lovable as a boy, was less so now. "There is too much of a man in him already. They always seek to wound."

Mrs. Wizzle, shaking her head throughout, later took Hillary aside to remind her of her own dear Mr. Wizzle. Hillary ought not miss the greatest joy on earth—true love between a man and a woman.

To all this motherly advice Hillary listened with a serious mien. Yet on her own, she merely laughed— at all the admirers, at all the games being played, and most of all at herself for having become this social butterfly.

"Any moment I shall be discovered," she warned herself. "I shall be inevitably unmasked as just Hillary and be thrown out of this enchanted palace. But meanwhile I shall bask in it all!"

Most astonishing was how easy it was to enchant. A mere smile did it. Or a direct look. Nor was there aught but pleasure in donning all her beautiful new clothes. The princess was always gifting her with a new dress or fine lace shawl or diamond earrings. Lady Gardener decreed Hillary could keep them all, for otherwise Princess Caroline would have been unspeakably hurt. Her Highness so enjoyed making others happy. But, Lady Gardener warned, Hillary must not accept anything but flowers, books, or items of sentiment from gentlemen. To do so would clearly be a sign that they had the right to expect a return in the form of some intolerable insult. Possibly several kisses!

"How many kisses for a bracelet?" Hillary had teased, pointing out the two pearl circlets on the Princess Caroline's arms that she was always absent-mindedly fingering.

"Too many. You would have to give your decency

for them," Lady Gardener assured her, but Princess Caroline interposed.

"These bracelets were given me by the prince as a wedding gift. To be true, Lady Jersey sold her decency to have them. For that man took them from me and gave them her, his mistress of the time."

"How did you get them back?" Hillary asked in awe.

"That is a long story. And you are not ready to hear it," the princess teased. "You still believe in love."

Hillary was uncertain whether she did or not.

"Love," the princess said seriously, "to many a gentleman is but a test of power. A gentleman values a lady and gives her a gift. She gives back gifts of kisses. It is all trading, buying, selling, and in some cases"—she looked down at her bracelet—"revenge." With a sudden shaking of her head, and in her loud voice, she said exuberantly, "Ah, do not listen to me! Charlotte found love. I pray you will, too. Here!" Making one of Her Highness's characteristic gestures, she pulled off one of the bracelets and gave it to Hillary. "Let this stop representing my hurt and another's deceit. Let it be on your young arms and represent just . . . beauty."

The lady giving and the lady receiving were actually giving Cupid one more chance to prove he existed. Count Guido was the first to attempt to be his representative. He took Hillary and his party to see his summer palace on the edge of the lake. It had twenty rooms, he told her, and she nodded. Then he said it in Italian as if she would understand the grandeur better. Hillary merely nodded again. Her own Holly House had thirty. Throughout the trip the count had fastened his eyes on the bracelet. "It is a

king's treasury!" he said with awe. "Surely I have
seen it on Princess Caroline's arm?"

Hillary admitted she'd been given it by her
Highness.

"She has a special love for you. Are you in her
will?"

Hillary was aghast. She was still too English not
to find such vulgar inquiry intolerable. But she
swallowed her ire. It was the Italian way to say
openly what one was thinking, and she saw in his
eyes that her value had risen substantially

Of a sudden a thought made her smile. Count
Guido was exactly the kind of fortune hunter her
father had feared would approach her. Yet the count
was a charming man, basically because he was so
open in his needs. Shortly, while showing her around
his palace, Count Guido took her aside to explain the
necessity of his marrying a lady of wealth. "My winter palace is more big than this summer one. Both, I
regret, need repair. And my sisters, they too need
repair—to their dowries."

"What does the lady receive for giving your palaz-
zos and your sisters all her money?" Hillary could
not help but ask, her eyes twinkling at his gall.

Count Guido was astounded. "Is it not obvious?
She receives *me!* What more could she ask?"

"But you supposedly receive her as well. Why
should you want more than herself?"

"Because I am special. I have a title . . . I have
history . . . lineage!"

"We all have that. My family is stocked with that.
What about love, count? Having heard so many different viewpoints on whether there is or is not love, I
must ask. You apparently think love is something to
be bought and paid for, reducing it to a commodity.

I daresay only poets believe in love for itself. Ah, heavens, you have disappointed me. I presumed from all your flowery statements you had some degree of affection for me."

"But I love with all my heart you! I ask you to be my wife! I give up my life in a duel to win you from any other man who tries to get you!"

He came close and would have grabbed Hillary in his arms, his dark eyes were afire, but Hillary pushed him back. "All this you would do for me. But what would you do if I told you I have not a shilling of fortune? That it is all tied up and given over to a gentleman—" She stopped herself just short of revealing her past secret engagement, which the princess had assured her was known only to Bartolomeo. "To a miserly uncle," she amended weakly.

"I would say I fight this miser man for you and your money and we would run away in triumph and wealth!"

"But if I did not want to take away my money from my uncle, would you marry me as a pauper?"

Count Guido bit his lip at that question. "This is a challenge to my love? I could say *sì* to you and mean it as this moment. But I have too much respect for you to be false. I, Count Guido, cannot marry a pauperess! But that does not mean I give you up. We could be together without marriage. I could buy you a small estate in the hills and visit you." His eyes lit up at that scheme.

Hillary, aghast, quickly pulled away a noticeable distance. "You would disgrace me like that? Poor love that!"

"But you do not know how I could love!" he insisted, catching up, and kissing her fully on her mouth while she struggled to get away. In a moment she was freed. A towering avenger, Bartolomeo, was there, pulling Count Guido away, so enraged his mustaches were quivering as he claimed, "Alfredo! You would touch this innocent angel! One who is under my protection! One whom the princess herself has ordered me to guard with my life. I have believed you honorable and you have shown yourself base! For that one kiss I shall take your life!"

And he lunged for his sword, but he was not wearing it. Count Guido was nothing loath to fight for the affront of being called base and for being knocked to the ground before the lady he loved. Both gentleman resorted to yelling insults at each other, and Hillary ran away from them to Victorine, who entered and calmly went up to both gentlemen and insisted that they not disgrace themselves any longer. "You embarrass us before this English lady? What will she think—that our gentlemen do not know how to honor a woman, but must fight in her presence? And I, Count Guido, I am nothing? That you yell before me?"

Both gentlemen apologized. Count Guido ran up to Hillary and fell at her feet in apology, crying that her beauty had driven him wild. Hillary accepted the apology and Bartolomeo accepted it as logical, for he too was driven wild by Hillary's beauty. He even sympathized with the count, so all were soon in charity with each other. But Hillary returned to the palace feeling disenchanted. With Count Guido, for his not being the lover he seemed. More with Count Guido's kiss, which left her as cold as his proposition. And even Bartolomeo had disappointed, for he forgave the count so quickly. Something too much of poseurs with no solid feeling in them, Hillary felt. Perhaps Lady Gardener was correct that she must return to England to find love. Next moment she shuddered at that conclusion. Not hardly! For what stood for love there was the cold, indifferent Viscount Wolverton and that was even worse! In truth Hillary was beginning to conclude that the undying love of Heloise and Abelard was more tragic for being so rare than for its ending.

Hillary was unable to sleep that night, wondering about her future living with an exiled princess. At first it had seemed romantic, as Italy had seemed so romantic. But at times reality was beginning to set in. She was not Angelica. She was Hillary Astaire and she would soon have to return to England and have to fight the viscount for the return of her independence. Remembering the cold, gray eyes as he vowed she was in his control made her shudder. The dawn expedition had wiped all thoughts of Wolverton from her mind. She was further distracted in the afternoon, when Mrs. Wizzle and she were invited to Sir Percy's, who was residing at the English consul's estate. They returned quite late, having stayed for high tea. Mrs. Wizzle enjoyed speaking to English people, after all the chatter in Italian, not to mention the princess's often conversing in French and German. They came up against more of a language barrier when, with a flood of Italian, a guard forbade them entrance.

"Is this the princess's subtle way of saying we have overstayed our welcome?" Hillary asked with some amusement but with a shock equal to Mrs. Wizzle's, who was threatening to have a spasm.

Lady Gardener was summoned, Hillary and Mrs. Wizzle relying on her ladyship's common sense. But almost immediately they lost faith in Lady Gardener as well, for she apparently had given those orders to the guard. And now her ladyship was sneaking them by the servants' back stairway, up to their rooms.

"What's amiss?" Hillary demanded when they were allowed to rest in Hillary's sitting room. "Has the Prince Regent landed?" she asked with an impudent grin.

"You are not far wrong," Lady Gardener said with a sigh. "I have been dreading that you would walk into him. I could not persuade the princess to send him packing. Instead what does she do but introduce him to Pergami and Victorine and invite him to stay to report all he would. She always outfaces her enemies! A brave soul, but foolish, foolish! And what shall become of *you?*"

"Forgive me, your ladyship," Hillary inserted. "You are beside yourself. I understand someone has arrived to threaten the princess, but why that should threaten me . . . ?" Hillary stopped speaking. Her own intellect had answered. "Oh," she concluded, and her face paled.

"Yes, precisely," Lady Gardener breathed.

"What! What? Speak, in heaven's name," Mrs. Wizzle demanded. "Who has come?"

"Viscount Wolverton, I expect," Hillary said calmly, and Lady Gardener nodded.

"We are undone!" Mrs. Wizzle exclaimed, looking about as if she would hide in the closet. Even Lady Gardener was flustered.

"But what, I still ask," Hillary continued coolly, "is amiss? So, he is here. Why should that concern me? I have sent him a letter breaking off our arrangement. Did you not assure me I need not marry him?"

"Certainly," Lady Gardener said, regaining her English aplomb. "I cannot believe I have allowed the surprise of seeing him to disorient me so that I was even set to hide you away. Such dashed flummery! Dear Hillary, your sense must always be relied on. What need we to quake! You shall simply explain to him that your feelings have undergone a change. You no longer wish to be his wife. He is enough of an English gentlemen not to wish to force you, I expect."

Mrs. Wizzle suggested that while that might be true, couldn't they rather wait in their rooms for a few days until he left? There was no need for an immediate challenge to the gentleman.

Ignoring both ladies debating this point, Hillary went to her bedroom to change her dress. On her return she was wearing her most fetching new gown. Walking past the ladies, still rapt in discussing the matter, Hillary exited into the hall. Both ladies were silenced. They stared. And then ran after.

"But where are you going?" Lady Gardener exclaimed.

"You're not going to . . ." Mrs. Wizzle begged.

"Yes, I am," Hillary said with a determined grin. "I am going to beard the lion. Take up the challenge. In short, I'm going to see the viscount and face him down." And with another grin she turned away from the ladies and lightly ran down the marble steps.

7

Lord Wolverton had changed for evening, and was the epitome of an English nobleman with his fitted pantaloons and elegant gray waistcoat the exact color of his hypnotic gray eyes. Next to Pergami and Count Guido and Sir Percy he appeared underdressed, for they were outdoing each other in fobs hanging from their waistcoats, stickpins, exaggerated collars, and effulgences of cravats that ballooned under their chins. Count Guido was in a flowered brocade waistcoat and jacket and he had rings on practically every finger, especially the two he used to put together and kiss, tossing that kiss to whichever lady happened to be passing. Bartolomeo and the princess were wearing matching shades of orange. That was Pergami's family color and his crest of an orange tree and a horse decorated the gentleman's waistcoat while Her Highness wore an orange sash emblazoned across her chest with similar Pergami embroidery on it.

Using his best man-to-man approach, the viscount edged up to a fellow Englishman, Sir Percy, and looking toward the two said confidentially, "It appears Her Highness has taken a certain Italian to her breast."

Not understanding the innuendo, Sir Percy replied factually, "Pergami is her chamberlain. His brother is also of the princess's entourage. His daughter and sister, too. Countess Oldi is a lady-in-waiting." He pointed to a rather rotund and silent Italian woman sitting on the settee with Victorine.

The viscount honored them both with the briefest appraisal through his quizzing glass.

"Everyone loves the princess!" protested Count Guido, standing near enough to have overheard. While his English was not perfect, his instincts were. "*Barone* Pergami," he stressed the gentleman's Italian title, "feels the privilege of being at this royal court. As do the rest of us. And as for his daughter, Signorina Pergami's beauty brightens us all."

To that Sir Percy was quick to agree, adding that the court had many *exquisite* ladies. In a trice the two gentlemen were engaged in a dialogue on the differences between Italian and English ladies. Most engrossing to the participants, but not the direction toward which the viscount had been leading them. He would have to be more direct. "But the princess must be rather lonely, I expect. Even a woman of exalted rank needs some *personal* affection."

Count Guido gave the viscount an affronted look. "You are implying, my lord?"

"I imply nothing. But we are men of the world, conversing together. I ask merely about the on-dits."

"By Jove," Sir Percy exclaimed, "you mean the rumors? Everywhere the princess goes she is followed by them. The lady cannot smile or have her hand kissed without everyone anointing the man in question as her latest lover. Rumors are rampant even about you since being invited to stay at her pink palazzo. The rest of us are not so favored. It would be blissful to be in such proximity to her entourage." He sighed. Count Guido nodded sympathetically.

Egad, the viscount thought, why all these calf's eyes? Why were these gentlemen acting as if being in the princess's presence was an honor devoutly to be wished?

Count Guido was now talking. "She admits Austrians into her circle, and we must accept them. It is enough they have taken over my country, but to break bread with them. It is not to be borne! And she lets them sit next to young women she should be guarding. I warned the princess to take two looks before welcoming more gentlemen." Guido gave Lord Wolverton a pointed glance, and then even more pointedly, asked, "You stay here long? Or you pass through in a wink?"

Wolverton grinned. "My plans are . . . flexible. Wherever I find pleasure, there I remain."

That answer did not satisfy. Both he and Sir Percy were quick to suggest other areas of Italy he would prefer. Sir Percy was recommending Naples. Even Sicily had its charm. Guido urged him to leave the Lombardy area where the Austrians held sway. Tuscany was more benevolent, and there was the charm of Pisa and its leaning tower. He even leaned on a slant to demonstrate that wonder in store for him.

The viscount could not help but grin. "I am not inclined to inclines. I lean more toward the beauty of Lake Como. Certainly the view of the Alps and the trees around here is breathtaking . . . and so romantic."

Both men bristled at that, assuring him the place was not romantic, the women very ordinary. The women however in Naples were known for their ample charms.

"And at this court of Princess Caroline, she keeps her eye on her protégées, so there is no need for you to imagine you can get away with anything with any one of them!" Sir Percy said, getting desperate enough to reveal the cause of their alarm.

Lord Wolverton looked once more at Victorine. Surely she could not be the reason for their dog-in-the-manger attitude. She was comely, but not strikingly so.

Count Guido had an inspiration. He would introduce the viscount to Victorine and of course Countess Oldi, her aunt. Perhaps the English lord would enjoy taking the two ladies for a stroll in the gardens? Even better a sail on a boat. The lake was quite near the palace steps.

Sir Percy was calling that capital! So warmly was the plan endorsed that the viscount could not help but grin and retort, "As both of you so wish for that treat, I should be the basest cad to deprive you of it."

All consternation, the two assured him they had already met the young lady and had many a walk with her, and they did not care to repeat it.

"That is not much of a recommendation," the viscount put in, his eyes sparkling at their obvious ploys.

"No, no, but we have had our share of that plea-sure. We now, gallant men that we are, share it with you! Yes? I introduce?"

"Some other time, my dear count. For tonight, since the princess has specifically invited me to be in her presence, I could scarcely be so rude as to absent myself. Not done, old boy."

The two gentlemen gave up and bowed them-selves away, leaving the viscount, while enjoying having thrown them into such a pelter, doubly anx-ious to meet the lady they were so clumsily attempt-ing to keep to themselves. At that moment the princess looked about as if searching for someone. Count Guido and Sir Percy moved toward the door, anxiously positioning themselves, rather like hounds just before feeding time. Then Pergami rose and exclaimed aloud to all, "But where is our darling Angelica! This evening is flat without her beauty!"

Count Guido and Sir Percy turned to see if the viscount had caught that and saw with dismay that he had.

So it was Angelica he was to be kept away from. Nothing could have more induced him to stay. Indeed, he might even rearrange his plans and remain at least a sennight if this Angelica seemed worth his while. For certainly he was failing to acquire anything tangible against the princess. Nor was he of a mind to do so, if she was being discreet. Only a blatant affair that had everybody smirking would have been worth reporting.

In a moment he'd joined Count Guido and Sir Percy and incorrigibly whispered, "What are we waiting for, old boys? Angelica?"

Sir Percy had to grin then. "I did not think such a known rake as you, Wolverton, would long be off the scent. Not when Pergami is making it all so obvious."

"She is a nonpareil, then?" the viscount asked, one Englishman to another.

Sir Percy could not help but nod. "If it were only that. But she is a charmer as well. She has broken my heart. Lord Peters left yesterday when she refused him."

"She refused me as well!" Count Guido interrupted. "But I, I am made of sterner stuff. I try again and again. She must love me. I am very lovable. As well as being a count!"

The two fell to disputing who most deserved Angelica, when their claims were interrupted by the footman opening the door. In a trice the gentlemen were on the run toward a blond lady just entering. Obviously Angelica.

Any questions were dispelled by the princess herself. "Angelica, my pet, leave those mens and come to me."

Breaking away from the gentlemen huddling about her, including Bartolomeo, all taking their turns in kissing her hand, the blond lady smoothly disengaged herself and glided toward the princess. There she was warmly embraced and responded in kind. Her Highness ordered her to sit at her feet on a cushion and immediately Victorine was there, sitting on the other side.

"My two beauties," the princess said with pride. "I bask in their loveliness. The waves of admiration for them come drifting up to me. Ah, lovely! I feel the wanting. . . ."

Princess Caroline's gilt chair gave the illusion of a throne. It was situated atop four marble stairs that led to the terrace behind her. Thus the gentlemen were forced either to stand or sit on the bottom of those stairs gazing up. From that respectful distance, insisted on by the princess, they carried on conversations ostensibly with Her Highness but aimed at the two young ladies on either side of her.

Wolf neared. He even took out his quizzing glass. But next moment he was standing stock-still. Egad, he recognized her!

Fate indeed had called him there. After yearning to catch one more sight of the beauty on the boat, he'd been granted it. Unquestionably, this was she. The same aura of pale blond hair, but now worn up in a mass of ringlets. Without the dawn shades of gold and coral shooting round her, she ought to have been a disappointment. But she was not. She had her own colors. A deep blue of eyes that could not have been noticed from the distance. Step by step as he neared, led on by his dreams of his dawn lady, he observed more wonders. A skin of alabaster, perhaps wanting more color. Yet there was natural pink in her exquisitely shaped lips. But it was the eyes that most enchanted, as their glance swept around the room, looking for someone. Unbelievable, but his lordship felt in his heart she was searching for him, as all his life he had been searching for her. Why not? She was perfection and obviously he deserved that. No other lady in his memory was so exactly worthy. Yet he kept his steps slow, fearing she would either dissolve like a mirage, or of a sudden douse his expectations. Stepping out of the crowd of admirers at her feet, the viscount drew her attention. There was not the smallest sign of surprise at his coming toward her. Not even when he brashly, ignoring the protests of the other gentlemen, broke through the barrier of the stairs and came up. One, two, three, four, and he was standing close enough to take the beauty in his arms.

It was the princess who held him off. "Just womens up here," she said coldly. "Only when I calls, gentlemans can come up. I protect my darlings from your advances."

"Surely all these other gentlemen are known to your ladies-in-waiting," the viscount interposed in his calm, confident tone. "As a stranger, I call upon the rules of hospitality and request at least an introduction."

All the while his eyes were boring into the blue-lake eyes beneath him. Her downcast glance called something to mind, but he could not quite grasp it. She stood up then, resolutely facing him, as if doing her duty. Her expression was almost like a challenge.

"I have seen you before," he said to her insistently.

The lady's eyebrows went up in question. But she deliberately did not speak.

"Yes, I thought it was in my dreams, but it was a waking dream. You were on a boat at dawn this morning, were you not? You are the spirit of dawn herself. Aurora manifest. Made up of all the colors of the lake and sky and blazing morning sun."

Hillary laughed. "You have a courtier's tongue, I see. And a poet's eye. If we have experienced in common a moment of splendor," she said in a soft, musical English voice, "do you not conclude we should allow it to remain untouched?"

"Angelica?" he inquired, withdrawing his breath. "But are you *English?*"

"Is the dawn English? Or is she English to the English and Italian to the Italians. But Greek at heart."

Walking away from him, she allowed herself to be swallowed up by the admirers at the bottom of the stairs.

The viscount had to admit there was nothing in her to disappoint. Her manners, her charm, even her repartee bespoke an intelligence that enticed. He had to acknowledge himself instantly struck. The French, as usual, had a word for it—*coup d'amour.* Standing there, Wolf came to his senses suddenly and bowed to the princess.

He interpreted Her Highness's pleased expression as assuming that his admiration for her protégée had neutralized him and his reports. She was not far off the mark, for he was thinking, blast the prince and blast his mission! One look at that lady, and he realized he'd found a greater mission. Mayhap the mission of his life . . . at least temporarily.

Wolf continued to observe the lady. Her white net gown of ethereal delicacy extended the angelic impression begun by her halo of light blond hair. Her laughter, her delicate movements as she ordered her admirers here and there, clearly indicated she was everyone's darling. Lured onward, the viscount attempted to make a space for himself about her, but Count Guido pushed him aside. Rather than fighting or shoving, the viscount held back. Actually he did not wish to be part of a crowd. He had more subtle methods of snatching this prize from the group's jealous guardianship. It ought not be too difficult, for his lordship had a history of winning the most sought-after women. Obviously this case called for every ounce of his expertise. His first rule of thumbing ahead of the others was to stand back and have the lady seek him out. He sought Angelica with his deepest glance. To which the lady responded with a laugh, as if they shared a secret. Then almost immediately she went to the princess and whispered something, and then to others, including Pergami, the count, and even to Sir Percy. What she was arranging, Wolf felt in his soul, was a way to be allowed to be close to him. Perhaps it was his excess of pride speaking, but he knew of a sudden that her discussion was about him.

Yet after her turn among the people, which concluded with Victorine and Countess Oldi, the beauty, without looking back, left from the same doorway as she had entered. Had she merely been saying her good-nights? And so early? Was she not to go in to dinner with them? Her actions threw him a leveler. They were not what he'd expected, nor been prepared for. Possibly it was a tactic to whet his interest. If so, it was prodigiously successful, for she'd allowed only just enough view of her to make him eager for more before leaving.

Count Guido was casting him dark looks, as if he was the cause of her departure.

"Scared her off, old boy?" Sir Percy asked with a grin. "She does not usually retire so early. Something you said to her, old chap?"

"Nonsense," Wolf snapped.

"Must have taken you in disgust," Sir Percy continued.

"That's a load of gammon!" Refusing to waste his time debating with this minor noble, the viscount instead asked for vital information. "Who is she? What is her background? What other name does she have but Angelica?"

Sir Percy turned red and was silent. When pressed, he answered blithely, "Who knows? The princess does not address her by any other name. She is more interesting as a mystery, I expect."

"The devil she is!" Wolf growled. "I do not care for mysteries. Nor do I permit myself to be kept out of secrets. I shall discover all there is about her, for I already know her future. And that is with me."

"Strikes us all that way, old boy. Join the group. But she is unattainable. Pergami and Count Guido there have already been rejected and others who have been here and left. I, knowing I could not possibly be worthy of her, am just content to be in her presence. I write her poems, and she is good enough to correct them for me. She has an exquisite ear for rhyme. But then what does she not do with perfection? I'd hoped to read her my new ode tonight. But you sent her away." With as much of a threat as this small insignificant person could put in his tones, Sir Percy concluded, "I would ask you to absent yourself, henceforth. Obviously she has not taken to you and would prefer your departure."

The viscount laughed aloud at that. "Not bloody likely," he said. "I am here and shall be by her side for all time. Let her get accustomed to me, she shall never be without me again."

8

Mrs. Wizzle and Lady Gardener were awaiting Hillary when she returned. Both had the same anxious expression.

"No," Hillary answered their unspoken dread. "He didn't recognize me. Everybody was calling me Angelica, and he accepted that. Furthermore, he was very anxious to court me, casting the most obvious lures in my direction. At first I assumed he was shaming me, that he knew me, but then I realized he did not. So I whispered to the princess and to all, that they were not to reveal my real name to Viscount Wolverton."

"Heavens! How long do you expect so many people to keep mum? While only a trusted few are aware of your past relationship with the lord, everyone knows you as Miss Astaire!" Lady Gardener countered with disbelief.

"Yes, but recollect, everyone addresses me as Angelica, or at the most, Signorina Angelica. Even servants. As if this, well, masquerade, was inevitable."

"Why not be honest and say *hoax,*" Lady Gardener said with disapproval. "It's too ramshackle by half: Not only will someone slip, but he shall on second viewing recognize you."

Hillary merely shrugged. "Well, until either of those events occurs, I shall carry on with my adventure. The longer he remains in ignorance, the more astounded shall he be when the truth is revealed," she continued complacently.

She was humming a bit in the pleasure of the evening, when Mrs. Wizzle finally was able to speak. In a small confused voice she put in her objection. "But he will recognize me. I have not changed."

"Yes, and he has already seen me!" Lady Gardener exclaimed.

Hillary refused to be deterred. She was enjoying herself too much. The memory of the viscount's first indifferent reaction to her at Holly House was such a contrast to the wide-eyed desire in his eyes tonight, she was loath to bring his admiration to an end. "He expects to see you, dear Lady Gardener, after all, you are the princess's lady-in-waiting. And if he links us, faith! what is to be shall be!" Of a sudden her mischievous smile faded, and she shuddered. Both concerned ladies pressed for an explanation. "'Tis merely meeting him freshly brings back the pain of his comment to me in England. It oft returns to terrorize. He claimed I was in his complete control—my wealth, my very body. And soul."

Lady Gardener's eyes narrowed. "That lord deserves a salutary lesson. What gall! What pride!"

"Overweening pride," Hillary agreed. "To be frank, it is his own fault that he does not recognize me now. He scarce looked me in the face at our first encounter. Although I own, my hair was covered with my mourning cap and net. Yet he paid me no heed, so absorbed was he in preening about and examining the snuff in his box. *That* had precedence to condoling a young lady still suffering from the death of the man she loved most in her life! I was alone and lost. And this stranger walked in and offered me not even *civility*. To a kitten orphaned, one would show some gesture of regard. Rather he made clear I was not up to his snuff—so much lacking that he would not deign to introduce me to his set. But it was his next assessment that cast me down completely, hinting that I was a disgrace not only to him but to my own mother's memory."

Her voice caught at that, and the ladies rushed to console her. She was like an orphaned kitten to them. And the cavalier treatment of his lordship offended them to the quick.

"If he could be so cruel," Mrs. Wizzle whispered, "he deserves more than a mere twitting!"

Riled before, Lady Gardener was now beside herself. "To dare to use my dear Millicent's name. Ah, we shall show the bounder! Let him squirm, I shall enjoy every moment of his being gulled. Indeed, I believe it shall do him good. For never has anybody humbled his pride. He has been cock of the walk too long!"

"Pride cometh before the fall," Mrs. Wizzle agreed, nodding. "But I must absent myself."

"Yes, dear Wizzie," Hillary agreed. "I espy you are developing a slight megrim and shall take to your room for a day or two. By then either someone shall

inform him or the brilliance of Lord Wolverton shall
finally surface to put two and two together."

The three ladies agreed, as did Princess Caroline
next morning when Lady Gardener discussed the
situation with her. So amused by the maygame they
would be playing on her husband's spy, the danger
was that Her Highness might too wholeheartedly
jump into the imposture. She was in accord with
Angelica that her having been introduced to all by
her pet name clearly meant this gulling of his lordship was preordained. But to ensure the secret
being kept as long as possible, the princess put out
the obligatory orders and bribes. Her only fear was
herself. Most likely she would give everything away
if she remained, being unable to cease giggling,
which must necessarily rouse suspicion. It would
be a most felicitous moment to take a trip to
Austria and France that had long been in the planning. In a trice, the princess ordered her trunks
packed. Her Highness was always off on the spur of
the moment. Once, Lady Gardener remembered, at
the start of Her Highness's own dinner party, after
looking round at the faces, she decreed them all
"monstrous fatigues" and before the soup course
was complete had called for their carriages, while
she went off to see a play. It was such behavior that
had pronounced the royal lady flighty. But the real
reason for Caroline's volatility was after being the
much-petted princess of Brunswick, she'd arrived
in England to find herself enduring years of cold,
superficial English civility. New people in new
places she continued to believe would greet her
with the affection she remembered. That explained
her eagerness to travel. But this time she had a
double reason. It would be for Angelica, for whom

she would go to further lengths than to another country.

But Her Highness did not escape before the viscount's confrontation, questioning her imminent departure. In a typical bold stroke, the princess invited him to come along. "You cannot spy without the lady you are spying on. Yes? Come to France and watch me. Who knows? I may discover a French gentleman and allow him to escort me in to dinner. *Tiens,* Frenchmen have a habit of pinching a lady's hand. To tell the truth, I have many a bruise from the Italians as well, but would not show you the bruise spots lest you report to the great Mahomet I have been attempting to seduce you. Yes?"

"No, madam. I am no longer interested in any of the regent's suspicions. I have my own reasons for wishing either to remain here or go with you, depending on whether a certain lady is to be in your company."

"Ah, you mean my dear Angelica! But what is this you are tell me? You are not to cast lures at my angel." And the royal lady shook her finger at him sternly. "She is a pure soul. No tainting, please."

"On my honor, I shall treat her as she deserves, with the greatest of awe and tender reverence."

"Hmm. Well, she is to stay here with Victorine and Countess Oldi to protect her, and of course Lady Gardener, so I have no fear that you will disgrace her. I shall in fact appoint Bartolomeo to stand guard. He shall do it with all his soul and devotion."

"Perhaps more devotion than you would wish," the viscount snapped, with a warning look.

"He shall not touch her. He is a kind gentleman."

"We are all gentlemen, madam."

"But not *kind*. Englishmen are cold and cruel and concerned only with their own wants."

"I want that lady," he admitted with an openness the princess could not but admire. "But she must want me as well. Love is not worth a jot if it is one-sided."

"*Nein!* Most men have one-sided love. They love one person always—themselves."

It was not in the viscount's interest to spar over that point, but rather, keeping to his objective, he said softly, "I have never before seen a young lady of such perfection. She humbles me, I admit. Does that sound like self-love?"

Her Highness was pleased at this change in the gentleman. His anguished expression reached her impressionable heart, especially as this young, magnificent-looking lord was moving closer to her in his need. Ought she to give him a hint of Hillary's identity? His gray eyes cast an impassioned appeal that made Princess Caroline waver, at which point Lady Gardener approached and the princess recovered enough to move away from him.

Flushing from the effect on her of his masculinity, she wondered how the sweet and untried Hillary could compete against such an experienced flirt.

"Whatever you wish, you must ask her ladyship," the princess said, stiffened by having Lady Gardener at her side. "I leave her in complete control of both my young ladies."

The viscount turned to face Lady Gardener's mulish look and realized he would have been more successful with the susceptible princess. That English lady would clearly be an obstacle in the race he'd set for himself. Nevertheless, he was ever best when challenged, he concluded with a grin. In the distance Angelica had come to bid adieu to the princess. The scene was one of many kisses and hugs. Upon the several carriages departing, Angelica walked back to the terrace to hold on to the last view of the carriages disappearing into the horizon.

"You are not being left alone," a voice whispered to her.

She turned and saw the viscount at her side.

He was momentarily without his polished pose as the close sight of her struck him breathless.

"I offer my services as your escort for a boat ride— this time to view the sun's setting," he said eagerly.

Hillary demurred, claiming she always preferred beginnings, some interims, but never conclusions. "That is why I do not care for marriage. That is such a sad conclusion, do you not think?"

The viscount was astounded. Never had he heard a lady not longing for marriage for herself and all her fellow women.

"I knew you were unique. Indeed, I have always found myself shying away from even the mere mention of marriage. We are in accord there, I expect."

"Also," she continued, playfully, "I find any union an ending. Especially for a gentleman and lady. They should just joust a bit, and then separate and *never be together.*"

"There are some unions that are deucedly pleasant. Say a kiss?"

"I have not found kisses living up to all that has been written about them."

"You have not been kissed by the proper person."

"Or an improper one?" she teased.

"Indeed, a very improper one," he laughed.

"Properly speaking, a kiss should never be exchanged without deep love. But who really loves?

Even Count Guido, who claims he wishes to marry me and kiss me, would he do so if I did not have a small independence?"

"He would if he were not blind. But all the men about you are blinded by your beauty, my dear lady. So you must be kindness itself to us all, for you have wounded us by mere sight."

Hillary laughed. "I gather you are highly accomplished in the practiced art of flattery."

"It is not art when it comes from the heart," he said seriously.

Shaking him off with a wave of her hand, Hillary refused to accept his earnestness. Rather she joined Victorine, who was rushing to relay some jolly news. Her father and Countess Oldi were taking them to see a miracle. Wasn't that exciting?

Hillary rejoiced with her friend. In a moment Pergami strode up all smiles.

"We are off!" he said, his voice bellowing to the mountains.

Countess Oldi was hurrying to keep up with his strides. The ladies skipped after, quickly donning their bonnets brought by the maids. Bringing up the rear was the viscount.

At the carriage Bartolomeo was astounded that the viscount had the audacity to assume he was included in the jaunt.

To his affronted glance, his lordship countered airily, "But I was given leave by the princess to pay my addresses to her protégée as long as I obeyed the proprieties." His eyes twinkling, he added, "And your very large presence should be sufficient for that!"

"But no! You misunderstood the princess! *I* am paying my address to Angelica!"

"Dashed fine, we shall pay them together and see which one the young lady prefers. Is that not sporting?"

The huge man frowned. "You make this a sporting bet? Is it not a disgrace to bet on whether a lady gives her favors or not?"

"Certainly that is a disgrace. How could you even suggest it? I mean we duel to be her champion."

"I do not have my sword!"

"We use wits, old boy. And while you may not have those along either, you'll have to make do."

While Bartolomeo was considering, the viscount had found his place in the large barouche sitting forward and gazing at the ladies sitting opposite him. Pergami lumbered in and sat next to the viscount.

"Aren't we cozy?" Wolf asked affably. Catching Hillary's amused glance, he had the presumption to wink at her. "Now," he asked expansively, "what is this miracle we are going to witness?"

"I expect," Hillary said, "the real miracle of this jaunt shall be squelching your audacity."

Wolf just grinned at his lady. "It is one of my most endearing traits."

"So you think," she said, but she had to laugh, as did he in sheer delight at being with her.

In fact his glance was unswervingly fixed on her face through every pace ahead, his grin growing wider and wider.

9

The ride continued long enough to fatigue Countess Oldi.

"Is it much farther, Papa?" Victorine demanded. "Auntie is beginning to feel the discomfort."

"We are almost there!" He looked at his sister. "You need to walk a bit? As the English say, go for a constitutional and relax the legs?" Then recollecting that not only did she not speak but could scarce understand English, he turned it to Italian. She shook her head, but said something, which caused him to look at the viscount and frown.

"Thank you for the consideration," Wolf could not resist interjecting, "but I do not wish to avail myself of a walk. Perhaps our dear young ladies would wish to? I should be most honored to give them both my arms."

"That should leave you properly defenseless!" Hillary quickly responded, her eyes twinkling.

"Not a bit of it," he reparteed with an appreciative laugh. "A gentlemen is doubly strengthened when he has a beautiful lady *in* his arms . . . or, somewhat less revitalizing, *on* his arm."

"Curious. I always feel revitalized when I'm at least an arm's length away from encroaching gentlemen."

"Encroaching! Merely because I wished to see the miracle? Once having seen one miracle, you realize, one develops a habit for them and cannot see enough."

Hillary looked down so he would not see her smile. She gathered he was attempting to flatter her blatantly and would not encourage him, not under the fulminating glances of Bartolomeo.

But the viscount would not let her ignore his meaning. "You do not ask what the first miracle was that I witnessed upon arriving at Lake Como. That suggests you already know. But I shall be specific, for I challenge this second one to come anywhere near the first. It was the view of a goddess of dawn on a boat—she was all shades of dawn—yellow, coral, pink, and then as the sun fully rose she was a particle of that very sun—all golden—a golden goddess everyone calls Angelica. But what is her last name? Or are you like Aphrodite and Aurora and Athena—known only by one name?"

"It is better to have one name and that a gentle one than to be entitled a predator."

His laugh startled the rest, who did not comprehend their byplay. "A wolf is not a predator. He is a noble beast. And quite faithful. Once mated, he mates for life, and if he loses his love will pine away for her."

"How unlike you he is, then. I have heard you prefer a pack of female followers."

"I am maligned. By the princess? Recollect she and I are on opposite sides of the royal duel. I'd be most obliged if you would believe not above half said of me by those of that camp!"

Hillary raised an eyebrow in surprise. "I think you fail to realize the obvious. Clearly I, too, am of the opposite camp. For I am devoted to the princess and can personally attest that the rumors against her are false . . . as you yourself must have realized within five minutes of being here."

The viscount, not wishing to commit himself, temporized, "One must not necessarily believe what is placed before one. The truth is often buried behind much pretense."

Hillary flushed, realizing that related to herself as well, and decided to test him. "But are you so discriminating? Do you always see the truth when it is staring you in the face? Or can you be gulled by the greatest blinder of all—self-absorption? Ah, yes, I daresay you might miss many a miracle before your very eyes while devoting yourself, for instance, to examining your snuffbox?"

The viscount was confused. Clearly she had some peeve against him? But what? He had never been so impolite as to turn his back on her to take snuff! Obviously something spread against him by Lady Gardener!

Leaning closer, he said earnestly, "You must not allow calumnies to poison your mind against me. Whatever was done to others could never relate to you. I would as soon look away from you as I would the most beauteous star."

"Gammon," Hillary countered, refusing to be reached by his courtly ways.

He would have pressed his point as he was now

reaching over to press her hand, when Countess Oldi garumphed loudly and gave him such a look, he remembered himself and instantly released the hand.

Egad, it was impossible to court her surrounded on all sides by jealous, suspicious guardians who, while not quite understanding his words, obviously fully understood his intentions.

In a few moments, just as the viscount was preparing for a second round in his game of bantering with the beauty, Pergami began to talk, feeling it was his turn.

Hillary agreed he must have his moment and gave him her full attention, and the English lord her profile.

Lord Wolverton was content for a while simply to gaze at it. He could not believe that each time he saw that lady, rather than not living up to his expectations, she always exceeded them. Today he was amused by her wit, as well as by the way she shone seated between the two dark ladies on either side. This despite her golden locks being covered, except for a few fluttering ringlets, by a wide-brimmed leghorn straw hat. It tied under the chin with a long blue satin ribbon that flirted with the breezes. That blue ribbon was ubiquitous as more of it belted her white muslin gown and wove itself through the ruffles of her parasol.

Countess Oldi was frequently ordering her to hold that fluffy umbrella up against the sun, but the young lady inevitably let it down to feel the wind. That pleased Wolf. He found nothing so boring as ladies possessing noticeably less beauty than Angelica's considering their looks of principal importance. One must not crush their dresses or disarrange their hair! These women were usually the kind who even in the midst of an embrace were concerned not only with their appearance but with appearances. Undoubtedly this young lady who wholeheartedly gave herself up to worshiping the sun on the boat and even now was abandoning herself to nature would make an ideal partner in pleasure.

Sensing his glance, Hillary returned it openly, without any subterfuge. She read his passion for her in his stare and was brazen enough to want to bask in it, taking a long draught, then, and only then, looking away. She shook her head as if wishing to shake away the memory, but he exultantly felt he'd made his mark. A slight flush in her face showed she was still thinking of him.

But next moment the baron's flatteries made her smile. A less experienced seducer might have been disheartened by that, but the viscount knew the difference between a tolerant smile and a disconcerted blush, and of the two he vastly preferred being the cause of the second.

The huge man, speaking loudly as if serenading from under her window although they were only a foot or so apart, was gallantly equating her to the glorious sights of Italy. Indeed, he claimed, the beauty of Italy had been enhanced by her presence. He could not believe an Englishwoman could have so much life in her. She must be "Italian at heart."

With amusement in her eyes, Hillary agreed that she felt at least half Italian. "For truly I only came to life upon my arrival here. Almost as if I were reborn and rechristened at Lake Como."

That was heartily approved of by the Italians. Bartolomeo repeated it in Italian for Countess Oldi, who embraced the young lady in response. Victorine had already embraced her, and Bartolomeo was almost an inch from doing so as well, when Victorine refused to give up her place, and so he wound up embracing her instead.

"Very prettily said. All the charm of a true ambassadress," the viscount approved tolerantly, but he was staring at her with some speculation. "What do you mean rechristened?"

"We are here!" Pergami exclaimed and stood up, indicating with his long arms and wide expansive gestures their destination.

A timely arrival, Hillary thought, and turned in expectation only to cast an astonished glance at Bartolomeo. Hurriedly he assured them that they would soon see it was worth the long ride.

The viscount was amused. In a country renowned for its vistas and monumental buildings, why had this bumbler brought them through miles of long roads, farm fields, and grassy meadows to a tumbledown old rookery? It was called Palazzo Simonetti and was shockingly ramshackle. Its occupants were a family of ragged Italians who had a most satisfactory discussion with Pergami that culminated with the passing of enough lire to warrant the most enthusiastic welcome.

"I will lead you all!" Bartolomeo exclaimed. "We do not need the guide, for I myself know the way and will show you this miracle, yes? It will be more amusing between us? *Sì?*"

Everyone but the viscount agreed. Countess Oldi objected to having to walk up to the second floor and needed her brother's arm. Victorine was positioned behind for support. The viscount moved quickly to have the leading of Angelica up the narrow, cracked steps, but she refused his assistance,

ascending on her own. That gave the viscount
pause. A lady would expect a gentleman to escort
her in that manner. Actually if a gentleman did not,
she would consider it a gross incivility, tantamount
to allowing a door to slam in her face. Yet Angelica
did not expect such gallantries. This made the viscount suspect she was somebody's beautiful by-blow
being given some respectability by the princess, who
never cared for such things, having adopted the
most unsuitable people. That conclusion was the
first chink in Angelica's armor. Not being worthy of
his rank meant he was free to dally with her. Even
her open ways to nature, which he had just found
so pleasing, signified she was too free and easy, or
in short, she was simply not of his class. Quite possibly that explained why her name was kept a mystery, for it might reveal the plebeian seed from
which she'd sprung.

Arriving en masse on the second floor, Hillary
turned to find the viscount gazing at her with a different attitude. But next moment she was distracted by the countess demanding they all fan her
to renew the breath she'd lost climbing. Having
done so, Hillary was free to turn back to Lord
Wolverton. His expression was unnerving, as if considering exactly how to make use of her. Her face
blanched, wondering if he'd recognized her. But his
next gesture showed that, far from remembering
the lady, he was acting as if she were not even a
lady. While leading her to the window where obviously the miracle was to be enacted, he held on to
her, as if they were handfasted. Indeed, as they
walked, she felt him closer than was seemly. His
body, with supposed inadvertence, bumped against
hers. With fixed attention Wolf waited to see her

reaction to that intrusion of her space. If she smiled, he would pounce. If she objected, he would bide his time.

Hillary did neither. Rather she looked concerned. "Are you feeling quite the thing, my lord? Perhaps the stairs were too high for you? I knew a lady who suffered just such imbalance the moment she found herself at any height."

Uncertain whether she was rallying or really sympathetic, the viscount could only deny and assure her of being quite in control of himself. The latter being untrue. She had clearly thrown him a facer! Once more he was uncertain of not only who she was, but what.

Meanwhile gathering everyone about him, Bartolomeo was insisting on their attention as he was ready to perform.

"Egad! Have we come all this way to hear *you?*" the viscount exclaimed. "I expect we could do that back at Lake Como."

"You were not asked to come! You push yourself in! You are not happy? You need not stay to experience this wonder with us. Wait in the carriage!" he boomed. But Lord Wolverton, smiling, insisted he would not dream of missing one word of the dear baron's. "I am riveted," he said silkily.

"Hmpf," the baron responded. Turning to the women, he smiled and said loudly, "Now, listen!"

Then putting his head out of the window, he leaned forward precariously. The viscount hoped he would fall. Countess Oldi and Victorine feared he might, and ran to pull him back. Distracted, the baron was forced to pull in his head to assure them he was safe and then had to begin all over again, leaning far, far out.

Hillary, having come close, noted that below them was a courtyard walled on three sides by tall buildings.

"Pergami!" Bartolomeo Pergami shouted down.

A loud, rolling echo repeated his name and went on and on and on, flooding them with the sounds of it. Nothing seemed to still it or wear it out. They were all awash in the repetition of his name. He pulled in and looked delightedly at them. Victorine and Countess Oldi were pleased, clapping at his performance with much gusto. Hillary was smiling, agreeing that it was certainly a prodigious echo. The viscount, raising one eyebrow, put out his hand to escort the lady of his choice back down the perilous steps. He was considering picking her up in his arms and seeing if she'd allow that familiarity, when they were stopped by the baron insisting the performance was not over. Now he had a speaking trumpet and through it he sent out a single but booming "Ha!"

In response they were suddenly overrun by laughter. "*Ha! Ha! Ha!* . . . *Ha!* . . . *Ha!* . . . Ha! . . . Ha! . . . ha—haaa! . . . haaaaaaaaaaaaaaa . . ." It couldn't be stopped. The echo was laughing and laughing, so loud and so long and such a flood of delight and jollity and so contagious that before they knew it, everyone was joining in. Bartolomeo had begun first and was by now convulsed on the floor. Victorine was giggling and hiccuping in her response. Even Countess Oldi was guffawing. Hillary was jumping into the laughter as she would the sea—laughing and throwing back her head. And still the ha-ha-has were swarming about. There was no resisting. Astonished, the viscount found himself grinning and then surrendering, laughing along, taking

Hillary's hands as they joyed in the moment, while Victorine danced about them. All were uncontrollably frolicking to the tune of the rollicking laughter.

When the echo finally stilled, they all looked at each other, tears in some eyes and others shaking their heads in disbelief at such a catharsis of mirth.

"Truly amazing," Hillary approved. "I have not laughed so long and so loud since . . ." She caught herself and altered what she was going to say. "Since I was a child. Surely this is good medicine for the most despondent souls."

"I admit it is unique," Lord Wolverton agreed. "Most enjoyable. Ought to take the starch out of the stiffest personages, I daresay."

"Yes," Hillary agreed. "What a capital solution for all the world's problems. We must bring the Prince Regent here to see if he could relax enough to allow the rest of us to live without exalting his royal self."

Unwilling to ruin this moment with their difference, the viscount switched to a political situation on which both agreed. "An apt response to the Austrians strictly ruling this region. They are in desperate need of the ease of a laugh."

Bartolomeo overhearing that stopped midguffaw. "It is not sufficient to give those devils a laugh," he thundered. "One must give them this!"

At that moment he pulled a pistol out of his belt and, going to the window, fired it.

"No! Stop!" Victorine had called, sensing what would come, and Hillary as well. Countess Oldi was merely confused, and the viscount amused.

But Victorine's fears were justified. An explosion of gunshots followed, as if they were in the midst of a revolution. The baron was standing satisfied at having demonstrated what he would do to the Austrians.

But in a moment, the local guards arrived, pistols out, seeking the culprit who had started the firing. All was confusion as Pergami and the echo continued the reverberating shots. Beneath the window, town residents were congregating in much alarm. Countess Oldi was overcome, and had to be led away by Victorine, while Pergami was rushing ahead to appease the guards with more lire and the people with a ringing, anti-Austrian speech, which brought cheers as loud as the sounds of shooting.

Hillary had covered her ears. She was astounded by the way the waves of violent sounds had alarmed her. Not that she felt faint. She prided herself on never being so weak, but she was overcome. Next moment she felt the support of the viscount's arms. He was holding her in his embrace, closely, fiercely, and as the shots had rung round, she felt the need to trust herself completely to this comfort. The penetrating gray eyes were so close to hers, she could not turn away. Then as his mouth sought hers and he kissed her deeply, she could only rest in the peace of that.

Then there was silence.

Hillary opened her eyes from the rush of pleasure and terror and delight and passion that had overwhelmed her to find herself looking into the triumphant eyes of the predatory gentleman. She knew she should pull away, and made a weak effort to do so. But he would not allow it. "We have been saluted. Our union has been blessed. We are meant to be one forever," he whispered, leaning over to take her lips again. But the haughty assurance reminded her of his eyes at Holly House. Further, he made quite an unfortunate use of almost similar words, words that had infuriated and goaded

Hillary for months. "Henceforth, you are mine. Your soul, your heart . . . your very self!"

Pulling away, Hillary rushed to lean out the window. "No!" she shouted decisively. And the echo accommodatingly rejected him for her, over and over and over again. "No, no, no, no!" while she laughed at his shock and went running down the stairs on her own.

The viscount turned to look out the window. The echo was still taunting him with its "No!" Unhurriedly he waited it out, and then, picking up the speaking trumpet, shouted the loudest "Yes!" ever heard.

From downstairs Hillary stiffened in reaction and some of her triumph faded. But then Pergami distracted her by reproachfully claiming he'd planned to shout her name and urging her to ascend to hear that tribute when the viscount appeared at their side. "A lady does not wish her name bandied about. Unless, of course, she is not a lady," he said, looking purposely at Hillary.

Undeterred by that insinuation, and turning to give her hand to the baron, the lady responded placidly, "Who and what I am is still a mystery. But what you are, Lord Wolverton, has been fully revealed. A true gentleman would never have taken advantage of a lady's senses being disordered by her alarm. Pity. One had such hopes that the reports about you were untrue."

Countess Oldi, arriving, had to be helped into the carriage, so Pergami overheard only enough to realize his beautiful Angelica was displeased with the Englishman, and that lifted his spirits considerably, so much so that as they rode away, he began to imitate the echo's ha-ha-ha, reviving their laughter. All were lightheartedly reliving the moment except the viscount, who was still recollecting Angelica's dismissal. Chagrined and chastened, he wondered if his assessment of the lady had been too hasty. She refused to give him even a glance throughout the ride home. Nor would she allow him to hand her down, but waited for Bartolomeo to have that honor.

"Nevertheless," Wolf whispered as she swept by, "we have kissed. Our souls have met. You cannot ignore that."

"Ha!" Hillary said shortly as she entered the palace, stopping to pronounce coldly, "All echoes fade at last and we are left merely to laugh at their memory."

Yet that night the viscount, musing over their shared passion, vowed he would repeat their kiss as many times as the echo had sounded . . . kiss upon kiss . . . kiss . . . kiss. . . .

10

One *acceptable passion* that Hillary had formed at Lake Como was for chestnuts. So many chestnut trees about, the people turned to their nuts as a free supplement for their meals. They roasted them, toasted them—ate them as snacks, added them to main dishes, usually with chicken, or sweetened them with syrup for dessert. Bartolomeo had discovered her weakness and arranged for Victorine and Hillary to take a drive through the thickest grove halfway up the hill in a glen behind the princess's palace. He was delighted that the viscount had not gotten wind of that excursion, but Count Guido had. That gave Pergami some competition, but another Italian as a rival was tolerable, especially one so young and uncertain how to really woo a lady. Far from tolerable was that English lord with his lifted eyebrows and cold gray

eyes and his reputation for winning the most
unattainable ladies. So it was with much relief that
Bartolomeo rushed his two young ladies into the
carriage. Countess Oldi refused to accompany
them, claiming she was still deafened from the gunshots echoing all night in her head. Propriety was
sufficiently preserved by the ever-willing newlyweds, Gina, the maid and Antonio, the driver.

At the forest destination, the two ladies ran
about collecting, until Bartolomeo claimed they'd
wandered too far from the carriage and he must
find Antonio to bring it closer. Not attending, the
ladies continued filling their straw baskets with the
fallen chestnuts, reddish brown and shiny.

Hillary compared the color to Victorine's eyes,
and Count Guido was astonished by the exactitude
of the shade. He had Victorine stand holding two
chestnuts directly under her eyes, while he made
the official comparison. Finally, when the young
lady had turned quite pink from his close personal
observation, he ruled it was true. She had chestnut
eyes!

Something had passed between the two as Count
Guido was examining her, and Hillary caught it and
was delighted. Not only would she then be rid of a
persistent and plaguey cavalier, but Victorine
would have an unexceptionable admirer.

To advance that relationship, Hillary announced
that she and Gina would explore the beckoning
watery sounds behind. Count Guido and Victorine,
absorbed in the discovery of their emotions for
each other, did not respond, so Hillary and Gina
wandered off. Around the bend was the delightful
surprise of a waterfall and its ripply pool. Hillary sat
down on the rock edge and watched the cooling

descent. Instantly Gina removed her shoes and
waded. Tempted, and looking about, Hillary considered doing as much. A shockingly unladylike action
to say the least, but with Gina urging her to join in
and no one about to observe, Hillary removed both
her shoes and stockings and, lifting the hem of her
elegant green gown, allowed her toes to touch the
sparkling water. She shrieked at the cold and stood
at the edge. Gina, having concluded her dip, was
returning to assure the proprieties between Count
Guido and Victorine. As no gentleman was in the
vicinity of Angelica, her chaperon services were not
needed. She was off.

Alone, Hillary looked up at the blue, blue Italian
sky. This small pond had made a hole in the cluster
of chestnut and laurel trees. One could see the sky
and in the distance the tops of the mountains hovering like guardians. The overhanging trees sufficiently shaded her from the sun, so she removed
her small chip straw bonnet that prohibited the
waterfall's breeze from cooling her head. Another
step into the pond caused her to lift her dress even
higher. Her blond hair was caught up by the wind
and fell out of the neat crown into a mass of ringlets
running wild around her head and flowing about
her like a golden cape. Ah, this was pleasure. To be
alone for the first time since coming to Italy. No gal-
lants, no guardians, no mother substitutes, no footmen, no traveling Englishmen to be entertained, no
natives judging her as not being one of them.
Naught but the waterfall, the trees, the skies, and
the mountains. She wished to gambol through the
water but knew her time was limited. They would
be seeking her soon. It would only be proper to
return before her absence caused comment. If she

were Eve alone in this paradise, she would dip without a stitch! Or since there was a limit to how bibli-
cally accurate an English lady ought to be, even in
her fantasies, she amended that to imagining herself stripped down to her petticoat with enough
skin unclothed to be reached and cooled by the icy
water. Then she would dry off by sunning on the
rocks until she could return to her existence,
soothed of all her wild, wanton ways. The night
before, she had found herself unable to sleep for
the feelings the viscount had roused in her. For
shame—not only had she let him kiss her without
castigating him for that indecency, but she'd
floated in the feel of that emotion, much as today
she wished to drift in the water. Of a sudden Hillary
reached up her hands to the sky, wanting to float
up there as well. Pleasure. Moments of pure, undi-
luted, self-indulgent delight.

"You are back to being a water nymph today, I
gather," came a soft voice.

Hillary almost lost her footing in her panicky
attempt to rush back to the safety of the bank. Lord
Wolverton was there, watching. He had caught her
pretending to be a nymph.

She laughed, embarrassed, yet wishing to carry
it off.

"What are *you* doing here? This is a secret place
where I supposed no one could find me."

"I shall always be able to find you. I merely follow
my longing, and it leads naturally to you."

He was reaching down to lift her up. She shook
him off, but he insisted on taking her hand and
holding hard. Allowing him to hand her up, she
soon discovered he was not being just gentlemanly.
Rather his lordship was using the occasion to pull

her directly into his arms, placing one hand through her curls, behind her neck, pulling her astonished face closer to his.

"You have the longest eyelashes I've ever seen. One is not aware, for they are so light until one has you this close. How many more wonders shall I discover in this face-to-face examination?"

Before she could reply or deny, he had kissed her again. The same surge of warmth surprised as it had that day at the echo. Having been cooled by the water, now she was thoroughly heated again. And then as he persisted, with kiss upon kiss, waves of feelings shook them both.

This handling was an intolerable insult, her brain was insisting. She attempted not to listen as the flooding of all her senses wiped out her sense of decency. But not quite. It woke her, broke her out of his arms, and sent her running barefoot back to the others.

First she came upon Gina. "I heard a noise," Hillary invented. "It frightened me. I forgot my shoes."

Bobbing a curtsy, Gina went quickly to retrieve them. A few feet away Victorine and Count Guido were picking flowers. Pulling a handful herself, Hillary used that as the excuse for her disappearance and disordered state. Gina was back with her shoes. That woman's usual sly smile had broadened, which made Hillary wonder if she'd seen the viscount. With all the indifference she could muster, she asked whether there'd been anyone else at the clearing. Gina, almost giggling, assured her she had seen no one, but that did not mean no one had been there. Hillary frowned at this deliberate obfuscation. But before she could properly fret about it, the baron was back, urging them into the carriage.

"Enough nuttiness!" he proclaimed. And only Hillary grinned, as the rest picked up their baskets of nuts and rushed toward the waiting carriage. Hillary dropped her flowers, not wanting any memory of the day.

As the carriage drove away, a tall, elegant Englishman stepped out onto the road. With a contented smile, he picked up one of the flowers the lady had tossed away and pocketed it. Bemused, he asked himself softly, "Is she real or a fantasy? Am I awake or asleep?"

Nevertheless while his gray eyes were inner-lit with the passion of the experience, his English sense was faulting the lady for her wild ways. A disapproving shake of his head belied the yearning the rest of him felt for the lady. She was such a paradox with the abandoned kisses of a ladybird and then darting away like a frightened, inexperienced miss. She had him floored at all points. Following the carriage on his horse, Wolf kept enough distance between them not to be readily observed. He no longer had a plan, he was just following her, needing to be constantly revived by the sight and nearness of her. Eventually the carriage stopped at another palace. This one was half in ruins. Bartolomeo was giving them a tour of what had once been a Roman site.

With an eager smile, Wolf descended, pleased he would have one more shot at her today. Alert and on the hunt once more, he intended to join their expedition and remind the fair Angelica whose she was. Not the young count's. Not the old baron's. Not anyone else's, but his. He had unequivocally staked his claim.

Hillary had often seen the Villa Pliniana from a

distance. The house of white marble with its magnificent colonnade gave one the sensation of walking back to the age of Roman glory. She wistfully wandered through the apartments, this time sticking closely to Victorine, although presumably the viscount had been left some distance behind. Still, it paid to be on guard. And she was, until the view from the terrace made her forget all but its magnificence. Stepping to the banister, she looked down at the silver lake, across to the mountains, and then directly ahead, catching her breath at the giant cypress trees like pillars upholding the sky.

"I could spend my life here gazing at this view," she whispered.

"I shall buy it for you," came a cool, crisp voice from just behind her.

Hillary turned in alarm. "You again!" The moment she'd relaxed, he appeared. "Blast you, are you a phantom? Good God, stop following me!"

Moving quickly Hillary joined Victorine, and the two responded to Pergami's shouting for their company. A fleeting glance back showed her the lord was no longer there, and Hillary relaxed. Next moment she looked again, having a dread sensation he'd been there only in her imagination.

"Why doesn't anyone live here?" Hillary asked.

"Only crazy people and English poets would like here," said Count Guido with a decided sniff of disapproval. "An English poet last year, Belley or Shelley, sought it, but he went to Livorno—cheaper there. Rich Italians want villas that do not fall apart with every step. Only English think ruins are romantic."

"An ancient Italian, Pliny, lived here," Bartolomeo interrupted, squelching the count for attempting to take over his position as guide. "It is all here as he created, down to the crazy fountain in the courtyard that flows every three hours. I check. It is quiet now."

Count Guido, still sneering, claimed naught in the palazzo was worthy of notice. But when Victorine noticed a mosaic mantelpiece, Count Guido decided to notice it as well, following after. Hillary was remaining close to Bartolomeo to ward off the sudden appearance of a certain British lord. But Lord Wolverton was content to remain hidden, for he was indeed attempting to throw Angelica off-balance by his appearance and disappearance. He wanted her shaken enough to reveal her true self. At first he'd been prepared to believe she was a lady of some consequence due to her position. But the prince had given him the names of several Italian investigators that the viscount intended to use if his own detecting failed. He flattered himself he was not such a slowtop that he could not soon see through the lady's disguise. Already he was suspicious of the wall of silence that sprang up whenever he probed into her past—so thick not even a fistful of lire could break through. Obviously someone had bought that silence. "Smoky," Wolf thought. That would only be the case if her background were not what it should be. Baseborn at the best. Possibly, egad, even a *courtesan* set up by the princess to entrap him and discover the Prince Regent's plans. But he would outfox them.

With a mocking gleam in his eye, he walked directly into Pergami, knocking the fellow aside.

Bartolomeo let out an oath. The viscount instantly bowed and offered a formal and flowery apology, wishing to be assured he had not injured the gentleman. Naturally the baron claimed he had not been hurt, this despite the viscount's having stamped down hard on his polished, booted toes.

"But are you certain, my dear sir, that I have not injured you in any way? It would devastate me if I were the instrument of bringing you even the slightest bit of pain . . . or discomfort."

Again Baron Bart assured him he'd escaped unhurt, but he was beginning to resent the overly solicitous attitude, as if the young lord were viewing him as a fragile, nay, infirm old man.

"It would take a ton of you gentlemans to bruise me," he said with a laugh, looking to Hillary for her agreement.

She was neither looking nor listening to Bartolomeo. The viscount's appearance had caught her complete attention. Her hackles had risen. She was one step from imitating the Italians and crossing herself in protection.

Lord Wolverton continued his elaborate charade. Had the beauteous Angelica been herself in any way discommoded? He suspected that she was rather peeved with him—what could possibly be the cause? "A lady of such obvious gentility who never goes beyond the line in her behavior would naturally be put out of countenance by the slightest deviation from dignity."

Hillary flushed at his blatant barbs.

"Actually I *am* rather disappointed in you, my lord," she said coldly. "A gentleman should be more considerate. I feel you revel in stepping on people's toes. Did you pull the wings off flies when you were young or do you still do so?"

His eyes twinkling, Wolf countered, "You wound me. I never disrobe even an insect. Unless it is a female. Then of course one must give in to one's senses."

Confused at the discussion, Pergami put in, "But how can one tell a female from a male fly?"

"Ah," the viscount turned to him and just keeping his lips from trembling, he said as seriously as he could, "But one can always tell a female of any species. She is the one who pretends to run away and always looks over her shoulder to see if she is being followed."

Forgetting his objective in wooing Angelica, the male in Bartolomeo could not resist responding to that with a loud guffaw.

Hillary was disgusted with both of them. Was this really their way of courting—by criticizing not just her but her entire sex? "You are mistaken. One can tell a female because unlike the male she is usually busy doing something, while the male is basking in his own self-importance, imagining that the woman rushing away from him is actually calling him to follow. That is why so many men wind up with smashed noses from the doors being shut in their faces."

Spotting Gina, Hillary requested that the woman accompany her to the carriage, for she was weary of seeing the sights. "Baron, I expect you will notice Victorine and her escort are no where to be seen. Despite your attitude toward women, I do not think you would willingly leave your daughter to Count Guido's unsupervised attentions—they have become rather marked on this outing."

Alarmed at that hint, the baron quickly bowed and went searching for his daughter and the seducing count. Hillary and Gina had descended to the lower level and were reaching the gardens beyond which was the protection of the carriage and Gina's husband, the driver, Antonio. But in the next instant, Wolf was beside her. It was typical of his audacity that he dared to signal Gina away, but what shocked Hillary to the core was that Gina obeyed him, despite her own orders that she remain!

"Ah, now it becomes clear!" Hillary cried with fury at being deserted and facing down the lord. "You've paid her! How else did you know exactly where we'd be!"

"The world loves a lover, especially Italians," the viscount said smoothly, shrugging. Taking her by the elbow he directed her through the courtyard to a bench.

"I will not sit with you!" she exclaimed.

"Come, you know as a gentleman I cannot sit while you stand, and I am most fatigued. Chasing you through this rubble has been the very devil!"

"You are the very devil!" Hillary exclaimed, but she sat, weary herself.

There was a pause.

He was shaking his head at her in disappointment.

"You have a sharp tongue, my beautiful Angelica—that is not in keeping with your appearance as a gentle angel."

"And you have a false tongue. Indeed, your every word, your every flowery courtesy and compliment but hides the thorns at the roots. I do not believe you ever speak without keeping your tongue in cheek!"

"I know in whose cheek I would wish my tongue," he whispered.

Hillary quaked at that and jumped up. "How dare you speak to me in such a vulgar way! This is treating me as if I were a common courtesan!"

"And are you not?" he asked boldly, his eyes daring her to reveal the truth.

That conclusion so astounded, Hillary's anger blocked out her fears, and she stopped to respond contemptuously, "Finally you have gone beyond the line of being forgiven. Much as I'd regret further burdening Her Highness, I shall speak to her when she returns tomorrow. She must retract her invitation. You have taken advantage of her kindness and of my decency. Be off!"

Wolf's words stopped her as she was leaving. "The curtain has descended on this charade. This flummery has reached a point beyond boredom. I have checked into your background. I know who you are."

Hillary's revealing glare of alarm caused the viscount to throw back his head triumphantly in a jubilant laugh. Her trapped expression was proof enough of his theory. "Now you are unmasked, my counterfeiter. No need to be concerned. I prefer my women undisguised."

"Who am I?" she said calmly, as if prepared unflinchingly to accept this moment. She was by now at the edge of the dry fountain and leaned against it, waiting.

"You are a woman accustomed, I expect, to being in a gentleman's arms."

At that Hillary laughed and turned away, but he caught her and held her in his arms, continuing feverishly, "Well, this gentleman wishes to give you pleasure for pleasure. You shall find it worth your while. If you want this villa, it is yours. If you want jewelry or pounds sterling, name the amount. I am willing to pay it, so much have you bewitched me."

Fully alive to the evils of her situation, for not

only could she not pull away, but neither could she reach the gentleman within him if he considered her a common cyprian, Hillary was momentarily overwhelmed. Still she struggled. It was of no avail until suddenly, miraculously she was rescued by the most unexpected savior.

A splash of water hit the viscount directly in the face. Then a gush of it. Shocked and well spattered, he stepped back, covering his face with both his hands.

"Pliny's fountain!" Hillary laughed, fully free. "Thank you, kind sir! Even from the ages past a true gentleman comes to a lady's rescue!" And seeking Pliny's complete protection Hillary jumped up on the fountain's rim, walking around on it.

Thoroughly soaked, she remained within its watery shield as the viscount attempted to pull her down, each time being pushed back by another watery rebuff. He stood back at length, watching her blithely skipping along the fountain's edge.

"Pliny has cooled your ardor, I observe," she said with a laugh.

"There is only one way to cool me down," he had to shout over the splashy sounds, "And I expect you know how!"

Raising her voice to be heard through the water's gushing, Hillary cried, "No, I do not! No, as well, is my answer to your infamous, immoral carte blanche! No, actually to whatever you may ask me. Simply insert that response. *No!*"

Wolf had stopped running round the fountain attempting to reach her, realizing with a shrug that the only way to catch the dancing water sprite would be to join her on the fountain's edge and lift her off. But that would necessitate a drenching for himself, which he was attempting to avoid, ducking and moving away. The elegant viscount was at last pushed aside by Wolf, who took charge, relishing the elements and leaping up into the thick of the eruption. Either her astonishment at this unexpected act or his touch unbalanced her poise, but next moment Hillary had fallen fully into the fountain's basin with a splash. Shocked, Wolf threw himself in after her. The water was just up to his waist as he stood, but she was prone and submerged. He got down on his knees to lift her, but she was sitting up on her own. The constant flow of water on their heads kept knocking them back down, splashing them, drenching them with water in their eyes, mouths, over their heads. Wolf was expecting hysterics from her, and when he heard her voice through the tumult, it took a moment to realize the sounds coming from her were not sobs but laughter! In vast relief, he grinned and sat down alongside the lady, both allowing the water to have its way with them. At last Wolf, holding on to the rim with one hand and hers with the other, pulled them out.

Soaked and dripping, Hillary was wringing her hair while the viscount stared at her sodden, clinging dress.

"You seem to delight in getting wet!" he shouted to be heard above the still-gushing fountain behind them.

"It appears to be the most effective way of bringing you to your senses!" she shouted back, still giggling.

"Quite the reverse! It has aroused my senses! Especially the seductive way your gown is sticking to your . . . eh, form!"

She put her hands over her ears, not wishing to hear him.

"I want you!" he cried, raising his voice to the top of his lungs to get her attention. That loud declaration alerted all in the palazzo. The count and Victorine came running. Bartolomeo was before them. "What has happened?" he demanded.

The viscount was too chagrined to say a word. Hillary was left to explain. "I believe you heard the viscount calling that he wanted you all. We are in need of your aid. His lordship is shockingly clumsy! As he bumped into you, my dear baron, he tumbled us both into the fountain just as it was making its eruption. I expect I, too, shall now be the recipient of his most profuse apologies."

The viscount bowed to that. Indeed, if he had had a hat, he would have taken it off to her, for she had arranged to make him look the most foolish and herself least culpable. A true lady would have cried out and fainted at his treatment and had both gentlemen challenging him to a duel. But obviously she was playing a secret game with him and wished it to continue—the duel she desired to engage in was the one between the two of them. Nevertheless, he must accept her account of the episode and did so by making her the most profound apology, bowing low.

"That's quite all right, my lord," Hillary said with a mocking smile. "You can't help being naturally clumsy. Rather clownlike, I expect. One shudders at the thought of you on the dance floor."

Smarting slightly yet with his polished address, Wolf claimed that he hoped she would give him a chance to prove how very agile he could be in close situations.

"No," Hillary said coldly, "You have had your last chance with me."

That pleased Pergami and even Count Guido, who had given up on Hillary for himself but vastly enjoyed an Englishman being given the same treatment.

"Henceforth," Hillary concluded as Victorine was helping her wring out her garments, "I request you gentlemen," she appealed to the count and the baron, "ensure that he remains miles away from me." Then turning and facing Wolf, she threw one word at him, "Touché!" And with a snap of her heels and a drip, drip, of her clothes she got into the carriage.

The two Italian noblemen hurried after the ladies, turning round in glee to view the English lord's humiliation, calling him clown and such in Italian, thanking Pliny for fixing the haughty English lord. And finally the viscount was alone at the fountain. He stared down at the whirling water. Recollecting himself and the lady floating in it, he smiled ruefully. It did her no disservice that she'd claimed victory. Easy conquest had become fatiguing. But one touch was not the finish of a duel. "Say rather, '*En garde!*' my lady," he whispered, and grimly resolved that with such a deft opponent, he could no longer fence with baited tip.

11

Lady Gardener and Mrs. Wizzle were gently but decidedly taking Hillary to task. What was all this gallivanting about with Lord Wolverton? Did she not know that she was playing with fire? He was certain to recognize her sometime. Did she not prefer to tell him herself?

Besides, Lady Gardener stated, "It is not straightforward. Their side is the faction that is known for its hypocrisy and deviation from truth, yet your not being open with the viscount opens us to the same charge—that we are shammers, lost to every vestige of propriety and decency!"

Moreover, Mrs. Wizzle added, "I am tired of hiding up here. I have not been able even to take a turn in the garden, except when assured he is gone from the palace."

The last appeal by dear Wizzie sufficiently moved

Hillary to agree to tell him. She was merely looking
for the correct time. What could not be admitted to
the ladies but only acknowledged to herself was that
the situation between herself and Lord Wolverton
had reached another level. While thinking about
him, Hillary spotted his lordship in the gardens. She
ran around the balconies until the gardens were
directly below. There he was indeed, strolling
amidst the roses and orange trees. She giggled at
her last memory of him all soaked. Now he was looking particularly dashing, in morning wear of top
boots and pantaloons. Actually it was rather heated
for such correct attire, but the viscount, up to his
intricately tied cravat, was every inch a Britisher.

A young maid, Rosa, just sixteen, was coming
toward him. Hillary could not help but hide behind
one of the pillars to observe that encounter. Rosa
shyly, nervously peeped at him with her big, black
eyes. Oft had Hillary noticed this twittery reaction
women had to him, as one would feel passing a
sleek panther. Not that she'd ever come face to face
with a panther, she admitted with a grin. Actually
on second thought, equating him to a panther was
too considerate. The viscount was more voracious
than that, she'd discovered. He was as named, a
wolf, seeking to gobble up as many damsels as
came into his path. She herself was just one of his
little treats.

Now the viscount was speaking to the young girl.
His soft laugh came floating up. Hillary was indignant, recalling his using that same tactic on her.
Rosa was eagerly asking if he wished something
from her. Oh, he wished something from her, the
knave! He stroked her cheek with a lazy, extended
finger. Rosa was blushing, Hillary could tell even

from this distance. But the viscount let Rosa go.
Whether he'd made arrangements to meet her later,
Hillary told herself, she was not a bit interested.

Wolf was indeed a large and powerful animal on
the prowl. Sleek on the surface yet deadly under-
neath. He could destroy with coldness, pride, and
lack of interest as she remembered him at their first
meeting. But he was even more deadly when he was
interested. Hadn't he attempted to reduce her to
the level of a wanton? Heavens, he had showed
more respect for young Rosa than for her! His
approach toward Angelica was blatant, with an
undisguised leer indicating she was a delicacy he
intended to partake of. No, nothing that light.
Rather his attitude was more that she was his life's
blood and he must drink her to keep alive, even if
she were left drained of all existence. No, too
gothic! Somewhere in between. But whatever the
style, his every glance told her unquestionably she
was his private property.

Sunk in thoughts of him, Hillary recollected his
attentions to the other ladies at the princess's
court and concluded his attitude was general to all
females. Obviously it was his direct, hypnotic look
turned on the princess that originally led Her
Highness to agreeing to his remaining. He was
dashed indiscriminate in his use of lures. As she
continued to watch him strolling, taking his morning constitutional, Hillary admitted to herself she'd
been a total widgeon to assume something unique
about his devotion to her. Obviously he gave all
women that same impression with his at-large dis-
tribution of glances, passions, even kisses! Blast
him, that was the appeal of a rake, she supposed,
making every woman feel she was special to him.

Yet that as well was the downfall of a rake, for once a lady realized she was rather part of a group, his wooing lost not only its particularity but all value.

What Hillary wanted was to be special to a gentleman as he would be special to her.

Suddenly the viscount looked up and caught her having unthinkingly come out to the balcony's railing. With his most polished bow and bright smile, he managed to suggest she was the answer to his prowling about. Quickly, eagerly, he signaled her to come down. But she shook her head and ran back into the palazzo and the safety of her own room, locking and bolting the door behind her. Why had her heart beat so wildly at his unexpectedly catching her glance? As if he had caught her in his arms? He had too much effect on her, she admitted with a groan. She must stay away from the gentleman. His intentions were clearly dishonorable. In fact, he had even spoken dishonorably to her. What would Lady Gardener have said if told the full extent of his lordship's liberties! In all likelihood she would have faulted her for not keeping a proper distance.

In an hour there was a knock on her door. If not the viscount himself, it was a letter from him. Ah, he was not so lost to propriety as to come forcing his way into her room. While with the princess, he kept to an outward show of gentlemanly behavior— hoping his note would lure her to a more accessible area. The thought of his touch on the note brought back the touch of his hands on her face, on her body. His lips had roamed over her face as well, heading toward her mouth and stopping there. Touching her own lips now, she felt them warm and throbbing as if just kissed.

Good gracious, that was her reaction to holding

his note. What would become of her upon reading it?

Tearing apart the seal, she eagerly perused the full page and was excessively disappointed.

More effective, more honest would have been one line asking her to meet him. Rather it was filled with his practiced gallantries. She could sense these phrases were well-used in his courtly career. Even the poems he quoted had no direct reference to her. Filled with allusions to her soft, endearing ways. Pure fustian! False to the core.

Quivering with rage, Hillary tore up the letter. Ah, he held her cheap indeed—thinking she could be won over by such insincere, all-purpose expressions! Was it too much for the gentleman to trouble himself to think of one particular expression directly relating to herself! As if he as the wolf had not bothered even to disguise his hairy paw as he reached for her. Well, piffle to him and his love letter.

She vouchsafed him no reply. Even when one more letter arrived, it similarly went into the fiery grate, this time unread.

The return of Princess Caroline brought Hillary out of her seclusion to greet her. There were gifts and hugs and expressions of being missed on all sides. Nothing better pleased Her Highness than to be told she was missed. She could not get enough of that. She got it from Bartolomeo in great effusion, from Victorine in greater effusion and in two languages, from Lady Gardener with dignified English reserve, from Miss Wizzle with a flutter, from Hillary with a tear in her eye that meant so much to the princess she must cry in return. Finally, the evening guests arrived and Count Guido brought her flowers. Sir Percy was there with a package of her favorite sweets. But the viscount outdid them all. He had bought a golden bracelet, "for her graceful arm."

She was delighted with it. Bracelets had always been her passion as everyone knew from her oft recalling that tale of the Prince Regent's bridal gift of two pearl bracelets being taken away and given to his mistress. Obviously the viscount knew where her vulnerability lay and had used her own stories against her. His gift had indeed won the princess's good opinion, for she was heard to use the words "consideration" and "concern" in relation to his lordship which Hillary could scarce tolerate. Even more effective was the viscount's exaggerated claim that he'd been counting the days of her absence. Hillary frowned at the blatant mockery in his voice, knowing he meant the opposite as the gullible princess graciously gave him her braceleted hand to kiss. Equally furious was Baron Bart not only at the viscount's advancement in royal favor, but that the viscount's gift meant he must now rush to buy an expensive present as well.

It was the second day since Princess Caroline's return and Hillary had still not revealed her identity. Lady Gardener warned, "The princess can never keep to a plan. She acts on instinct. If he cajoles her, as he is doing, she will confess everything to him about you. Is that how you wish it disclosed?"

In truth, Hillary did not know how she wished it discovered. On the very evening of her return, the princess had taken her aside and urged the truth. "His lordship is a knowing one. What you English say, 'up to every rig and row.' And he has spies. He will discover. You had best discover yourself to him first. Make him guess, if you wish to play that game. But you direct the game, yes?"

"Be honest," Mrs. Wizzle implored, wanting to be let free of her confinement. But Lady Gardener's last words had the most potent effect. "Tell him tonight. Or I shall on the morrow!"

Therefore when the viscount urged a stroll in the garden after dinner, she agreed. After so long keeping her distance, he was surprised. At once his suspicious nature concluded it was a new ploy of the princess, since this change had occurred directly upon her return.

As they seated themselves on the veranda, looking at the blue of Lake Como and the dim outline of the mountains, a peace engulfed the two. He recalled his first sight of her on that lake. She had seemed like a dream then, now when actually in his arms and feeling her wildness, she was an obsession. Whatever the stakes the princess was playing for, he would top her and take this lady as his prize.

"You have received my letters," he said softly, assuming that, as with all ladies, she had been won over by his flatteries and apologies. "If I have been too impetuous, blame your beauty that has caused me to forget the reverence due you."

She turned her eyes from the beauty of the lake and viewed his taunting gray eyes. His mention of those letters was not helpful to his cause, rather the reverse. "I did not quite understand the message in your letters, nor indeed in all your advances, my lord. Are you asking for my hand in marriage?"

The viscount laughed aloud, his first natural reaction. He caught himself enough to carry on more diplomatically. "Why talk of marriage and such a confining state when there is the scent of orange blossoms in the air?"

"Orange blossoms more likely lead to thoughts

of marriage. Or are you trifling? In short, what are your intentions in this pursuit? Be honest instead of boring me to tears with your copied sentiments disposed in the fire as befitted their tawdry, meaningless mumblings. I ask you openly, what is your objective?"

Smarting under her insult, the viscount stared at her, his eyes narrowing, his senses alert. She was always a challenge, but this must be the princess's attack. He was to ask her to marry him, and then what? They would announce her as a courtesan, and thus discredit all his testimony for the prince? No, he would not fall for that crass maneuver.

"I regret that you have experienced such a lapse in memory, my dear Angelica. I have been frank with you as to my objectives. I will take you under my wing for a while and teach you the delights of love as we have already experienced them. But as for marriage, I daresay that is too high a price to pay for so suspect a commodity. Frankly, I have never found a lady worthy of my name. And assuming I did, she at least would be a lady."

In a blaze of temper, Hillary found just the way to tell him after all. "Ah, you wish a lady, such as your conveniently forgotten fiancée?"

The viscount froze her with his stare. "The details of my private life are not open to all, and certainly not to one of your stamp."

"Am I so worthless? What does that say then for a gentleman who wished to spend so much time in my worthless presence? Not much, I expect. You are such a complete sham, as well as a rake. Dishonest to the core. I pity any lady who would be forced to be in your company for above a few moments. Thankfully that shall never again be inflicted on me!"

She turned to reenter the salon when he grabbed her. "You may tell your princess I have not fallen for her simpleminded game of setting up a courtesan to disgrace both myself and my prince. But why allow yourself to be used in this sham? It cannot be as profitable as my offer. For I shall devote my life to making yours comfortable and . . . filled with pleasure."

He attempted to take her roughly in his arms, but she pushed him away. "There is not a convenient fountain here. But the lake is just beneath the balcony. If you persist, I shall give you another soaking."

He gave a small, intimate laugh. "If you recollect the soaking was mutual. I am not adverse to both of us jumping into the lake and finding a boat there . . . and laying our wet, cool bodies on the bottom where we could be rocked together, heated together, exploring the joys and rapture of love—together."

For a moment his voice hypnotized her as did his stroking of her white, bare shoulders. "What about your fiancée?" she insisted. "What would she say if I wrote her and told her of your actions?"

He stepped away as if he'd been slapped. "Good God, is that the second plan in your maneuvers? Believe me, it will not wash. Miss Astaire would not understand a word of what you say. Nor actually would it matter, for I am not really interested in her thoughts. Only in her obedience and assuring my lineage."

"Ahhhh!" Hillary exclaimed, as if he had taken off a mask and revealed such a monstrosity beneath, she could but recoil. "You are worse than imagined. Heartless, yes, but not just from indifference as one assumed, but from a cruelty and selfishness that I feel will never be expunged. Out of my sight, you vile thing! Ah, yes, I do have some news that might reach through those thick layers of self-regard and conceit. I have been informed that you are not, in effect, engaged. Rather that that poor, deluded Miss Astaire has broken your engagement long since and gone her own way. But as well as being a toplofty libertine, you are not even aware of your own business. Why haven't you read your letters? You might discover you are free to find some other poor, helpless lady to gull into accepting you, until she begins to see the rot at the core and shies away. As Miss Astaire did. As I do!"

And with that, almost sobbing her hatred and her fury, Hillary succeeded in pushing past him, seeing a flash of his astonished face and then finding herself in the salon. Lady Gardener was at her side in a moment.

"Did you tell him?"

"I told him enough for a man of intelligence to understand. But perhaps we are expecting too much from an English lord of the Prince Regent's camp. They must needs have things spelled out. If he has not grasped it himself by tomorrow, I give you leave to spell it out to the gentleman in large block letters."

Baron Bart was at her side and anxious to teach her to play billiards. She and Victorine joined him in the game room. The viscount followed, staring at the lady as if she were deranged, and yet he could not half stop following her about. At one point, while laughing over Sir Percy's remarks, she turned, and found his gray eyes fastened on her every expression. Observing however that there was pity in his lordship's glance as well, she laughed harder, much more than Sir Percy's poor remark merited. The viscount assumed she had gone over the edge, Hillary realized with amusement. That was more convenient than believing in the truth of her remarks. She stopped laughing abruptly and returned his stare. Her own eyes filled with some pity but mostly disdain. Then quite deliberately and with cold resolution, she turned away from him, refusing to grant the privilege of another glance, although his gaze remained fixedly yet suspiciously on her for every moment of the evening until she retired for the night.

12

It was impossible to believe what Angelica had told him. Egad, she was a tricky madcap—wild to a fault! How could she invent such a tale and say it to him with a straight face, as if she had some secret knowledge? Obviously she was just attempting to get a rise out of him in order to laugh at his gullibility. She was a constantly changing young lady like a chameleon who left him not only flummoxed but unable to credit his own senses. But she had gone her length with the mention of his fiancée. It showed a mean-spiritedness he would not have expected. Was that in retaliation for his asking her to be his mistress? Dash it, she should have been flattered, actually. Hundreds of women, nay even thousands, would have envied her that opportunity.

Despite his assuring himself there was not a whit

of truth in her flummery, he sought to reassure himself by sending his valet, Marston, to Venice. That was the last place his secretary, Mr. Curtis, had been ordered to forward his mail. He had intended to give new directions once he was settled, but he had lingered in Lake Como longer than first assumed. Yes, Angelica was the lure that had held him there, entrapping him into following her about like a great gawk, unable not to be in her presence. Even on the very night after her outrageous ploy—so obvious a hoax it had whiskers on it—he was unable to cease being her shadow. Her easy, open manner with Sir Percy pierced him through until he was just short of calling out that slowtop! If she preferred Sir Percy, who had a hint of shop in his background, so be it. Let her keep to her like. Like to like.

Easier said than felt. For every time she let that fumbler take her hand to escort her over the minor obstacle of a mere two stairs from the dining room to the hall, he felt a gnawing at his vitals. Dash it, he was unable to wrench himself from following that lady. He told himself his riveted attention was merely investigative, hoping to spot her reporting the failure of their latest stratagem to the princess or Lady Gardener. But Angelica obviously had other things on her mind, such as flirting quite shamelessly with Sir Percy.

If Sir Percy's reading her a poem had not been sufficient gall for Wolf to drink, she added a chaser by joining Baron Bart in a game of billiards. Thus must she hold her cue, the baron instructed, and had the audacity to put his big paw on her delicate hand to perfect the position. Even his daughter, there as the ostensible chaperon, ought to have been disgusted at the blatancy of her father's approach and her friend's compliance, but she was there apparently merely to applaud each pocketed ball.

The next day the viscount, set to cross-examine that angelic lady, was brought to a standstill on hearing that almost the entire court had gone on a picnic, including Angelica and the princess. He bribed several outriders and stable hands to find their destination only to receive conflicting directions that sent him driving fruitlessly about, until he came across them just as they were all returning, well amused and well fed—while he had not even had his tea.

There was always the hope of cornering the lady at dinner, except Angelica was slightly out of curl due to the touch of the sun and remained in her room. The princess sent hourly to inquire how she did and received satisfactory enough reports to be easy. But Lord Wolverton was far from comfortable, not only had his waiting been for naught but he'd been roped into an interminable game of whist with the baron, the princess, and Countess Oldi. As was the usual practice with all royalty, the rest allowed Her Highness to win, until Wolf committed the solecism of forgetting to watch his cards sufficiently and won one hand. Then he purposely won again and again, until everyone was in his debt.

"Let the game end," he announced, picking up his winnings and looking piercingly at Princess Caroline, who seemed to be the only one awake to his private meaning, for she said with a half smile, "But the game between man and woman, she is never finished. One must always be hurting the other. For what? For the pleasure to take control?

There is no control of one person over another. There is only death. As my daughter died. As I shall die. And you. Why then must we fight, fight, fight? And nations fight? It is foolish beyond permission."

"There is something in what you say, Your Highness," the viscount said softly with a slight bow, and took his leave. "At the same time," he whispered to himself, "there is nothing in what she says as well." And smiling at his own witticism he left, if no wiser, at least richer.

Marston returned the next day having ridden hard through the night with a pouch containing a pile of letters from Mr. Curtis. Eagerly the viscount shoved aside all his social correspondence in his search for what he was certain would not be there. But it was. By heavens, a letter from Miss Astaire. How the devil had she known?

Taking a deep breath to control himself, Lord Wolverton unstuck the wafer, which seal he observed with distaste was in the most common style for note paper of a musical note. How blasted unoriginal was that chit. He hoped the contents within would be more intriguing.

Shocking was the word, he had to admit. Good God! She was crying off! Giving him the slip in no uncertain terms. That provincial! That ninny had dared to jilt him—Viscount Wolverton! One more read through. It was so. But why was it so? He recollected signs of skittishness. A young lady obviously afraid of marriage and gentlemen, bred in a remote estate with not a hint of fashionability or spark to her.

The lord's first reaction was to discount her refusal. Miss Astaire did not have the power to overset the signed agreement! And what the devil was Mrs. Wizzle doing? He'd placed her there as a guardian to ensure that the young lady did not get into a muddle. For, blast her, Miss Astaire had appeared as if she needed her hand held simply to walk across the room without tripping or coming acropper. Often during the last year he'd found himself concluding that he'd been too precipitate, and wondered how *he* could break off. And yet. And yet her very ineptness had attracted him. He would so have relished making her over into the image he wished.

Another reading of the letter and that attached to it by Mr. Curtis mentioning his trip to Holly House, disclosed the information that the young lady herself had instructed the letter be mailed post haste to Italy. The viscount was nonplussed.

How the blazes had Angelica known of the existence of such a letter? And how know the contents of a *sealed* letter that all this time had been in a pouch in Venice? Impossible to have found out from this end, regardless of the princess's spies. The only possibility was from the other end—or Miss Astaire herself—which meant that goosey creature had made her jilting universal knowledge. Quickly the viscount tore open his social correspondence. No hint of his having been given the slip, even from a most renowned tattler. To the contrary, all contained juvenile jabs at his soon being leg shackled. Against his inclination, the viscount began to recollect Miss Astaire in detail. He could only envisage an enshrouded mouse of a girl. Not up to her mother, who was such a diamond and said to have overshadowed even her companion, Lady Gardener.

By Jove, that was it! There, the connection with

the princess. Lady Gardener must have continued correspondence with her friend's daughter and obviously that was the source of the knowledge of his jilting!

Smiling at having so easily unraveled the puzzle, the viscount was congratulating himself when an unbidden flash of Miss Astaire came back. He remembered her all in black clothes and cap, and she also had, if he recollected correctly, dark tresses hanging down her back. Only the blue eyes had a tinge of familiarity. But most English ladies had blue eyes.

A most dreadful thought possessed him. But he dismissed it. Yet it had snagged on to his consciousness and irritatingly clung. No, there was no possibility that Angelica was Miss Astaire. Her name, if he recollected was Hillary. That impersonation would require a lady with a great deal of savoir faire and necessitate the entire princess's court being engaged in the conspiracy to hoodwink him. Too massive, too monstrous to be believed.

He dismissed it. It would not remain dismissed. He took it out again and rethought it, only to banish it from his mind with almost a growl.

Angelica was at breakfast, eating her favorite figs and chestnuts. The baron was peeling the chestnuts for her as if she were a child, and she was laughing in gratitude. The viscount's piercing stare caused a bit of the nut to go down the wrong way. She easily coughed it away. Nevertheless the baron made a big scene of calling for water, tea, honey to soothe her throat. None was needed. She ate an orange next, archly ignoring Wolf as he silently sipped his tea all the time focusing his glance on her. But his stare did not have an ounce of passion

in it this time. Rather it was one of outright speculation. The juice of the orange went down her fingers
and she delicately wiped them. The baron made
some allusion to wishing he could be the orange in
her hand, and she just laughed. She had a way of
dismissing all her admirers with what was, he realized, a queenly air. Something only a lady of quality
could accomplish. Actually the closeness to
Angelica demonstrated by Lady Gardener was
uncharacteristic of that lady, who was usually quite
jealous of her standing. If Angelica were a common
lady or rather a lady of ill repute, would her ladyship taint herself to accept her to her bosom? He
had explained that by concluding that it was in
keeping with her having accepted the highly
improper princess as her leader. Why cavil at a lady
the princess wished introduced into her society? At
Princess Caroline's direction, Lady Gardener had
accepted Bartolomeo Pergami, a soldier of fortune,
and his entire family. She had even been affectionate to young Victorine Pergami. How surprising,
then, to go another step and accept a young lady of
the shabby-genteel set, even possibly one of the
muslin company, and turn her into everyone's petted, sought-after darling?

Her Highness obviously had her own rules about
everything. Was that not in keeping with the headstrong way the princess had refused to accept her
husband's will, eventually bragging that though
she'd lost a prince's affection, she'd gained a kingdom's love, instead.

Since joining Princess Caroline's entourage, the
viscount had been shocked at how important it was
to the pathetic royal lady that everyone love her.
People must always pay her homage and compli-

ments—even caresses were permitted—anything
that demonstrated caring. That very attitude had
convinced the viscount that the princess had acted
if not immorally at least improperly with Bartolomeo. For that fellow was vulgarly free with his
hands and kisses. All was forgiven here in the name
of love. Indeed, Her Highness's eyes had often
scanned his own expression expecting it to turn to
adoration, and was delighted when it did—for one
lady of the royal court. What in blazes was this? A
court of love? Kisses were thrown across the room
as people entered. Gifts and compliments showered all the ladies, but particularly the two young
ladies that ruled there. Most especially the angel of
the set.

Like a midsummer's madness, everyone breathed
in the elixir of love. And the center of everyone's
attention if not passion was Angelica. She floated
by them as if dropping particles of desire. Yet paradoxically she seemed pure. Would she be called
Angelica else? Didn't she seem to bless each one
just by her presence? Often she was surrounded by
the Italian children, those petted cherubs of the
court, playing games with them. Young or old,
English or Italian, everyone sought out Angelica.
She was Princess Caroline's dream of herself, having the beauty, charm, and even royal airs Princess
Caroline lacked.

While Her Highness looked always slightly out of
kilter, Angelica was perfection. While the princess
spoke in a loud voice that shattered, Angelica was
soft toned and soothing. While the princess was old
and tired, with obvious false curls to cover her
graying locks and overly rouged cheeks, Angelica
had a superabundance of glorious, sunlit hair that

caused all the Italians in the streets to stop and gape at her. Her skin was flawless; her eyes like the deepest part of Lake Como on a dreamy morning. And her lips . . .

The viscount shook his head—he was losing the track of his intended thoughts. Roughly he pulled his concentration back to his ingenious point, that the princess had fashioned Angelica as the lure to gather all the adoration around her and soak up some of the reflected parts onto herself, so needy was she of it. The Prince Regent, although demanding unending praise, dashed well did not go so far as to want love. That was a woman's thing. Perhaps because she'd been so deprived of it by her husband, who'd greeted her on her arrival with his mistress at his side and his heart dedicated to his common-law wife, Mrs. Fitzherbert.

Flummery! He was falling for the princess's propaganda, blaming the prince for her neediness. One could not constantly hear her sobbing stories and not be somewhat influenced. Apparently even he. That had to be watched. For in truth every English lady ought to withstand her husband's having a mistress without complaining so loudly. Just wasn't done!

That was what bothered him most about the princess and her influence. She continually did and said and wore things that were just not acceptable, encouraging those around her to do the same. What she could not do, her young protégée, Angelica, did for her. Such as attaching all, including the prince's representative—or his august self. Egad, he'd come panting after her. When he would not go whole hog and propose, they'd come up with this scheme to humiliate him.

Angelica laughed, and he looked up from his untouched breakfast. She was eating figs now and Bartolomeo wished to peel them himself and give them her from his own hand. And she allowed that! Brazen hussy! No, impossible for her to be that well-brought-up English lady. She was probably still at Holly House. He must write to Mrs. Wizzle.

There was the key, he thought, and straightened up in delight—Mrs. Wizzle! If that young lady had dismissed her ere heading out to Italy, Mrs. Wizzle would have written to him. And there had not been a letter from Mrs. Wizzle in the pile. He'd looked most particularly, actually expecting one, as a report. No, this was not Miss Astaire! Angelica was radiant, glowing with life. Miss Astaire was enshrouded with death.

Count Guido and Victorine were heard in the garden and Bartolomeo, recalled to his duty, went to supervise. Angelica loitered at the table. She was now eating grapes. One grape plucked and gently placed between her berry red lips. And another. Another. They slipped in. All was done with such delicacy. Eating as if she did not need to swallow, but merely sipped her food like dew from a flower. She was enchanting. He could spend hours watching her every motion. Adoring her.

Damn her, that was her aim! To attract! To spin him into the princess's web. And yet he could no longer struggle. Whatever they wanted from him he would give—egad, just to be able to put his lips where the grapes were and slide softly into her sweet mouth.

"What do you want from me?" he asked hoarsely, surrendering.

Hillary looked across the table at him, as if surprised that he was there, or had the effrontery to speak to her. Although obviously she had remained there to allow him that opportunity. He was besotted but not a fool. He saw the maneuvers but was helpless to parry them. He wanted to be caught—if being caught meant being close to her. One kiss, he thought as he came close, changing his seat for the one Bartolomeo had abandoned and watching her closely as she ate yet another grape. Then, ye gods, he was unable to resist. He followed the grape with his mouth and tasted the grape on her soft lips and plunged into her startled mouth.

He was wild for her. When Hillary pushed him off, he could do no less than follow her. She ran for the garden where Bartolomeo and Victorine ought to be. They had gone somewhere else. Perhaps to the back veranda to watch the boats on the lake. She turned to run there, when Wolf caught up, taking her from the open garden area to the orchard, which was dense with fruit and leaves and pulled her down under one of the trees. Her body struggled in his arms, but he would not surrender her.

She slapped him so hard he felt his eyes water, and loosened his hold on her. She did not run away, confronting him, saying with so much fury he could not but recognize her sincerity. "You profane me with your touch, you—you dirty wretch! You libertine!"

"And you are a teasing wench!" he growled, still attempting to get control of himself as he lay sprawled. "You think it is quite correct to inflame me, but not to bear the results of that lure? What are your conditions to have you? I accept every one without reservations. I have never wanted a woman as I want you, nor waited for one as long. Money,

position, even, confound you, marriage, if that is
what it will take!"

Hillary stopped to stare at the befuddled gentleman at her feet. He was slowly rising, giving up on
his attempts to pull her down on the ground with
him. He assumed he would win her now through
negotiations, and part of his old hauteur was
returning. Nevertheless she grimly shook her
head.

"What are you refusing? Even *marriage,* egad?"

"Are you not engaged?" she asked with a fixity of
eye that let him know he could no longer pretend
with her.

"Apparently not. As you've discovered, probably
through the offices of Lady Gardener, my fiancée
has written to . . . eh, cry off."

Hillary took a deep breath, almost a gasp. "You
have read her letter? And you *accept* her refusal?"

"Yes, yes, what the devil does she matter?" He
winced hearing himself so completely humble. He,
who had never had to stoop to win anything. This
was chastening indeed. Yet he would press on to
press her to him as he abjectly concluded, "What
does anything matter but you?"

"You don't wish to marry me," Hillary said softly.
"You are simply being led by your . . . unbridled
lust. That is not what I wish in a husband."

The viscount received a complete shock. "You
are refusing me, when I have condescended to
accept whatever you are . . . even if . . . if . . ."

"If?" Hillary coaxed, her eyes dancing at his
white-faced astonishment.

"If you are what I believe . . . a decoy of the
princess's. Taken from a lower level and like the
Pergamis raised and given honors you do not rate.

She has set you up to win me, for the purpose of revenging herself on the prince."

"But why should she and I do that to you, my lord? Unless you were the prince's spy, which you denied."

"I am not his spy. Odd's blood, I am the eighth Viscount Wolverton, not some menial to be hired!"

"Yet you would do it as a favor to your prince. Stop by to nail down incriminating information against her?"

"If there is none, why are you so afraid?" he said, his disdain returning after its minor eclipse.

Hillary walked back to the open garden. The roses and their scent enveloped her and then she felt herself being enveloped by Wolf's arms.

"This is going beyond endurance!" Hillary exclaimed. He was behaving with such presumption she no longer felt the need to consider his feelings. "How many times must a lady refuse before it sinks into your paperskull that you are being refused?"

"We have passed that. I have agreed to your terms," he said, drowning in the sparkle of her blue eyes inches from his own.

"There are no terms you could ever meet. I want true love. You must give me that to win me, and that, my lord, you are frankly incapable of ever giving anyone, for all your love is reserved for yourself!"

Astonished as the viscount was at that estimation, he would not have relinquished his hold on the lady if he hadn't heard voices nearing. Several courtiers were appearing and they surrounded Angelica with delight. She merely tossed them a smile and broke through their encrusting her to hurry to the marble stairs, seeking the seclusion of her rooms.

Ignominy beyond belief, he was following! Hillary realized, hearing sounds behind her. The only recourse was to attempt to outrun him.

At her door she rushed in, for he was almost atop her. Indeed, Wolf charged through the door after her, dismissing her maid with a harsh command. Hillary quaked at the wildness in his eyes. "We have nothing more to say," she said in alarm.

"We are not going to be conversing," he said breathlessly.

"Hillary, dear, what's amiss?"

Hillary turned and ran into the arms of an elderly lady. That woman held her close and asked what had alarmed her, and then looked beyond and saw not only what but who had alarmed her, and she herself gasped. But she clasped Hillary tighter in her arms.

"Mrs. Wizzle!" the viscount ejaculated.

The dear lady drew herself to her full height of five feet two inches, and said haughtily, "You are well aware, my lord, that a gentleman does not force his way into a lady's chamber. Do I really have to send for the footmen to have you removed?"

His eyes went from Mrs. Wizzle to Hillary, who was now standing calmly staring at him.

"You aren't . . ." he began, choking with disbelief, affront, humiliation.

"I am," she said coldly. "Hillary Astaire, your one-time fiancée. Now, by the grace of God, set free."

"The devil you are!" he mumbled and turned on his heel and left.

13

Lady Gardener was relieved to hear the subterfuges were finally over. Anything that smacked of deceit was inimical to her. Mrs. Wizzle, who had been looking forward to the viscount's knowing the truth and thus being able to explain herself to him in person, now was reluctant to approach him. His fevered glare had thoroughly alarmed her. It was so totally unlike the suave, indifferent lord she'd met in England who had always been a perfect gentleman.

"He was like a wild beast," she whispered to the princess, who had summoned the two ladies and dear Hillary to a meeting on that matter.

"Ah, but all men are beasts at the heart. They put veneers, like clothes, and pride themselves on perfecting those coverings, but strip them, and voilà, the beast appears, wishing to strike all soft and beautiful things, like my Angelica."

Lady Gardener did not comment on that. The late Lord Gardener had always been a perfect gentleman, regardless of the occasion, and she still regretted the loss of his dear companionship. Nor did Hillary and Mrs. Wizzle dismiss the viscount's reaction as typical of all gentlemen. Mrs. Wizzle had her dear love as a shining example and Hillary of course had the perfection of her father to hold as a beacon.

"There is something particular in the viscount," Mrs. Wizzle insisted. "Never have I seen a gentleman so completely forgetting all proprieties. He forced his way into her rooms and had her by the arms and if I had not spoken . . ." Unable to complete the charge, she stopped. Then with a deep breath, carried on, "He was nigh onto offering her an intolerable insult!" She was still shaking at the fury of his expression, which had hit her like a blow.

"Ah," the princess exclaimed, her eyes glittering. "He has not . . ." She was unable to ask the question. Mrs. Wizzle had wanted to ask the question, but had not had the temerity. Lady Gardener had no such delicacy.

"Has he ever made improper advances?" she demanded.

Recalling not only his kisses but other intimate embraces, Hillary could only answer yes, but looking at the frightened faces, realized that to do so would create a difficulty for them all that could not be easily overcome. The princess would have to have somebody challenge him to a duel for her honor. Mrs. Wizzle would faint and blame herself for allowing the young lady out of her sight. Best not to sink them all into such distastefulness. Therefore Hillary quickly assured all three mothers that she had been quite untouched. "He did gaze at me with some heat, and I believe kissed my hand a few times."

The princess pooh-poohed that. "Kisses we must accept and indeed they are very pleasant, especially when they come from such a beautiful man as Lord Wolverton. He is called Wolf, you know, but that is no excuse for wolflike behavior. Not with my dear lamb of a child. Not my angel girl. He should know when to draw the line."

The next person to see the viscount was the princess herself. She called him to discuss his position there, prepared to instantly dismiss him. He surprised her by being on the offensive.

"Most shocking business. For a pledged lady to masquerade under another name and go about as if she were not pledged!"

"But she was not masquerade! From the first we call her Angelica. It is my pet name everyone pick up. I cannot abide Hillary! Too hard a name for such a delicate young lady. To be truly true, when you arrived, she and we expected you to recognize her within hours. I was most flummox to return from my trip and hear you had not. He is jesting, I said. He sees through. But Lady Gardener claimed you could not because of your head."

"My head?"

"Yes. She said there was something fishy about it. Ah, yes! A cod's head!"

"How observant of her."

"I did not press, for Angelica found your courting a lady who had already rejected you . . . amusing."

"Vastly amusing," he said with a freezing stare.

The princess was disconcerted. "If you are offend, I daresay you ought not remain here. I must protect my childs. Her experience with men is small. Except for you, who treat her very ill. The gentlemen here would never presume on her innocence. English young ladies, I say, need seasoning. Thus, their seasons. Angelica did not have that— you push in before. She was so cloistered, she never even had a wardrobe of gowns. Never had her hair up. *Mein Gott,* she did not even know the very basic . . . eh, relationship between a man and woman. I explain to her, and she cried. I did, too, when my Mama told me. But not as much as when I spend the night with the prince."

"Your Highness," the viscount reproved, shocked and feeling himself flushing like a maiden. How dare she speak of such matters to him? Did she have no delicacy of mind at all?

"Ah, I forget you are not a friend. One must not say these things to you. From one of *his* camp. It would be best if you . . ."

Sensing that he was about to be given his congé, the viscount quickly interrupted. The last thing he wished was to be dismissed without the opportunity to punish Miss Astaire. Actually he had sworn to make all these dear, dear women regret they'd ever reduced his pride to nil. To procure the needed access, he must sound humble. And contrite. It went against his grain to do so, but he did. "I have come here to make a full confession to Your Gracious Highness. The prince *did* suggest I visit you. Disturbing reports had reached him. I was to observe and write if there was cause for alarm."

Her fright at that was prodigious. "That great Mahomet! That vile, vile pig of a person!" she was exclaiming.

The viscount made haste to speak soothingly to her, for her eyes were bulging. "It is actually in your interest that I have come. For I can report back everything here is *above reproach*. All rumors are strictly malicious!"

The princess's purple face slowly cleared at that. "Ah, you are as beautiful a man inside as you are beautiful without."

"Eh, precisely," the viscount responded, amused at how easy she was to gull.

"You see what a cruel man he is! How he always look to hurt and never to love. Why would anyone want to be with such a man? He hurt me and more, he hurt my daughter." As her tears began, the viscount, uncomfortably, quickly intervened.

"You have no cause for tears, Your Highness. I have seen nothing but admiration for you from everyone hereabouts."

"That is true!" she exclaimed, her mind happily diverted to the more joyous present than the agony of her past. "And I have my Angelica. She has become like my daughter. She laughs like her and is wild like her. But I admit, Angelica is more lovely. To see her is to take one's breath away. The gentlemen all love her at sight. I have had so many offers for her hand, she could have been married twenty times. But I say no to each one. None of them worthy of her. Not in position, not in the heart. Angelica needs a man who has *a heart.*"

"Without doubt," Wolf replied unemotionally. "That is always a handy organ to have about."

The result of the conference was that the princess

welcomed him to stay and never, ever return to that cruel, poor excuse for a prince.

"We have a new supporter," she announced to all at dinner. Lady Gardener was not immediately convinced. Mrs. Wizzle, always believing in redemption, was delighted and shyly said as much to him. Hillary was anything but pleased. She eyed the lord coldly and looked away.

"You'd hoped for my dismissal," he said after dinner, while Victorine was playing the harp.

"I'd assumed as a gentleman you'd realize you were overstaying your welcome," she said with an icy manner never used to him before.

"But I am widely welcomed by all. I am the new member of your team. Do we have a secret password when we meet?" He leaned closer, conspiratorially, and said with a mocking tone, "I say, are we planning treason or simply how to gull the prince? You are, after all, the past mistress of gulling others, are you not?"

Hillary stared at him no longer in disdain but in alarm. "You intend to make trouble, I gather. Speaking of gammoning people, you assume that having appealed to our dear princess's kind nature, the rest of us are not aware that your object in life is always to harm."

His smile faded at that. "Quite the reverse, I should say. My attitude toward you, Miss Astaire, has always been one of protection. That was so the moment your father came to me distraught at leaving his daughter on her own. He and my Uncle Sherwood coaxed me to forget my own interest. Which I did. Despite my reluctance at marrying at all, I kindly accepted you as my future mate."

"How magnanimous." Hillary flushed and then

doggedly carried on. "I can only say that the kinder part would have been to abstain. Obviously my father was not himself. You said 'distraught,' which shows how obvious it was to the most undiscriminating. That alone should have stopped a gentleman from taking advantage."

Annoyed at her twisting his benevolent act into one of selfishness, Wolf responded with some disdain, "You cannot have been correctly informed, my dear lady. I suggest you discuss the situation with your attorney. Your father was of sound mind. It is outrageous, not to mention unfilial, to suggest otherwise. He pleaded with me to 'help a dying man to peace.' It was only due to the generosity of my heart that I reluctantly agreed. Even after, I gave you a full year's grace. I have been naught but noble in thought and deed and been rewarded with ignoble treachery and deceit!"

Hillary surprised the much aggrieved gentleman by laughing in response. "Well, then, you should be delighted to be free . . . as am I. Mayhap next time you are forced into a good deed, you'll recollect the results of this one and rein in your overgenerous nature."

Wolf stared at her with a sudden shaking of his head. "Where did you get that waspish tongue? You seemed so gentle, such a lady, when I first met you."

"You did not meet me," Hillary said blithely. "You met the top of my head. You spent most of your time staring at your snuffbox and discussing the merits of various sorts of snuff. Mayhap if I'd put a snuffbox on my head, it would have done the trick! I said to myself, if he recognizes me, then I have maligned him as a haughty, uncaring, toplofty, stiff-rumped lord, awash in self-consequence. But you did not. As little as you spared me a glance did you spare concern for my circumstance. Your manner to a recently bereaved young lady was cold to the point of cruelty. Any future connection to you terrified me to the bone. My only thought was to be free! I was and am deeply grateful to the princess for her protection from you."

The viscount's face was flooded with cold fury. He wished to retaliate and did so. "She had no authority. Once your father accepted, legally I could keep you to it, if I wished. But why should I wish a lady who breaks faith so easily? That is not my idea of a wife."

"Nor are you my idea of a husband. So since we are obviously not what the other wishes, but rather vastly unsuited, I expect you ought be grateful to me for rescuing us both."

"Possibly I might have allowed you to break the agreement if you had made your sentiments clear."

"I did make them clear and you merely threatened me."

"*I?*"

"Indeed, you told me I was already yours body and spirit and that you could do with me as you wished."

"What a delightful thought," he said, still smiling but coming down off his high ropes at that tempting picture, adding, "I certainly did not realize when I said it what a pleasure was in store for me."

"Or displeasure for me!" Hillary snapped.

"We have both given ourselves pleasure since then," he whispered.

The harp solo was concluded and the princess was calling Hillary forth. Relieved to be away from him, she moved with alacrity to the pianoforte. She began with a joyful Italian melody that was much applauded. Her voice, like all the rest of her, was a joy to audience. It had a pure, tinkling sound like that of a bell on a clear morning. After that she sang a sad song of lost love in English, and had Lady Gardener wiping her eyes discreetly, while Mrs. Wizzle sobbed for her love. The viscount was astounded.

All those weeks since he had come, Hillary had never offered a single performance, perhaps fearing he would see a well-trained lady and recognize who she was. Evidently she had stopped singing only since he'd arrived, for Sir Percy was exclaiming how they had missed her evening performances. She and Victorine then sang a duet in Italian, which entranced all the gentlemen with the contrast between the dark sober lady and the glowing blond, smiling one. It was like viewing a sunset and not being certain which shade was more lovely, but *oh*ing and *ah*ing at both.

Evening tea was being passed around, and the viscount was unable to find a spot next to Hillary. Every moment caused his hackles to rise. The lady was his, and he'd let her go, much as if one had given away a coin thinking it was a sixpence and discovering afterward it was a rare gold coin of inestimable value. But he had feelings about her above chagrin. After publicly being made an object of humor by the young lady's ploy, he owed her retribution. He owed her tit for tat. Step one of his plan, that of winning the princess's approval and remaining in the lady's presence, had succeeded. Step two was to use his well-rewarded charm to have Miss Astaire join his other conquests, so he might advance to step three—retaliation, or, jilting her in turn. Yet his past success with ladies, he realized, had depended on his uncaring heart. One had to be uninvolved so to manipulate a relationship. The best revenge on another, the viscount recollected having read, was to have a happy life. He should have been grateful to Miss Astaire for breaking the engagement and gone on to find a lady of his own set, who suited him, he told himself. That would have been possible if he were not wild for Angelica, if she did not send his pulses racing by just her presence.

In short his heart was not in any plan, either of retribution or forgetfulness, for it was entirely taken up by adoring the lady. Every morning he swore he would keep to his vow of settling with her. Yet while attempting to duel, his emotions deflected each sword's thrust. Egad, she had made a weak fribble of him! If she were still Angelica, he could retaliate and achieve some appeasement by taking her in his arms. But as Miss Astaire, he could not touch her. Nor could he forget having touched her, and how her lips had warmed to his. The realization that she had not been an experienced lady made her response even more of a compliment. As well, he admitted with some self-reprimand, it made him more of a cad so to play on an innocent. But, egad, she was *his* innocent. She was *his.* Obviously he'd felt that even back in England when he had said she was his—body and soul. That was hyperbole, and completely out of character for him. And yet, he must have felt it then to say it. Certainly he felt it now. Her every smile at Sir Percy and the baron cut across his skin like a knife. He must have all her smiles, all her touches . . . and God knew, all her kisses!

Sir Percy was leaning close to her pale golden head, and it took all the viscount's civility not to challenge him for encroaching. Odd's blood, next moment that fool focused on a lock of hair at her neck and surreptitiously touched it, so light a stroke, she did not even feel it. Nor had anyone else observed his bold act. Sir Percy was red from his daring. It was clear he had been contemplating that attempt for hours. Nerved himself to it. And this success caused him almost to fall in exhaustion to his seat, relishing the pleasure.

If he'd been so overcome by the mere touch of her ringlet, the viscount thought, smiling at last, what would he do at the touch of her lips? Obviously Sir Percy's reaction proved he had not had such favors. She was chaste with all but him. Possibly because she knew, while he didn't, that she was kissing her affianced husband. The legitimacy of their passion in no way lessened it. Nothing could, even her attempt to illegitimatize it by tossing him away. It was there, so strong he wondered she could not sense it wafting toward her.

But obviously she did. For at that very moment she obediently looked up and met his glance. Delighted, he bowed to her, with a locking stare that made her quickly turn away.

Shy away, turn away, run away . . . she would not be free of him, the viscount concluded. She was wrong to have said they were free of each other. They were not only tied by legal contracts and social acceptance, but beyond that by the passion that he and Angelica had exchanged. Passion was the leading string he had tied about her and now he held it loosely with just enough slack to let her think she was free. But soon he would pull her back and see her squirming, struggling, but returning to his arms!

Almost in reaction Hillary approached the baron, as if his large and imposing form could make a protective buffer. But the viscount would not permit her escape, himself obstructing her path.

"We are connected, Angelica," he whispered. "You are mine not only by your father's will and your responsibility as an English lady, but by your own heart."

"Fustian!" Hillary exclaimed, unaffected by his use of guilt and such. "I'm not the shy little maiden you terrorized with such twaddle when last in England. I've learned a lady can say no. And I have said it to you. Indeed, I've made it prodigiously clear I am *not yours,* neither as Angelica nor as Miss Astaire."

"Under whatever guise, you shall always be mine."

"Oh, pooh!" she said, quickly walking on, straight to the ebullient welcome of Bartolomeo.

"Angelica, my angel," he cried. "You must sing with me now!"

And she did. Determinedly. Never once looking at his lordship. Thus establishing her freedom. But upon leaving the room with Victorine, she noticed Wolf was smiling as if saying he'd enjoyed both her performances, that for the general audience and the one for himself.

14

Lord Wolverton must be two men, Hillary thought. One earned his reputation for capturing a score of women, was vital and rakish and on the prowl—in short, the man they called Wolf, who stalked Angelica, looking at her as if his very next breath of existence depended on touching her lips one more time. The other was the viscount, that bored, indifferent lord whose self-consequence and opinions were all that mattered to him, so filled with starch he would scarcely unbend to make a lunge at her as would the wolf.

The viscount was the one she had first met, who had come to her estate and wounded her self-esteem. The viscount was sent by the prince to destroy her dear princess. The viscount was the snuff taker who obviously felt she was not up to snuff. Stuff him!

Now there was a third one. The wolf in him was suppressed. In the sennight since he'd realized who she really was, he no longer grabbed her or dared to kiss her. Yet, unlike the viscount, he was not indifferent to her presence. This new gentleman eyed her every move, and yet was holding back, as if expecting her suddenly to come running to him.

In truth Hillary had a tendre for the wolf. Again and again she found herself looking past the lordly covering for the wolf within. Often, she'd spot evidences of him. In a glance. In a gesture. Even in a warm smile. Mostly she felt him in there, lurking. On the surface his words to all were smooth and polished, but she heard an undertow of jeering. Especially in discussion with the princess or Lady Gardener.

The night before at table, his confession that his time in Italy had taught him the gentle sex must always be treated with tenderness had almost reduced Princess Caroline to tears. He was describing, she claimed, her ideal, precisely how she'd attempted to create her court, where men and women would be loving and gentle to each other. Like the fairly tale world by these fellows Grimm she'd recently read.

The viscount had responded with typical mockery, "My grim thoughts, precisely." And he had the audacity to look to her to share his amusement. Rather she took up the salt shaker and, dropping a grain in the palm of her hand, very deliberately blew it at him. He guffawed at that. Grain of salt, indeed!

It really was at times as if they were holding hands under the table with no one the wiser. Hillary knew she had to stop reacting to him. After all, he

was not only her enemy but the princess's. She
sensed, nay, knew his threat, and chastised herself
for making any response, even unspoken.

All her life Hillary had claimed to want a *gentle*
man. Well, Sir Percy was that in spades! He had
been near to collapse one day when she gave him
the privilege of holding her hand. His hand trembled so much she spared him further agitation by
removing hers. Thinking of Sir Percy called him
forth. He'd come to join in the princess's idea of a
picnic on the veranda. Sheets were to be spread on
the marble floor. Her Highness and staff were collecting choice cushions to throw about.

Mrs. Wizzle was looking forward to it, as was
Hillary. Lord Wolverton, obviously viewing the
entire event as childish, nevertheless sardonically
claimed himself enchanted by the prospect. Hillary
gave the lord her most withering stare, to which he
responded by assuming a most innocent expression. Their communication was cut off by Mrs.
Wizzle's cry that Hillary needed a shawl against the
sun, for her white frock was almost backless. With
pleasure Sir Percy offered to run to the lady's chamber and request one from her maid. Mrs. Wizzle followed after him, certain he would not bring the correct one. So for a brief interlude, before the return of
the two and the coming of the rest, Hillary and the
viscount were alone. She pretended not to be aware
of that, walking about the trellised, ivy-twined railing. It had a wide enough top to sit on, but of course
a lady would never do so. Hillary sat on it.

"You might slip off," Wolf said, coming close.
"But then, danger appeals to you. You are inches
from falling down to the rocky shore beneath, near
twenty feet."

"I like heights. They go to my head," she said with a laugh, looking down and then out at the lake.

"You go to my head," he whispered, being Wolf again, gently touching those bare shoulders and stroking across her back.

"There is no need for you to simulate a shawl. Sir Percy is bringing mine."

"Have you ever granted Sir Percy the favor of touching you?" he asked harshly, his hands going around her waist.

She looked up at him, so close. He was staring down, as if her next words were of prodigious importance. Hillary pushed him away.

"Sir Percy is too much of a gentleman. I expect you could learn a great deal of gentility from him. Who gave you leave to touch me?"

In relief Lord Wolverton laughed, claiming he was merely holding her so she would not fall. "I am being your protector. That, after all, is my right."

"No, it is not!" she exclaimed, her blue eyes glowing with her fury. "When will you accept the fact that you have no hold over me?"

His lordship stared at her as if she were meaninglessly railing at the rail, which confidence peeved her so much that she exclaimed, "I did not tell you all about Sir Percy. He *has* touched me. I allowed him to hold my hand last night in our stroll, confident that as an honorable man he would discipline his emotions. Which he did, being more concerned about my feelings than his. Unlike some people."

"Shocking, isn't it, the way some of us give in to our emotions? I knew a lady who jumped into a pond just to enjoy the sensation . . . who sought to become one with the dawn on the lake. Impossible to credit, but she also gave kiss for kiss when in the arms of her husband-to-be."

That return to her thrust hit home indeed! Smarting at his quiet amusement, Hillary rushed to retaliate, but before she could, the others returned. His the last hit, Hillary begrudgingly conceded, not realizing she was giving a home thrust just by walking away from him and greeting Sir Percy with delight.

That timid lord was all atremble at the privilege of putting the shawl round her shoulders. Lady Gardener, just arriving, nodded her approval of the shawl, but felt Hillary's head should be similarly sheltered. At that moment Mrs. Wizzle walked in with a pink, wide-brimmed straw hat and was applauded by Lady Gardener for her forethought. Hillary allowed the two ladies to arrange the hat and shawl. Only after much primping were they both satisfied.

"You allow them to play with you like a doll," the viscount whispered with disdain.

Ere she could rejoin, there was the usual commotion at Princess Caroline's arrival. The picnic could now officially begin, except that Her Highness claimed they were waiting for the baron and Victorine. There was much good-natured bantering about Victorine not making an appearance until Count Guido did. But the princess did not smile, distracted, and next moment let out a cry of indignation. "What have you done to my darling Angelica!" Rushing to the astonished Hillary, Her Highness quickly removed both the hat and shawl. "With these shrouds how can my darling enjoy this picnic? She must feel the breeze! Ah, look, the hat has disarranged her coiffure. It is fallen. Sofie, bring me my brush . . . in the bag."

In the next moment, the princess was taking

down Hillary's pins and brushing her hair. The pale golden locks were flying every which way, as if they had a life of their own.

"Egad, she is a beauty," Sir Percy whispered, his breath choking as he stared at the wonder of that loosed hair, now revealed as long enough for her to sit on.

Near him the viscount heard and agreed. But he resented the princess displaying Hillary's tresses to all. It was as if she'd undressed the lady! They all treated her as if she were their personal plaything. Confound it, how did Miss Astaire allow such . . . such intimacies? In the next second, the lord realized that rather than resenting it, Hillary was responding to the princess's treatments like a delighted child being stroked by her mother. She held on to the princess's arm for a moment and even leaned her head against the flat, august chest. And the princess hugged her tightly.

Blast, the viscount realized with a start. They cared for each other. Truly. He realized Miss Astaire had never had a mother, and indeed had been recently orphaned. Obviously this young miss was a loving creature who readily responded to all affection.

The viscount was on the mark. Hillary did care for the princess. Mrs. Wizzle was a dear but too much of a governess, who earned her affection but not adoration. Lady Gardener was too strict and often disapproving. One could respect her but not feel entirely at ease in her presence, having always to live up to either an image of her mother or of a proper English miss. But the princess forgot all barriers and treated Hillary as if she were a child—her child. It compensated for the years she'd not been treated thus by anyone.

What a needy little creature she is, Wolf thought. That made a great deal less of her responding to *his* affection. Was she like a kitten that would cuddle up to anyone who would pet her? Just in time he recollected that she had withheld herself from Sir Percy. That was obvious from the famished expression with which that lord followed her every gesture. So Hillary did have some discrimination, after all. She was correct when she chose him to respond to, but idiotic in her affection for that flighty princess. Yet he had learned something of the depth of the young lady's devotion to Her Highness.

During his musings, he noted Sir Percy closing his eyes dreamily and putting out his hand, stroking the air before him. Without doubt the poor, besotted cawker was imagining he was touching Miss Astaire's hair. The viscount smiled in derision, and yet, yet. He himself was longing to stroke those pale yet glowing tresses!

The princess had finished brushing a hundred strokes, and tenderly arranged the locks about the young lady's shoulders.

"You do not need a shawl when you have your hair, more beautiful than spun silk, more colors and gleams than a Norwich shawl!" Her Highness, her voice breaking at a thought, concluded, "I always combed Charlotte's hair for her, when we were allowed to be together."

Hillary came close to the lady, whispering, "I know what it is to lose the person who is everything to you. My father died even a shorter time ago than Princess Charlotte. There is no assuaging that grief, but to remember that one day we shall see them again. And in the meantime, you have so many people who love you. All your court and . . . and me."

At that the two embraced away their sorrow.

In disgust the viscount turned away, leaving the scene. He'd lost his appetite for the picnic. By Jove, he had to get her away from that princess. If he had taken her to himself before these ladies had won her over, he would have been the *only* object of her affection. It would have been easy to win her love, and egad, so damned rewarding. Each day she was becoming closer to that royal lady and might very well decide, as had Her Highness, that marriage was not something she would want, and especially not to one from the prince's faction. Here in this halcyon world in Italy, he could blend in with them, but if they ever returned to England, the schism between the Tories and the Whigs, respectively the prince's group and the princess's, was deep indeed. Almost insurmountable. He had to win her in Italy and make her his before the conflict came to a head.

He must plan! He must plan!

15

Resourceful fellow that he was, an ingenious plan came readily to the viscount's mind. It was the simplest maneuver ever devised. He would tell the truth to the princess, or frankly, that he wished to ask Miss Astaire once more for her hand in marriage. That royal lady was not averse to marriage proposals in her court—Angelica almost weekly received at least one. But to him the princess stipulated that he must not too forcibly press his case and further accept rejection with restraint. The viscount gave full assurances of being on his best behavior, so the princess urged Hillary to go for a stroll with "this charming Englishman, who has turned his coat to us."

"Turncoat indeed," Hillary said coldly.

"Changed sides, Your Highness," the viscount gently reproved. "My conversion is due to your court having the most exquisite beauties." And he bowed pointedly to both ladies. The princess was flattered. Hillary stared blankly at him.

"Drivel," she said and walked away. He rushed after.

"Why don't you believe me? It was not I who duplicitously pretended to be someone I was not."

"Ha! You are masquerading this very moment. Who are you? The cold, haughty viscount? Or the wild man of feeling? Who are you? Are you sincere in your conversion to our side or not? Who are you? Do you follow me because you really care or because you cannot forgive my affront?"

"I asked you to marry me when I thought you were a courtesan—is not that enough proof of caring?"

Yet Hillary had a sensation that under the words lurked a trap. "You were not in earnest then. You meant merely to possess me. I have heard you are a renowned collector. Your horses are the talk of the ton, as is your insistence each be the most prime article. Even with such small items as snuffboxes, I note you never have the same one twice running. Yes, I expect you are a collector of all things from horses to snuffboxes to hearts."

He smiled tolerantly at her evaluation, not offended in the least. "Yes, I collect prime articles. And of women you are the most supreme example. Don't you want to join in my collection? To be the shining star of it?"

He said the last softly, and she felt a bit breathless at his cajoling, but she blinked away the effects of his gray glare and concluded, "I join no man's collection. I detest collectors. I am unique, and I want a gentleman who is aware of that."

"But is not that just what I said? You must have a connoisseur really to appreciate you."

"Pity you do not understand. I would wish a gentleman who had not spent his life glorifying himself. What else is a collection but an attempt to say to the world, 'I have the best because I am the best'?"

"Correct. I am," he said with an incorrigible grin.

But Hillary would not be laughed out of her point. "I mean what I say. I seek a gentleman who puts himself second and the woman he loves first."

"That is *your* pride talking. Quite colossal pride, actually, insisting on being of first importance. Your very demand to Count Guido that you be loved for yourself and not your money is vainglory. Miss Pergami, I gather, understands the count's need for financial support and is encouraging her father to meet his demands. A far cry from you, who would not humble yourself even to keep your father's word. In sum, you ask not just for marriage, not just love, you want a gentleman to become your total slave? Consider, are *you* worth that?"

"Probably not," she said, grinning at last—actually overcome with laughter at his image of her. "Quite true. I am not a jot worth it. Yet, widgeonlike, I intend to wait for a gentlemen who believes I am—at least in the beginning. Then if we are both subsequently disillusioned, we can say we had a lovely month or so of delusion to remember."

"I will not give you delusion, nor illusion. Simply truth. I want you. When you are prepared to accept your position in life as a wife, you will find I have offered you the highest you can seek."

Hillary sighed. "Not enough," she whispered sadly, almost forlornly. "I'll continue looking. And I suggest you leave our company and keep on with your search. The summer is almost over. We are, the princess tells me, soon going to relocate south to Leghorn on the Mediterranean. There is an Austrian she wishes to introduce into our court there. I have hopes that he will have, as the princess promises, a more devoted nature than other recently attending gentlemen."

Even about that last reference the viscount remained sanguine. Only when alone did he grimly admit he had botched the proposal. He should have made it less of a demand and more of an appeal. But egad, if she wanted total surrender, he had too much pride for that. Indeed, he wished for *her* total surrender, and obviously she had too much pride or romance for that. Now what? Now, he must act. Since she was using the oldest stratagem—jealousy, introducing that Austrian to humble him—in return, he must do the same to humble her. Indeed, if jealousy was to be the weapon of choice, he could not but win, that being his specialty. Whenever a current flirt had showed signs of overconfidence, he'd instantly switched to another rival lady to chasten the first. He'd assumed Miss Astaire was beyond such tricks. But since she was not, he was nothing loath to give her a much needed comeuppance.

Unfortunately there was not a plentiful selection at court. Therefore, he grinned, he must make do with what was at hand and began paying his attentions to Victorine. The lady was flabbergasted, resistant. Then, resembling her father's opportunism, she began to respond to his lordship, especially when Count Guido was about. Confident of his conquest, the count now found himself having to defend his territory.

As for the viscount, not only did courting Victorine give Hillary her due, but gave him the perfect excuse to be always in her presence. He congratulated himself again and again on the success of his strategy. Indeed, within a few days all the court was whispering about Lord Wolverton's shocking change of favorites. He hoped Hillary's nose would be more than tolerably out of joint and tried to be as blatant about his new preference as possible. Upon Victorine's gushing over his favorite snuffbox with the mother-of-pearl covering, he instantly gave it her.

Hillary warned her that a lady never accepted anything of appreciable value from a gentleman. Flushing, Victorine rationalized Hillary's statement as jealously due to her having stolen her beau. Wanting the box, she kept it. The viscount had found the perfect way to a Pergami heart. One bought oneself in. He gave her brooches and bracelets and won kisses and evening strolls and the threat of a duel from the count.

With the cool autumn hard upon them, Princess Caroline could dally no further at Lake Como. It was her policy to move south for the winter, but no further than Tuscany, near the Mediterranean. The palazzo being rented, all that was required was to make it suitable for a princess of her special tastes. To ensure that, Her Highness must supervise personally, and left immediately, taking along Lady Gardener and Bartolomeo. The latter addition caused the viscount's generally lifted eyebrow to go even higher, but he was no longer interested in that situation. Mrs. Wizzle and the rest of the court were to depart the next day. But before leaving that area, a small nucleus of the party was to accompany Count Guido for a tour of Milan. That group included the two young ladies as well as Countess

Oldi, who had been persuaded to supervise the trip by the count's including in the itinerary a visit to his principal palace. The count's object was to give Victorine a view of what she might lose by continuing her shocking flirtation with the viscount. But the Englishman wiped the smile from the count's face by promptly inviting himself along.

Ere her departure the princess had given Hillary a new pet. It was a white kitten with blue eyes, almost the color of Angelica's, which explained Her Highness naming it Angel. The animal caused a last-minute delay of the Milan trip by jumping from Hillary's lap and going exploring. Hillary refused to go without her. Actually she did not wish to go at all, for she resented being in the viscount's presence as audience to his latest sham. She did not have an iota of belief in his affection for Victorine. Yet hinting at those suspicions offended her friend to the quick. Indeed, the young Italian lady attributed Hillary's reaction fully and unequivocally to jealousy, especially since Victorine had now gained two of Hillary's ex-beaus.

To prove the falsity of that charge, Hillary stoically accepted a sennight ahead with a most disagreeable assortment. Besides the two gentlemen who had once been her courtiers, now both panting after another, it consisted of Countess Oldi, who was naturally devoted to her niece and spoke so little English and Hillary so little Italian that they could never converse beyond gestures, and Victorine, of course, who was decidedly cool since their disagreement. Angel was taken along as her only comfort and friend.

Never having been but a few days in London, Hillary found Milan exciting. The white marble cathedral was dazzling against the blue sky. She wished Sir Percy were there, being so well versed in all architectural matters. She had to make do with the guide. When the party was outdoors again, Hillary hung back for a last view of the imposing structure, unable not to exclaim, "But is it better than Westminster?"

"No," the viscount could not resist replying. He had been looking at her, hoping to see chagrin at his desertion, and saw rather her face in rapture. So had she viewed the lake at sunrise. He turned round and saw the cathedral through her eyes and admitted its magnificence.

"If you had followed my advice and gone to London," he said sharply, "you would have seen Westminster Abbey and many of our London marvels."

A retort died on her lips as her eyes widened at the sight of a tall form completely covered in ghostly wraps of white flannel. Most startling was a visor of net across his entire face, even the eyes. He was rattling a wooden box. She eagerly questioned Countess Oldi.

"Penitent," was all the older woman said, and shrugged.

"As penance for his own sins, he asks alms for masses of the souls in purgatory," the viscount obligingly explained, and then with a gleam of mockery could not resist asking, "Do you not have a fellow feeling with the poor sot?"

"I?"

"Indeed, for your many deceptions. And desertions."

"Piffle. My list is quite small next to yours. You would need a lifetime of penance just for what you are doing to poor Victorine. She and the count were near to an agreement. If you are not in earnest, you have one more sin on your soul. Rattle your box, my lord. I will give you alms."

Laughing at the appropriateness of that, the viscount added with his usual sangfroid, "I never apologize for my acts. Nor ask for forgiveness. Certainly would not demean myself to do penance. That is so blasted Italian. An Englishman would never expose himself to comment on the thoroughfare."

Hillary, grinning at the thought of the viscount in such a costume, responded, "Actually I think it is rather generous of him to humble himself so."

"Not exactly in your line, one would have thought. But if you wish one can suggest several ways to humble yourself in expiation."

Hillary ignored his innuendo and his closeness, swiftly moving away. At that the viscount took a moment to collect himself and recollect his strategy, moving rapidly back to Victorine. But such lapses recurred. Visiting the Ambrosian Library, the count was attempting to impress Victorine by translating the love letters of Lucretia Borgia and Cardinal Bembo on display. Countess Oldi halted him midparagraph, concluding it was too "warm" for young ladies' ears, which left both ladies disappointed. They were directed instead to look through a glass cage where a lock of hair from that infamous woman was preserved. The viscount could not help but indicate to Hillary that it was not quite as blond as hers. "I expect all perfidious women are blond, and all sincere ones," he said, turning to Victorine, "brunette."

That could not but be received with approval by all, since Hillary was the only blond lady there. "I wonder why they do not have a lock of Cardinal

Bembo's hair. We could then comment on the perfidy of dark-haired gentlemen," she responded.

"He was probably bald," the viscount whispered.
Both could not help but laugh at that deflation. Once
more the two had to remind each other to part. That
was most difficult since they found they not only
laughed at the same things but enjoyed the same
views. Reaching the count's palace, Hillary had a talk
with herself and decided she would give Victorine an
open field. Complaining of a cold, she secluded herself in her chamber for the entire visit. Victorine,
realizing her aim, was warm again to her friend, and
reported every night how the two gentlemen were
vying for her attention. She had never enjoyed herself as much. Hillary, watching Angel scratch about
for something in the corners, was reminded to ask if
the viscount had come up to scratch and proposed.
Victorine admitted he had not, but Count Guido had
lowered the amount of dowry he'd wanted. It was
within her father's means, and when she returned,
she would have either the princess or her father
question the viscount as to his intentions, and if he
was not sincere, she would accept the count before
he changed his mind. She dashed out with a blown
kiss. Dejectedly, Hillary sat down on the settee, soon
joined by Angel, who'd lost whatever had been
sought in the corner. "What say, Angel, dear?" Hillary
asked with a laugh as the cat settled in her mistress's
lap. "Have we been wasting our time in empty corners? I expect both of us will be happier at Leghorn.
There with the sea so near, we shall have a plenitude
of new fish to catch."

Angel was alert at the suggestion, ears up, but no
fish appeared, so she forgot the promise and cat-
napped.

Hillary's thoughts were of the Mediterranean Sea and wishing she could dip a certain lord in it up to his patrician brow. Angel meowed in objection to Hillary's sudden clenching of her fingers through the kitten's white, silky fur. Laughing, Hillary made amends by stroking softly and apologizing, "Pardon. I ought not even be thinking of that lord, who shall shortly be returning to England . . . unless his interest in Victorine is not mummery." Yawning, Angel signaled that she had not a single concern about his lordship's single state.

"You advise me to forget him, I presume? You are appalled as am I by his shallow, philandering nature. Blast him!"

Angel was moved by something in her mistress's voice to rush up and lick her face.

"Thank you," Hillary laughed. "At least you are faithful . . . and loving." And she hugged the animal back.

Their journey to Leghorn would take them past Pisa. Hillary's inclination was to stop for a view of that inclining structure, but Countess Oldi insisted the princess had waited long enough for their attendance. Yet while Pisa was to be passed by, another delay was approved, Count Guido's detour through the smaller ridge of the Apennine Mountains. Pressed by the viscount's competition, the count wished to win points by showing off another of his holdings, a vast field of vines and olive trees. How could Victorine and Countess Oldi object to this obvious flaunting of his eligibility, when both were quite eager to be convinced of that very thing?

As the carriage went up a narrow path cut into the mountain, the count was happily preparing them for the view. "We go to the top," the count insisted, "because my lands are behind and can only be seen if one looks from there." So the carriage continued higher up the path, while Countess Oldi, swallowing her terror, merely asked Hillary to change places with her, as she refused to watch how near to the edge the carriage was veering. The count laughed and assured the dear women of the generations of travelers who had successfully climbed this very road. Quasi-reassured, the women at least forced themselves to ignore the swaying of the coach making spiral turns up the mountain. Victorine concentrated on the compliment, but she could not help but wish, as the carriage rocked, that the gentleman had simply sent her flowers. At last, mercifully, the count leaned out and called the coachman to halt, indicating they were at the lookout point.

When they were handed down from the coach, the two Pergami ladies were more than willing to follow the count away from the road's edge to the comparable safety of the mountain itself, and they hurriedly leaned against the rocky mass. "Here," the count said proudly. "You stand here and lean, and you see the beginning of my lands. Peeking from the peak, yes?"

Victorine obliged and claimed she was much impressed at whatever she was supposed to have seen. Countess Oldi refused to lean or look, keeping her eyes closed. Hillary was too awed by the nearer view to follow them back. Instead the lady went directly to the edge of the road and looked down.

The coachman was muttering that they should be moving on. There was not enough room if anyone else came along the road. The count ignored him, continuing his description. By then the countess and Victorine were attempting to cut short his oration. The coachman sat on the carriage steps worrying that the horses were beginning to fret. He shouted something to that effect, but no one but the viscount paid him any mind.

Lord Wolverton was a noted horseman, and he, too, was disturbed by the horses' antics. He shouted to the count that they should immediately descend because of the horses' fidgets.

"*Stupido!*" the count called back, laughing. "These animals, they are used to heights. They trained for it. My opinion is . . . it is *you* that is fidget," he said with a sneer. "You do not like to look down, my lord? Me, I do! I am more accustomed than you English to this platitude."

"Quite so," the viscount retorted with a grin of amusement. Hillary was unable not to smile at that malapropism, but her expression altered at Wolf's next comment. "Nevertheless something is wrong with these animals. They are sensing something. It never pays not to respond to an animal's sharper instincts." Uneasily he looked about.

At that Hillary paid heed to the atmosphere. It seemed heavy, as if pressing. Yet the view once more attracted, and she returned to the edge, exclaiming at the vast panorama. There were so many other mountains and hills about, as well as streaks of green treetops, that Hillary felt as if she owned the entire world. Close to the horizon she could see a speck of sea, and her heart jumped. Ah, the Mediterranean where the princess had assured her they would bathe together. But a sudden jolt interrupted her happy expectations. Turning to warn the others temporarily rescued her. For Hillary had stepped back and when she'd been shaken, she landed on the edge. But that was not sufficient.

At that moment everybody understood the warning the horses had been sending. The jolt, as if a giant had bumped into the mountain in an attempt to dislodge all who dared come upon it, sent the carriage rolling over the rim. The shrieking horses and driver were dragged along and dashed to pieces as they went tumbling down.

Those screams nudged the rest out of their shock. The count threw himself in front of Victorine, flattening her against the mountain's side. Countess Oldi was sobbing and crying out, "*Terremoto!*"

The count grabbed for her as well, pushing her against the rock. "Hold on," he unnecessarily ordered both ladies.

Closer to the edge, the viscount had been thrown to his knees. He was just rising. His first reaction had been to search for Hillary. Before his stunned eyes, he saw her teetering on the edge. "Move back, by God! It's a bloody *earthquake!*"

In a mad dash, Wolf was scrambling toward her, reaching out just as she was out of his reach. He could do naught but stand at the ridge and shout. Yet his voice was blotted out by the sound of rocks falling after the lady, as if to crush any last hope and bludgeon her body into oblivion.

She had gone over in a blink and no one had heard her scream as she fell. Hillary was nowhere in sight.

16

There was silence for a breath, and then
screams coming from Victorine and the countess.

"You are safe," Count Guido was assuring the two
women. "It is just a slight one. We have had these
before. But another could come. They pair themselves. Best if we were off this high point to a wider
road." He looked round, himself fearful of getting
too near the edge lest he be tossed over as he'd
seen the coach and driver go. Moving slowly, the
count was halfway toward the stunned viscount on
the edge.

"Careful," the count cried out. "Another could
come and throw you over. Move back."

Turning round, Wolf's face was white and strained.
From head to toe he was shuddering in impotent
rage. Next moment he opened his mouth but naught

came out. His head kept shaking in wordless denial. An unspoken No . . . *No!*

The count could not understand the agony of the man over the loss of the coachman and horses. Sad, yes, but not enough to destroy a gentleman of his class. And then he looked about. A sudden remembrance overtook him like an icy draft. Where was the beautiful Angelica? Nowhere. Hoarsely he gasped, "She was in the coach?"

The viscount still did not respond. He'd turned round again, scanning back and forth.

Count Guido's warm sympathy and affection for the beautiful lady overcame his practical good sense and he stood next to the viscount on the edge. Casting a hurried glance, he noted a wheel lodged down in a crevice, but no other sign of the coach. "There is no hope," he said softly with tears in his eyes. "It is *molti, molti metri* down. There would be nothing left of the coach."

"She was not in the coach," Lord Wolverton was just able to say. Some dim hope stirred in the numbness encasing him.

"Ah! Thank Deo! Up here?" And he looked about, still seeing no one.

The same toneless voice answered, "No, she was standing here. I couldn't reach her. She went over."

A deep sigh from the count. And then he could only say, "It was quick. We must think of that. But how to tell the ladies! The princess!" Shaking his head he went back to the ladies, who were by now composed enough to let go of the rock face and stand at least a step away from it.

The viscount heard screams behind him and then sobs as the count relayed the message. Moments passed. Wolf was reliving that split second. The nub was that he'd been too far away from her. She had gone over before he could straighten up. Yet, yet, if he had lunged! Could he have grasped her . . . pushed her to the side and kept her up there with him in his arms?

A cry came up, ripping through him. For the first time in his life, his lordship did not consider his appearance before others. The cry was one of sorrow, yes, but mostly of fury at himself. Damn him to hell, why hadn't he moved faster? Why hadn't she been a step back from the edge? He might have reached her then. Or if only he had been standing beside her! Confound it, why, oh, why had he let her go to the edge, while he like a cawker had stood back admiring her enjoying the scene? Ah, he had been careless with her, and she so precious. He had allowed her to roam about, risking herself, knowing how wild and unthinking she was. He should have put himself between her and all harm. He should have . . . made himself her guard, her protector, and positioned himself always between her and all danger. But he'd almost felt as if nothing could touch her. As if she were not mortal and would float over lakes. An angel with wings, she'd seemed, who could rise above all mortal harm.

The count was back, urging him to follow them. They were going to a lower level where they would be safer in case of an aftershock or a rockslide. The viscount was just standing there still in his daze. The count clicked his tongue at him, and then, shrugging his shoulders, warned, "We shall leave you here. We leave. We go . . . now."

Victorine behind was pleading with the viscount to escort them. He was not responding, standing perilously at the edge, staring down. Countess Oldi exchanged glances with the count. They whispered, quickly concluding he was to be left to his own devices for they must immediately leave. But Victorine ordered the count to bring him along.

"How can I take him? He wishes to stay there!" he snapped, forgetting he was talking to his love.

"Grab his hand. He will come," she shouted. And the count, muttering, once more walked back to the edge and without saying a word, pulled at the viscount's arm. The lord jumped and nearly went over, taking the count with him, but they righted themselves. The count was so furious that he'd nearly lost his life for the imbecilic English lord that he began shouting and cursing and pulling him along until the viscount was well back; and then he shoved him toward Victorine. Her sobs woke some chivalry left in the numbed aristocrat, and he let her take his arm as he escorted her down, while the count followed with the almost prostrate older lady.

They walked. There was no point talking. Only Countess Oldi kept muttering prayers. Occasionally Victorine cried out to God. Count Guido cursed. The viscount remained silent.

When they had reached the level where the road was wide enough to extend to a plateau, the viscount dropped Victorine's hand. "I must go back," he whispered. "You're safe here."

"There is nothing . . . to go back to," Victorine said, sobbing. "We must go forward. There!" she pointed to a peasant and a cart. "We must get that."

The count was before her. He'd already brought out enough lire so the peasant was more than willing to give his cart and himself as the driver to take them down to the town. Behind him a gig approached. A young boy of fourteen had come too late to join in the largesse. He stopped to stare and congratulate the driver on the good fortune the *terremoto* had brought him. When all the survivors had piled into the cart, Countess Oldi began having hysterics and Victorine had her hands full with her, and so was unable to observe that the viscount had not joined them. The count did, but had lost interest in that gentleman's welfare. He had done more than was called for, risking his own life to bring him to safety. If the idiot would go back, let him!

The viscount waited until the cart had disappeared and then, turning toward the waving youngster in the gig, he managed half in Italian and half in gestures to convey, "A lady has fallen over the edge up there. Is there a possibility . . ." He could not finish the question. The young boy looked at him with the curiosity and delight one gives to others who are experiencing a tragedy. This was even more sensational since it was a young lady.

"She fall?"

"Yes."

"Ah, sad. Was she beautiful?"

"The most beautiful lady I've ever seen."

That delighted the young man. He nodded. It had to be so for it to be a truly memorable tale. "And you loved her?" he continued, to make the story complete.

"And . . ." The viscount, still half-dead in shock, gasped out the truth, his voice breaking, "And . . . I loved her."

The young boy's cup was full. He would tell everyone he had seen a stiff English gentleman cry, sink down onto the ground and cry. What else could a man do when losing the most beautiful woman ever?

He, too, would cry. In fact he joined the Englishman in tears.

The Englishman recovered first. "We must get . . ." His mind blanked out and then clicked into place. "A rope . . . a long, heavy rope . . . several to tie together . . . and bring your gig." He reached into his pockets and brought out more lire than the youngster had ever seen. Ah, this *terremoto* had made it his family's lucky day as well.

"And nails," the viscount said with a steady voice.

"Nails?"

"No, pointless. Just the rope, blast you!"

The boy shrugged. "No use. Even a mountain climber could not . . . Too far down!" He stopped talking as the Englishman was not listening. The dazed man was just walking on, back up the mountain. His dark hair was blowing in the breeze, covering his eyes. He did not brush it away. His cravat was askew, and he did not straighten it. He merely walked.

The young boy shrugged. There was a wild glow in those unforgettable gray eyes, he told his mother as he collected the ropes and nails and hammer and everything else he could think of, all the time shaking his head and exclaiming, "He thinks he can climb down to her. Or do you think, Mama, that he is going to throw himself over as well? I should like to see that!"

His mother looked up from the money in her hand and blessed the *terremoto* and her son. "Go with my blessings," she cried, and added, "but if he jumps, ask him to empty his pockets first, for your brothers and sisters. And do not get too close if he starts to foam at the mouth. Mad with grief is good. But if he is just mad, you be careful."

The boy, uncertain how to tell the difference, nevertheless agreed to keep a wary eye, and set off with great anticipations for more drama.

Just before the earthquake, Hillary had been holding Angel in her arms while standing at the edge of the mountain, gazing at the encircling chain of smaller mountains. Closer, there was a valley of trees. Then looking directly down she saw a sheer drop and quickly looked up, steadying her balance. A bird in the sky swayed oddly as if it had lost a wing, unable to soar. It gave one small shriek. Angel in her arms was mewing wildly. Those were two signs. Within her as well was a warning sensation that made her instantly step back.

She was in the act of turning when the mountain shook. That was the reason she did not immediately go over. Rather she was hanging half off, half on. But the tremor had been so strong she was finally shaken off and tossed out into the air. The mountain had heaved its back and all on its edge had gone down. She'd been clutching Angel with one hand as she fell. Instinctively Hillary reached out with the other hand and grabbed on to a bush. It had broken her fall.

As if fate were cruelly toying with her, Hillary hung there, suspended. She gasped but still did not scream. All her energy and composure was needed for her rescue. The bush was already straining under her light weight. Looking wildly about for some other support, she spotted below, but to the extreme left, a ledge that was wide enough to rest on. Her instincts told her to jump for it. Her fear told her she would be jumping off to her death.

The sky was all around her. Oft had she looked into the heavens, convinced her mother and father were up there. Now in her most desperate state, she appealed to them. Oh, she knew they could not rescue her, but they could do what they'd often done, give her calmness and the ability to make the correct decision. At that, like a wave, she felt an ease going through her body, telling her she was loved. Angel in her arms was crying. It was up to her to rescue her cat and herself. She had no one else she could count on. If she could only get herself to move.

The bush made the decision for her as it cracked some more. Now it was clearly leap or fall. Recollecting the axiom, "Look before you leap," Hillary looked hard at the ledge, fixed it in her sight, and then with a deep breath threw her light body across and down to it. She fell exactly in its center. Angel was either jarred or jumped from her hands. But that was providential, for Hillary needed both hands to stop herself from rolling over. Huddled, gasping, crying, she rested, afraid to risk another motion. But she got up on her knees and crawled as far back as she could and sat with her shoulders against the rock. The shelf was three feet wide and long. One could sit but not stretch. She got her breath. When her heart eased from beating so loudly, she was able to hear a meow. Angel had also crawled to the back of the ledge, but was wary of coming to Hillary's arms from whence she'd been tossed about. Thank you, she seemed to be saying, she would stay on her own four feet.

Very well, Hillary concluded, resigned and too shattered to coax the animal. "Oh, my God," Hillary cried then as her mind had a moment to realize what had happened to her. Worse was assessing her predicament at present. She began to tremble. "Stop it!" she shouted at herself. "Stay calm!"

She dared not look down, knowing how far that was. Yet, after a while, hoping to find another larger ridge that might lead to a path, she forced herself to look below and gasped at the distance down. In despair she looked about. There was no other ledge. The only place of safety was where she was. It was ages-strong and would hold her, as long as she did not fall asleep and roll off. Next to the ridge there was what she'd first thought was another bush. But on closer examination it was a small tree, growing sideways and up. It would be safer yet if she could hold on to it. But that meant risking movement. She had to move, for her brain warned her there was the threat of a gust of wind knocking her down. Or the mountain shaking once more. She had to hold on to something. Steeling herself, she shifted her weight toward the tree, inching, to ensure that neither she nor the mountain became quite aware of her effrontery, fearful that if the mountain realized her intent, it would throw her off again. Yet after two more shifts and the mountain not reacting, Hillary concluded it was no longer interested in her. Emboldened, she risked a larger shove and another, and eventually by that pattern, reached the tree. Immediately, she put her hand through one strong branch for added security and sobbed at that small victory. It gave her the excuse to rest. And just breathe. Just be.

With terror temporarily receding, Hillary's body demanded attention. She'd known all along she'd been hurt—whether while falling, landing, or jumping. Somewhere along, a muscle or ligament in her shoulder had torn, for her arm hung limply. There was a sharp pain whenever she moved it, bringing tears. Both her knees hurt, but she could move her legs as well as the other arm. That would have to do. Ignoring pain and terror, she closed her eyes, hoping when she opened her lids she would see some way out of her predicament.

Life had dealt Hillary two gigantic blows—first her mother's death and then her father's. Both times she'd first reacted as Angel did—turning her stomach up to the world, showing she was defenseless and assuming fate would finally forbear to hit her again, only to learn quickly that did not serve. Fate struck at will, regardless of supplication. Eventually to survive one had to roll back on one's feet and stand up and climb out of the dilemmas on one's own. As she'd done by taking care of Holly House and dealing with the empty chair behind the fireplace and the chess pieces that never again would be lovingly stroked. And her own hair that he would no longer touch and kiss. Even when Hillary had hardened her grief, she was struck again by the appearance of the cold stranger and his haughty demands. But similarly she'd overcome that forced engagement by once more taking her future into her own hands. She'd come there to a happy time in Italy . . . only to meet her death.

Shying away from that conclusion, the next moment Hillary forced herself to face up to it. If she were to die there, at least she'd had the pleasure of travel and meeting the princess, who loved her, as did Mrs. Wizzle and to some lesser extent, Lady Gardener. And forgetting false modesty, she'd also discovered the joy of being admired and the delight of embraces. Kisses were not annoying and simply breath-stopping. She'd been taught by Lord Wolverton's kisses, one could drift into a pleasure zone of peace and fulfillment. Blissful to have felt that before one died. Inevitably Hillary began thinking of the viscount, wishing both had been less interested in dueling to win than in joining to love. What an intolerable waste of feelings . . . and now life!

Of a sudden Hillary recalled that she'd been standing in front of Lord Wolverton when the mountain had shrugged her off. Could he, too, have been tossed over? If so, why could not the two have gone over together, possibly clasped in each other's arms? Better yet would have been for both to land on the ledge. His strength would certainly have been most useful. She recollected the few times he'd picked her up. He was, she owned, powerful. Her father had said he boxed at Jackson's Saloon and added something about his "stripping well." That was boxing cant, she assumed, but the phrase was shockingly indelicate, she had felt at the time, although it became more palatable, even intriguing, after that same lord had held her in his arms.

Dear God, if they were only together here, somehow he would lift her to safety, Hillary felt. But instead she languished, her mind wandering, while the sun stared her in the eye, telling her it would soon blind her or drowse her and she would slip into its arms and burn in a blaze.

Actually that would be a rather lovely death. Blazing into a good-night. Preferable to diminishing in sheets and darkened rooms. Up there on a mountain, she would end by blending into the beauty of nature and the sky and the earth.

Curiously, once having accepted its not being

too ill a way to die, Hillary lost her fear of being up there and stopped cringing. Indeed, the moment she agreed to die up there, she sought for ways to live. The tree that she was holding on to could be used to climb, couldn't it? But she wondered what it led to, for she could not see above her. The jump had taken her to the side of where she'd been previously. There might be another ledge above hers that would be closer to the top, from where she could stand and scream.

She screamed anyway then, surprised she had not thought to call for help all that time, but she'd been so certain anyone about would have been shouting down to her. Nevertheless she cried for help in English and Italian. Then she called different people. Victorine and Count Guido. She skipped Countess Oldi. And at last she called to him. Called him Lord Wolverton. Viscount. And again and again, Wolf, because it was short and the sound carried and because it was to the wolf in him she was appealing. To the wild animal that would be able to climb across the mountain and pull her up, seeking her out and saving her, as if she were his pledged mate.

Hearing a howl would have been comforting. But Hillary had to grin. She was thinking in mythic terms of a man turning into an animal. Actually if he could so metamorphose himself, it would be vastly preferable if he'd turned into an eagle. Even better if she could turn into an eagle and fly off. For in real life only one person was so dedicated to one's survival, and that was oneself. She stopped wasting her time crying out and cried her disappointment.

Then she heard someone else crying. It was Angel, who had forgiven Hillary's dropping her and was cuddling. "Well, it's you and me together, Angel," she whispered, comforted by the return of the furry thing. It trembled in her lap as she trembled in the mountain's lap. When she had a little more energy, she would attempt to climb the tree, she promised both herself and Angel. But for a moment she had to gather strength, and closed her eyes to do so.

It was high noon and the sun was burning Hillary's lids, so after a small doze, she opened them. With a groan she recalled where she was and stopped herself quickly from stretching. Her right shoulder and arm were now a symphony of pain—sharp and dull with overtones of jabs, as the arm hung useless. She could not even pet Angel. Or shrug the kitten off as it climbed up that arm to her shoulder and landed on her head. She shook the animal off and the offended Angel jumped from there to the tree. Good, Hillary thought, stay there. Much as she loved Angel, she couldn't hold her or help her. "You're on your own," she whispered, "as am I. I hope you do better than I have."

Angel blinked once and turned her blue eyes upward. Then slowly, digging in her claws, she climbed the tree, meowing as she went.

Lord Wolverton had torn off his cravat and was lying flat against the road, leaning his head over. He had done that at various places, hoping to see or hear some sounds, some life.

The young boy, Michele, had arrived with the rope. The viscount got up and approached him. Michele stepped back, warily remembering his mother's words about the man being mad, but the

viscount ignored him and went for the ropes. One
was the strong, long rope Michele used to climb up
to the barn roof. It had an iron clip at one end that
was to be attached to an iron opening. The other
was a substantially longer rope that was to be used
to fence in their farm. The gentleman accepted both
ropes, but after a brief glance, dismissed the rest of
the boys's hurried offerings, including the nails and
hammer. Lord Wolverton was walking about searching for an outcropping of sufficient strength and yet
thinness to tie one end of the rope. Michele helpfully looked about with him. Both found nothing.
Michele shrugged. The viscount concentrated.
Above, the mountain had several promontories.
Egad, that was it; rather than climbing down, he
would climb up, to secure the rope around the
promontory. Of further benefit was that the higher
position ought give him a better view of the situation below.

Heartened by finally having a course of action,
Wolf went speedily toward the peak and began climbing up.

"Wrong way," Michele called helpfully, but when
he was ignored, he simply grinned. His mother was
correct. The Englishman was off in the head. His
woman fell down, and he climbed up. Simpleton!

But in a few moments Michele grasped what the
climber was doing. He was quickly and efficiently
tying the rope around the pointy part of the mountain that looked to Michele like an outstretched arm
of God indicating heaven. While the Englishman
was efficiently positioning the longer rope, Michele
was helping by cheering from below. The viscount
did not respond either to the jeers or cheers. He
was concentrating on tying several standard double

figure-eight knots. Before attaining to his dignities as Viscount Wolverton, he'd climbed the bell tower to remove the clapper at school. All for a lark! He had used a rope then and had young lads of the age of that boy below cheering and jeering. But, egad, he had done it. There was nothing he could not do. As long as there was something one could attempt. He stood up, delighted that he'd had the memory of himself climbing the tower. It seemed like a gift to tell him not only that he could succeed but that he should do so.

Holding to the rope, Wolf leaned over the edge. His breath caught. There was a shelflike extension down there with a small tree growing at its side, its top almost reaching the road below. Wolf could descend back to that road and hang himself over and attempt to reach the tree. His logic pointed out that the ledge was not directly under the spot where Hillary had fallen but rather to the left. But his heart told him that was the only place she could be. If she was not there, he would henceforth see her only in his dreams. But his love, his instincts, his will told him she was not gone from his life. In a moment he was awash in assurance.

Signaling to the boy, Wolf had him stand directly in line with the ledge as a marker. Michele moved as directed, but when the Englishman started to descend he ran forward to greet him.

Enraged, the viscount cursed the young boy out thoroughly, but since it was in English, the youngster did not take offense at being called a sapskull and gudgeon and blithering idiot. Once more the viscount positioned him, signaling that he was to remain precisely at that spot. Michele remained standing there stiffly while Wolf climbed down and came directly toward him. The boy had the sensation that the Englishman meant to push him over, yet so glowering was his expression he could not disobey and move. The viscount placed a rock as big as his head in that place to mark it and dismissed the boy.

In relief Michele ran back to the horse and gig and got in, ready to ride off if any more threatening gestures were directed toward him. But apparently he had served his function and was forgotten. Now Wolf was back to lying flat and looking down. From there, though closer, he could not see around the jutting edge even to sense the ledge below. But he knew it was there, he had seen it. Standing up, he tied the rope hanging from above around his waist. Similarly he tied the shorter rope with the hook around his hips. Secured, he lay back flat on the ground, only this time hanging perilously over. From that position he could hear the branches rustle. Extending his hand he was disappointed at not being able to touch it. From above the tree had seemed closer. But there was a significant space. Damn it! His hand hung there for a while as he rethought the situation when he was startled to feel something soft and furry land on his arm.

"Egad!" the viscount exclaimed, straightening up and bringing up with him a white kitten. "It's Angel! Her blasted cat." The blue-eyed kitten shivered, clutching to the viscount and attempting to cuddle against him. "Where is she, blast you? Don't tell me God has such irony that all this was done to rescue *you!*"

The kitten looked abashed but delighted to be rescued anyway.

"Yes, but she was holding you! If you landed there, she must have as well!"

In a whirl he dropped Angel, who ran toward Michele. The lad was amused and delighted they'd rescued something, and with a cheer scooped up the animal into the gig. Once again the viscount was back to lying down by the edge and leaning way over. This time he called a name.

"Angelica!" And then when there was no response, he attempted, "Miss Astaire." Then in despair, "Hillary!"

"Help!"

"*Good God, you're there!* Hold on!"

Hillary shook herself. A voice had called her name. It was *his* voice. Surely not a fantasy. He called again, and then she knew it was so. He was close. She felt a sudden loosening of the terror encasing her, a surge of joy. Her Wolf had come! She sobbed a bit, and then, her mind clearing, she concentrated on the facts. His sounding so near meant the tree led up to the road. Momentarily she was chagrined that she'd not had the gumption to climb it earlier on her own and rescue herself. But she'd made one attempt and been unable with her injured shoulder to pull herself up. There was so much pain from her arm and head as well. Yet now, newly charged, she shoved herself with all her might toward the tree, landing fully on it and holding hard with her good hand. Half on the ledge, half on the tree, she hung there. Once more she heard her name and attempted to answer. But she was using all her energy to hold on. She was looking down and panic began spreading through her again, until she heard his lordship's cool, superior voice calling, "I've got your blasted cat!"

That was so typically Wolverton, it surprised a small laugh out of her and brought her to herself again. She rejoiced further at the thought of Angel's safety. Perhaps that meant she was next to be rescued. Buoyed, she made another attempt to pull herself up higher.

"I'm on a ledge down here by the tree," she managed to cry out.

"I know. Stay there."

The familiar matter-of-fact tones calmed her. They challenged her. She must climb up to where Wolf was waiting. She climbed. Pulled. Inadvertently her glance went down, and she saw her death there. Then she looked up again to safety. The pain in her injured arm threw her off-balance and the other arm was hurting as well from the tightness with which she was holding onto the trunk in a rapt embrace.

Possibly he was planning to climb down on that very tree, but heavens, it was too weak to support them both. She whispered that, but he did not respond. For a moment Hillary had the dread that he had left. That he had never been there. "Where are you?" she screamed. And quite close to her, almost at her side, came his quiet voice. "Here."

Her eyes were foggy, but her other senses were clear. He was there. Almost close enough to touch. He was climbing down. There was a rope attached to him. As always, he appeared to know exactly what he was doing. He nonchalantly swung the hooked end of the rope hanging from his hips toward the tree. It held on, and he pulled himself behind her. She felt his body covering hers. His mouth was at her ear. He was breathing lightly but with some exertion as he disconnected the hook and tied that end around her waist.

Pulling hard, she felt herself becoming part of his body. Lashed together. For a moment that gave her an overwhelming sense of security. In his fierce, clutching embrace she and he moved as one. Hillary's arm and shoulder were shot with fresh pain as he clasped her, but she almost relished the pain.

"Just hold on to me," he whispered. "By gad, I've got you now, and I'll not let you go!"

She was appeased by that. But the next moment her heart jolted and she cried out as he pushed them away from the tree's safety and swung them back and forth on the rope, like a pendulum. Her heart beat loudly in terror as they were suspended in air, the two of them hanging in space.

"Enjoy it!" he said with an excited laugh, sounding as if he could climb without a rope—fly if need be! His confidence assuaged her fear, and she relaxed.

"Quite a unique experience hanging here, would you not say?" Wolf was speaking conversationally, attempting to keep her from going into a swoon, for her face was white and her dress torn half off, and her shoulder, he gathered, was of no use to her.

"Are we going to die together?" she asked calmly, almost in acceptance.

"You can be certain that henceforth, my darling, we shall be doing everything together. For I have you close. We are one."

She felt that was so, as he methodically hauled them up. He found a crack one place and another and lifted them both up, using the rope only when necessary so as not to strain it too much, keeping it for security only. She attempted to help him, but he told her sharply to let him handle it, and indeed, she had only ruined his rhythm. She let him reach and pull, reach and pull.

Michele could not resist coming to the edge. He let out a "Bravo!" upon seeing the gentleman holding a beautiful blond lady whose long hair was flying with the wind so that it seemed the Englishman had fished an angel out of the sky! What a story that was! Wanting to be part of it, and forgetting his mother's warning, he lay down on the road as the Englishman had done and extended his hand, but he was swiftly told to go to the devil. "I'm bringing her up myself. You're in the way, blast you."

The lady was smiling at him and even laughing softly. Wolf had brought them up to the level of the road, where they teetered. He took the slack end of the rope with the clip that was holding them together and attempted to toss it onto the edge of the mountain. It caught on a crack and began to slip. Michele ran and stepped on it and pushed it into a deeper crack where it held. Then thrilled with his assistance, he began pulling the couple up, crying out to the world, "I'm fishing angels!"

"Stand off, you idiot! You're unbalancing us!"

Michele stepped back. On his own the grim-faced Englishman climbed over the edge, dragging the lady with him. They were both on solid ground, but still near the edge. Taking a breath, the exhausted viscount was just able to whisper to the boy, "Get the horse and gig." Then untying the ropes, he laboriously stood up, and pulled the half-conscious lady farther onto the center of the road. She was securely back on the mountain at last. Wolf smiled his exaltation. He'd fished an angel! His angel! "You're safe," he whispered soothingly, but with a crack of relief in his voice. "And I'll keep you safe."

And then with a murmur of thanks to the mountain he lifted the lady and carried her to the gig, placing her in. Angel pounced on her inert body. The viscount jumped in after and scooped Angelica into his arms. Again and again he kissed her, trying not to let her see the tears spilling down his cheeks as he murmured his love for her. That was when he sensed an audience and looked up, spotting Michele watching with a big smile, as if it were the concluding scene of a carnival act. In fact he was just beginning to applaud.

"Confound you, idiot! Get us out of this place. There could be another shock any moment!"

Not understanding the gentleman's English, Michele sat there grinning until the Englishman spat out one word in Italian. But that word sent the boy jumping onto the gig and swiftly directing the horse down toward safety. The word was *Terremoto!*

17

Everyone was attempting to blot out her experience, Hillary acknowledged as she lay on a Grecian settee of pale golden silk, carried for her convenience every morning out onto the balcony. She, who had never been demanding, found herself unwittingly exploiting them all. A mere allusion to her trauma and everyone was quick to give her what she wished.

The first request had been to move her from the room the princess had lovingly prepared at the large palazzo in Leghorn. Not that Hillary was ungrateful for the fresh satin hangings chosen to match exactly the yellow glory of her hair, nor the selection of delicate French furniture that Hillary had preferred. But the view sent her shivering.

She who had once loved to gaze at mountains, the higher the better, with their tops touching the tip of the sky, now found them looming and laughing and threatening future terror. Here, bless God, the Apennine Mountains were not directly atop her as they'd been so magnificently at Lake Como, but yet, she wished for no mountain view at all. During the carriage ride to Leghorn, her arm and shoulder immobilized by swathes of linen, her other hand held tightly by Lord Wolverton and her head in Victorine's lap, Hillary had occasionally wished to be lifted up to see how close they were to Leghorn.

"Can I see the sea?" she kept asking, as if the wide expanse of that other massive wonder of nature could wipe out the first terror of nature, its mountains.

Victorine was stroking her hair and assuring her they would see the sea shortly. Count Guido was cursing himself for having brought them up to that peak. Victorine and Hillary assured him no one could predict a *terremoto,* therefore no one could blame him, although Lord Wolverton looked as if he did.

"How could we assume you were not in pieces?" the count continued graphically, justifying himself for above the hundredth time for not staying and joining the viscount in her rescue.

Hillary winced at any reference to her moments hanging on the ledge and attempted to turn the topic. But it was the only one in all their thoughts. Angel on her lap had undergone the same ordeal, but the kitten did not seem to have been noticeably reduced in spirit, unlike Hillary. Everyone was much struck at the change in her. Gone was the laughing, teasing romp of a young lady. Now Hillary was languid and nervous. Sudden sounds made her jump. Constantly Victorine had to hug her to reassure her that all was well and she was safe.

The viscount was chafing that he could not hold Miss Astaire in his arms. He would certainly do a better job of it than her young friend, who carelessly moved about and let Hillary almost fall to the bottom of the coach each time. Nor were Victorine's constant tears helpful. Nor her cries of, "I thought I'd lost you!" The only comfort for Hillary was the large, well-sprung coach, sent by the princess, filled with satin pillows for Hillary to rest against. Nevertheless, with each jarring motion there was pain. Confound it, his injured lady needed strong support from the swaying. Yet Victorine insisted Hillary would only feel "safe" in her arms.

It was on the tip of his tongue to say Hillary's safety had come about only through his arms—which was where the lady should be at this moment! Blast that Pergami woman—once more she'd let his dear one fall, causing a spasm of discomfort on Hillary's beautiful face. That was the last straw. Wolf leaned forward and said firmly, "She needs a stronger arm, Miss Pergami, than your delicate grasp. I think it would be best if you let me . . . support her for a while."

Victorine had looked at him in conflict. As delicate as Hillary was, she had become a weight, but then, Victorine's love would not let her relinquish the duty. Nor her guilt. They had flown off the mountaintop and sought safety while Hillary was clinging to its side. There was the look in this English lord's eyes that constantly reminded of his having gone back, climbed down, and pulled Hillary to safety. His every word intimidated. As now, when he sternly claimed he alone knew how to hold and protect her friend. While Victorine was considering her reply, the viscount took the decision and Hillary out of her hands.

There was a gasp of outrage from Countess Oldi. Hillary was an unmarried lady. It was not permitted that he embrace her!

The object of both embrace and discussion, Hillary did not vouchsafe a word either way. In any case the point was academic, for Hillary was already being firmly supported against Lord Wolverton's strong chest. She smiled in relief at the greater comfort. Indeed the viscount lifted her up so she could get some air and further he held her so securely that his arms and body cushioned each shock.

"Yes, that is better. Thank you," she whispered.

That ended the discussion. Still Countess Oldi could not help but send scandalized looks in the direction of the couple. They looked intimate. The count wished he could have volunteered to support that beautiful burden for a while, but somehow, from the expression on the viscount's face and the memory of the count's own desertion, he dared not suggest it. Almost did he open his mouth to speak, but Wolf, seeming to sense what he would say, warned him off with one fierce glance. The count sat back and talked to Victorine. Countess Oldi was distracted by that conversation, which centered on Princess Caroline's reaction. When the princess's own coachman had arrived with this deluxe conveyance, he'd revealed the scene at Leghorn— screams, fury, despair at the first message of the lady's death, and then screams, joy, and delight at the second message of her rescue. But there had been that in the princess's tone when ordering him to drive her precious daughter back to her that suggested *his* life depended on that safe arrival.

Clearly that boded ill for them, suggesting, as they feared, the three would be blamed for Hillary's experience. Again and again they rehearsed how best to present the matter to Her Highness, hoping they could speak first before the Englishman. For who knew what *he* would say? He might even suggest they'd run to protect themselves, ignoring Angelica's cries for help. The moment, after all, had been one of terror for them as well.

Meanwhile Hillary rested in the viscount's arms. He occasionally talked soothingly to her, introducing only happy thoughts that she could dwell on. He had a boat at Leghorn and would soon take her out on it. She would see nothing but miles of blue, blue Mediterranean. Hillary had smiled at that picture. It blotted out the mountains, cleansed the terror. He had her secure in his arms and would protect her henceforth, he assured softly.

Of course she felt safe in his arms. Whenever the moment of dread came back, he was there to whisper it away. He soothed with a strange new gentleness, stroking her hair and keeping her so enveloped in his muscular strength that she felt eased enough to doze.

The moment of Hillary's arrival at the princess's palazzo in Leghorn was necessarily one of much emotion. Her three mothers ran up to the coach before it had even stopped. Almost did they pull the young lady apart in their eagerness to hold her in their arms, anxious to reassure themselves she was alive. Even the servants were standing round to catch a glimpse of the lady who had come back from the dead. A miracle woman blessed by God. Some reached to touch her as she was carried by, but Lord Wolverton would not permit that, nor Bartolomeo's attempts to take her from his arms.

The princess kissing Hillary a dozen times

impeded the viscount's smooth carriage of her up
the stairs. Lady Gardener was insisting everybody
give the lady air and stop hovering over her, while
Mrs. Wizzle merely held on to Hillary's dress, which
hung over the viscount's arm, just to continue the
connection. With smiles and returning kisses
Hillary reassured them all that she was alive. Yes,
she was. Indeed.

As the days passed Hillary did not cease to be
cherished. They'd allowed her a sennight of quiet
repose before wishing to be told every detail of her
story. To assure she would not have to repeat it
endlessly, the princess arranged for one recital,
whereupon she was carried to the princess's own
salon by the baron. Of course several doctors, one
ordered especially from Rome the moment the
princess received word Hillary was injured, had
already each examined the lady. The diagnosis was
that Hillary was in shock and must rest to forget
her ordeal. Her shoulder was not dislocated as the
local doctor had ruled, mauling it further with vain
attempts to replace it and reducing Hillary to tears.
Rather the muscle was torn, which meant the arm
must be immobilized to heal. The princess was
loath to have Hillary arise too soon from bed and
risk reinjury of the arm, and gave the doctors a
most pronounced stare during that discussion.
Adroitly sensing the instructions desired, the
Roman doctor, a polished practitioner, spoke up.
One could allow arising from bed occasionally, if
she immediately rested on a couch. "If possible she
should be supported in her small walks by a loving
arm." The ladies fought over whose loving arm that
would be. They compromised on taking turns while
she took her daily turn in the garden.

The surprising reaction was Hillary's, who at one time would have laughed at all this coddling. But that adult Hillary had been pushed aside by a frightened little girl who wanted everyone to be around her for protection. They must give constant assurances she was safe, that the ground would not suddenly shake and toss her off her balcony, that the mountain would not come looking for her, deprived of her sacrificial death, and fall atop her as she lay on her settee. That was the reason for Hillary's asking for a change of rooms. The princess castigated herself for not having thought of Hillary's understandable dread and immediately ordered everyone to stop their activities and come outfit a room on the opposite side that looked out on the sea. Was the sea a preferred view? Hillary agreed that would be most comforting, and so the change was effected with all dispatch. There were still some mountains visible but rather than looming above, they were safely in the distance like a decorative border on the horizon. Hillary had become leery of all heights, not only of mountains. That young lady who had scandalized the viscount by sitting on the balcony's edge, who had laughed at Victorine's shying away from the highest windows, now herself remained on as low and level ground as possible. She hugged walls and always positioned her chair with a strong, safe structure behind her. That was the preferred position on the day she was to tell her adventure to the most select members of the court.

Hillary recounted her plight with English understatement that only found favor with Lady Gardener. All the rest were excessively disappointed— especially when she reduced most of the drama to a two-sentence synopsis. "So I leaped from the bush that supported me and landed on a ledge from where Lord Wolverton rescued me."

More details were demanded. How had she kept Angel in her arms? "I was holding her when I fell. To her belongs the credit for saving her own life, for she kept clutching on to my hair." Hillary's sense of humor was reviving, and her eyes were laughing while patting the yawning Angel on her lap. "Yes, Angel was of immeasurable assistance," Hillary carried on. "For she kept meowing in my ear, reminding me it was my duty to find some safe ground for her. Obviously it was incumbent on me to leap to the nearest ledge. Which I obligingly did."

"A true English heroine," Lady Gardener decreed.

"Angel or me?" Hillary asked.

"Both," her ladyship pronounced.

Mrs. Wizzle just continued to cry. The princess was thanking God, certain all the love everyone had for Angelica had lifted her up and floated her to safety.

"Not quite. I mean I would not say I exactly *floated*. Nothing that graceful."

The count denied that, assured she had done that as she did everything, with the height of grace.

Victorine exclaimed that Hillary was most brave, for she herself would not have been able to let go of the bush.

"Actually, I had no choice. It was cracking under my weight." There was enough of the old Hillary to laugh then.

But no one else laughed with her, still in the horror of the moment. Wolf would ordinarily have understood her approach and grinned along, but he had been denied the sight of her for a maddening week while the ladies confined her to bed and

now he was just hungrily gazing at her, feeling too
much to react to her words.

Basically the viscount was angry. She was his!
His by every right known to man and God! Her
father had signed the agreements that made her his
wife. He had loved her as Angelica. And later,
although he'd made a beginning attempt to serve
her tick for tie, in his heart he was only waiting for
her to acknowledge his right over her. But then on
the mountain, feeling he'd lost her, all ideas of right
and other such idiotic emotions were swept away
by the sensation that something vital had been torn
out of him. He knew he loved her with all his heart,
just when it seemed he'd lost her forever. On the
ride to Leghorn, he'd whispered to Hillary they
must henceforth always be together. Drowsily she'd
smiled at that, whether agreeing or not he could not
be certain.

Intermittent with his thoughts, Wolf was basking
in the sound of her beautiful voice. The words were
not registering until his own name caught his attention.

"And in typical heroic style, Viscount Wolverton
swung down on a rope. He rescued first Angel and
then took me up. We hung there in the air, swaying
on the rope. Most elevating. Then my lord simply
climbed us both up and over the top. He brought
me safely up to the road again, from whence I'd
been tossed hours before. Which must mean, I
expect, I owe him something . . . such as . . . my life,"
she said with a gentle smile while giving him a teasing glance.

"You are my life," the viscount answered, for
once oblivious of all bystanders and allowing his
true feelings to be revealed.

That was too blatant for the ladies. They all stood up and insisted Hillary had tired herself relating it all, and she must rest. Bartolomeo was chosen to carry her back to her room. The viscount and his declaration were swept aside in the bustle, in the hopes both would be forgotten.

In her bed, however, Hillary remembered it and put it with that moment when she'd looked up and saw him climbing down for her. Her heart had known then as her heart spoke now. And she at long last listened and admitted. They were one.

Still the next day Hillary had a renewal of doubts. For admittedly, of late, she was not herself. She cried at the smallest gesture of kindness. It was as if her experience on the mountain had turned her inside out so her emotions were on the outside, easily reached. The coming of dusk brought tears. The sweep of birds, wild laughter. All life was achingly, yet frighteningly, beautiful. Being placed in a situation of terror had ripped off her surface of invulnerability. That was the negative. The positive was, face to face with death, she had awakened to the reason for living—to love all about without reservations. Was it any wonder her feelings for the viscount rose so strongly?

"You know you belong to me," he whispered when he'd snatched a few moments alone with her on the terrace.

"The Chinese claim that is so. I remember my father telling me that once one saves another person's life, one is responsible for that person forever after. Something about having interfered with God's plans for them. I often have the sensation of having fooled the mountain or God—for sometimes they seem interchangeable—that actually I was meant to have been dashed on the rocks along with the coachman and the horses. . . ." Her eyes began to relive the terror again.

"Stop seeing that! You were not meant to die! You were rescued from the earthquake *by the mountain.* It held on to you long enough so I could rescue you. We are each other's destiny," he insisted, and Hillary smiled, her terror blocked and balmed again by the soft protection of his gray, intense gaze.

"Your eyes are like fog," she said with a laugh. "They cloud the terror, but it is there."

He cursed, forgetting she was a lady and forgetting how visible they were to the rest, and held her tightly in his arms. "I shall shield you from all terrors, even of the mind and memory. In my arms you are safe. As you were safe when I took you in them off the mountainside. God and the mountain wedded us together. That is a unity no one can put asunder. You felt it then. You feel it now."

She felt it. The strength of his support flooded through her. She rested against him, hearing his racing heart. He was bestowing kisses on her forehead that somehow slid down to her lips—kisses different than those she remembered. They were all gentleness and caring in every caress. She gave herself up to him completely, as she'd trusted him on the mountain.

"You are mine forever," he insisted. "Say it."

"I am yours forever."

He was exultant. "I will tell the princess tonight."

For a moment Hillary wondered what he would tell the princess, and then realized she had pledged herself to him, again.

He was discussing their marriage. Something in Hillary warned her that she had allowed herself once more to stand too close to the edge and been swept over. Yet his arms reassured her. She gave up thinking and allowed the viscount to take over her life. The old Hillary warned and screamed but was unheard in the soothing pleasure of their embrace.

When informed, Princess Caroline and Lady Gardener could not believe Hillary had agreed to marry him.

"He rescued you. Like a tale," the princess said. "But life does not end in a rescue. Or in a kiss. Life is the *afterward*—when the kiss is over, and the man's lips kiss others. When the rescuer-hero goes back to being himself or that very man you ran from."

"He's changed," Hillary exclaimed. "He loves me so much. He cherishes me. He will stand between me and all harm. He has promised."

Lady Gardener scoffed at that. "No man can do that. No person, actually. It is between yourself and fate. You rescued yourself—by clinging to the bush, by risking jumping onto the ledge, by holding on to the ledge for hours, even though you were in concussion and with a torn arm. Even on your own you began climbing the tree. His lordship merely gave you a hand up, as any gentleman should."

The princess agreed, dismissing the viscount's actions. "Gott sent him back. He was His instrument. A stranger would have been as good. It is Gott's will that you lived. Accept the life He gave you and cherish it. Do not throw it away on a gentleman you refused before."

Hillary was confused. The ladies began to instill doubts of her feelings for the viscount. Except Mrs. Wizzle, who believed the two were meant to be together. "You have changed him," she said with a smile. "You have taught him love."

"Yes," Hillary admitted, smiling happily and keeping her promise. Lord Wolverton was her fiancé once more.

Hillary and the viscount as an engaged couple were permitted to be alone together at the palazzo, as long as they remained within hearing of a distant maid. But for outings a chaperon was still needed. Victorine came along when, as promised, the viscount took Hillary for her sail on his boat from Leghorn harbor. The expanse of the Mediterranean met all of Hillary's expectations. She relaxed, enjoyed, ran to the rail and pointed out the mist-covered islands in the distance. The viscount named each one. Elba drew particular attention. "How maddening for Napoleon when he was stationed there with France so near and yet so far away," she observed.

"That is exactly how I felt when you were in my sight and not in my arms," the viscount said, and Hillary smiled, of late enjoying his every flattery. No longer did she distrust his love. He had proven its depth. She made some remark about the pleasure of sailing together.

"There are many pleasures ahead for us to share," he whispered, and Hillary felt her skin tingle, for he said it affectionately, with such a happy anticipation, the promised passion was not something degrading as she'd once feared. It would be, as were his kisses of late, tender and true.

Another letter came from Sir Percy, who had written her many from Milan. Skimming through it, she acknowledged that his despair at her near loss proved his love. She was regretting his pain when the viscount interrupted with a request to see the letter.

"I have that right," he said seriously. And his eyes showed glints of steel she remembered from before.

Nevertheless the new Hillary handed over the letter.

"Egad," he exclaimed, "this is a love letter. Why do you permit this? Or has it once more slipped your mind that we are pledged, so you feel free to encourage a score of gentlemen!"

Hillary's hackles went up. For the first time since her accident she stared at her savior with some of her old impudence. "I have written to him of our engagement. I have told him there is no hope for his love. I merely allow him to relieve his feelings. For, recollect, he loved me before you ever did."

The viscount denied that. She insisted. "You ignored and despised me at first meeting. Wished me changed to be worthy of you. Blew snuff in my face. Made me feel unworthy in comparison to your many diamonds, while Sir Percy, at first introduction, looked at me as if I were the brightest diamond of all."

"You were . . . you are," the viscount shot back, still attempting to understand why the lady always opposed him. The sweet pliant miss of her recuperation was fading. The independent Miss Astaire was reawakening. He stared at her determined expression, and laughed, returning her letter. "Very well, if one gentleman's devotion is not sufficient, read all the declarations you seem to need. I had hoped ours was deep enough a love for you not to need addendums."

Ruefully Hillary admitted he had made quite a point. "It's just that I don't know how else to tell him there is no hope. I have used plain English."

"Perhaps I can be of assistance. Allow me to answer his letter and he shall get my message."

Sighing, Hillary handed him the letter. He had that right, after all. His love was enough for her. "But you will be gentle?" she asked.

"I am always gentle," he said in shock.

Hillary laughed at that, and he smiled softly. "At the appropriate moments," he amended.

But his kisses were no longer gentle. There was a return of the passion she remembered in Wolf. Enjoyable, of course, but disturbing. The demanding, mocking man who had attracted Angelica was reemerging. The one who always somewhat alarmed her. That man might eventually demand payment for his rescue. Or had she already given it to him under his gentle guise?

18

Wolf developed a habit of taking Hillary with him wherever he went as if she were already his wife. Sailing, visiting, and of course shopping for Christmas gifts for the court. Shawls were decided as the most suitable gift for all three of her mothers—in a variety of colors. For the other ladies-in-waiting, such as Countess Oldi, he and Hillary purchased fans. The gentlemen received fobs to hang from their waistcoats. This joint selecting of items completed the picture of them as a couple.

While recuperated enough to do her daily tasks, Hillary still found it trying to spend hours shopping. She had a footman with her at all times to pick up items, for her arm, which had been too long immobilized, had now frozen into place with a shorter reach. She could not fully extend it, and it was rather weak in even lifting a teacup. As for her hair, she who had always preferred arranging her own was grateful for the princess's large staff. Count Guido, Victorine, and Hillary's maid came along to make the shopping outing respectable. At Pisa, Victorine thoughtlessly recommended they all climb to the slanting bell tower. Hillary turned white at the thought of its height of eight stories. The viscount instantly denied any desire to be so elevated, commenting dryly that only the most bird-witted sought bird's-eye views—he preferred to see his fellow creatures on a level plain.

Hillary laughed at that, grateful Wolf was taking blame for the party's missing that tourist's treat. Still, her eyes twinkling, she could not help giving him a slight return thrust. "You have changed indeed. Or is it that being so elevated yourself, a view from on high would hardly be a novelty?"

The viscount merely bowed, admitting he had been rather high-and-mighty all his life, but since meeting her, she had cut him down a peg or so and now he was more on a par with his fellow man and woman and would do his level best to remain so.

Casting an ironic glance, Hillary let that go, although she would not have done so previously. But his hovering about her and spending hours discussing whether Lady Gardener would look best in blue or green, as if it were the most pressing of his concerns, could not but please, and had Hillary smiling graciously. To which he responded blatantly, "Is my docility winning points with you, by Jove? Do you really wish so pliant a husband?"

"Not if he is pretending to take an interest in my concerns," she warned, and he laughed and responded, "But how could you imagine I would not wish Lady Gardener to look her best? As for Mrs.

Wizzle, I have found just the shawl for her while you've been wasting all this time on the princess." He held up a chintz shawl in a brown circled pattern on a reddish background. "It recalls her complexion, does it not?"

Annoyed at that aspersion on her friend's freckles, Hillary tossed that shawl away and chose a soft, pale blue that matched her gentle eyes, she said pointedly.

The viscount was showing signs of his old humor, apparently. He could not continue forever, she concluded, in his softer mode. For a while it had been nigh unto having a fourth mother with his constant coddling—sitting at her side in the coach, supporting her arm, covering her from breezes, and practically carrying her off and on. Even now he kept a sharp eye to see when she was fatigued and protected her from heights. The viscount left her only for a brief time to do his personal shopping while Victorine and she were occupied being shown the newest in fabric. When his lordship returned, Hillary could not help but wonder at all the packages the footmen were carrying. For how many other people was he shopping? she wondered.

On Christmas morning she discovered the number—one. All the gifts were for herself. The rule that a lady could only accept items of trivial worth and no personal apparel, he had ignored, explaining that it was not relevant in their case, as she was his fiancée. Lady Gardener agreed he ought to have bought her the diamond ring, but the jeweled tiaras and the pearls en parure, consisting of necklace, brooch, and eardrops, were excessive. The fur lap robe unnecessary. Only the lace shawls, fans, reticules, and parasols were in the realm of acceptability. But, heavens, the lace robes for nightwear were patently shocking! Even Hillary had blushed and would have returned them to him, but found it more embarrassing to bring attention to those items. She merely opened her eyes wide and put them away in the bottom of her trunk.

But they had made their point, for she thought of them whenever the viscount gave her one of his most searching glances. She had given Lord Wolverton a snuffbox with an etched wolf in its cameo top, which she could not resist upon spotting. It had delighted his lordship so much, he assured he would throw away the rest of his collection, for hers was the one that really depicted him at heart.

"I hope not," Hillary laughed. "I've presumed you a lamb at heart of late. Indeed that is who has won me."

"But you know I am a wolf in sheep's clothing, else you would not have found this appropriate for me. The wolf in me is there, my dear heart, remember that at all times."

Hillary felt a tingling through her veins at not only his remark but at the intensity of his voice. It was not unlike the kisses he had given Angelica. But upon his coming closer and their stares stirring each other, he quickly stepped back, recollecting in time to treat her with honor, appeasing himself with a gentle kiss on the palm.

"You have me eating out of your hand," he admitted ruefully, "but recollect, a wolf never nibbles what he develops a taste for. He wolfs it down *whole*." His eyes had a spark of laughter, but as well an admonitory taunt that flicked across her skin in the most tantalizing way. Her alarm lasted less than a moment, for Lord Wolverton immediately reverted to his recent gracious, considerate self, making her every wish his command. In fact, he prided himself on anticipating not only her wants but words.

"You're thinking you would wish to join that group," he whispered as Hillary was watching some Italians on their way to a family swim in the ocean. "I shall buy you a house by the sea and wall it round so you may bathe at your convenience and without outraging propriety."

"Yes, but . . ." Hillary began, unable to explain. It was the openness of the Italians and the whole family bathing and laughing together that she admired— the *family* of it. She who had always had so little of a family, and had held on to her father buckle and thong would have loved to have had at least five siblings. Being always near a loved one would leave one less in a panic than when there was only one person in one's heart.

"You want family outings?" he remarked, staring at her and guessing her thought. "But first we must have the family, what?"

Hillary flushed and rose to stop him from speaking in that improper manner. "My lord, I believe we should join Lady Gardener. She is beckoning."

"You little coward," he said gently. "Why need you the protection of her ladyship? Indeed, since you are giving a perfect imitation of her yourself, I might as well be having this conversation with that lady. In fact, I think I will. I shall ask her ladyship what her opinion is on the number of children you and I should have and whether we could have a family bathing hour? What say?"

Hillary was unable not to giggle at the thought of

Lady Gardener's outraged reaction at being thus addressed.

Laughingly, lovingly, Hillary and Wolf continued their relationship. They had come to an armistice in their duel. With no one else had Hillary ever laughed so much, the lady acknowledged, although she suspected he brought out the most improper side of her. On the other hand, she had softened him and opened him to enjoying the other people of the court. There was always whist of an evening and the viscount won continuously from people who could ill afford it. But of late he always found a gracious way to return the winnings afterward.

"If you are going to return the sum, why not lose to them in the first place and save their face?" Hillary had snapped, irritated by that streak in him.

"I must always win," he said seriously. "To own it, I have not the smallest objection to returning the spoils. I play not for gain but triumph."

She shuddered at that and looked at him deeply, unable to accept her next thought.

"No," he said softly. "I am not seeking only to win you. I shall never give *you* back."

Laughing and flushing, Hillary denied that had been her thought. But it had been.

Another disconcerting moment occurred on one of her rare outings without the viscount. During a carriage ride with Victorine and Baron Bart, the baron spotted Lord Wolverton at Leghorn's dock, escorting a man to a nearby ship, and pointed both out. "Antonio from Lake Como," Bart exclaimed, and Hillary recollected that Antonio's wife was Gina, one of the maids there. It was prodigiously curious. She planned to question the viscount about that rendezvous, but all resolves were forgotten in the excitement of that evening's surprise.

Princess Caroline received a note that made her gasp. Then her face flooded with sadness as she called the court to attention, and solemnly announced the death of her father-in-law, King George III. All were requested to pray for the soul of the poor man who for over ten years had been lost in madness, wandering through his palace under watch. When in his right senses, he had always supported the princess against his son's worst attempts to discredit or even divorce her. Most especially had he stood buff against the prince's orders to forbid the lady from seeing her child. As long as George III had had his reason, she had been safe. Caroline's tears flowed and she was not ashamed.

It was Bart who said what had been in everyone's thoughts after the prayers.

"But what does that mean, my dear princess? You are then no longer princess? Yes?"

Lady Gardener said it first, with much pride. "Your *Majesty*," she said, and curtsied.

"Heavens, I am the *queen* at last!" That newly exalted lady could only gasp and shake her hand. "But poor England. For now that great Mahomet is the king."

The entire court was all atremble at the realization that their dear, exiled princess was now the queen of England. Her Majesty was uncertain what to do, but only for a moment. For she did what she usually did. When in doubt, she traveled! The king had died on January twenty-ninth and she had not heard of it until the middle of February. She must travel instantly to Rome to consult the ambassador as to her standing. Thus to all, she gave her first command as queen: "Pack!"

Without more than necessary delays, the court had packed and packed themselves into carriages and headed for Rome. It was not till they'd settled in that Hillary had a spare moment to discuss the situation with the viscount. Her Majesty had left Hillary at their lodgings to rest, while she and Lady Gardener reported to the consulate to receive final instructions on her position.

The young lady was all delight and anticipation. She could not, however, help but note that of all the party the viscount was the one not jubilant. "What is it?" she asked.

He attempted to pretend he did not understand her question, putting her off, but Hillary insisted he be direct. So Lord Wolverton frankly admitted, "I am appalled that all of you are so unaware of the realities. Does not the princess—"

"The queen," Hillary interposed quickly.

He shrugged. "But that is the crux of the matter. The queen if you will . . . but not unless the *king* wills. And he certainly will never permit that. This has merely brought the matter to a head for all of us."

Hillary did not want to be told that. Did not want to believe that the happy plans were daydreams, and rather there was a battle ahead. She stared sadly at the viscount, who disconcerted her by not smiling in reassurance, but swiftly turning his eyes away. Before she could probe further, the queen had returned.

Her Majesty's white, strained face clearly announced that Wolf's prediction was justified.

"There is to be *no official recognition!*" Lady

Gardener said explosively to all the waiting court. "The embassy has given orders that Her Majesty is not to be treated as consort!"

"All at a direct command from that—that man in England," the queen said, trembling with shock.

Bartolomeo was cursing the gentleman when the viscount touched him lightly on the shoulder, "I say, old man, you are insulting my king."

Everyone gasped. Turning and staring at the viscount, Her Majesty protested, "But you are with us now . . . you have said as much." And Hillary echoed that with her heart and eyes.

"Whatever side we take on your *personal* relations, my dear lady," the viscount said calmly, "it is a certain fact that my king, indeed, every Englishman's king, is now George the Fourth, and I expect you, of all people, being royal, would wish that he be honored as such."

"Indeed," the queen agreed with a flush, silencing Bartolomeo with a look. "But also I wish he to honor me as his queen. Which I am."

The viscount bowed to that, and the moment passed. But Hillary's heart was beating in suspicion. And when a message from the queen's friends in England arrived, they were all summoned for further details.

"He claims I am not fit to be crowned with him!" the queen announced, her voice breaking at the ignominy of that. Her court hummed with fury as the lady piteously concluded, "I am not to return to England. I am alive! He treats me as if I were dead."

"But what should keep you from returning to England and demanding your rightful place?" Lady Gardener asked, refusing to be cowed.

"Ah, you forget the threats! The moment I set

foots in England, he shall put me on trial for divorce and to take my titles. He claims to have much evidence against me."

Her face crumpled into her handkerchief, and all were silent while she recovered herself.

The men about her were muttering, touching their swords. They wished for a fight. Lady Gardener did as well. Mrs. Wizzle looked at Hillary in despair, but Hillary was looking only at the viscount. He had what she remembered as his haughty "snuff" expression. He knew this! she realized. Her mind was in a whirl of dread suppositions. The queen's next comment distracted her. What most offended Her Majesty had been the order to the clergy to omit her name from the liturgy.

The Italians did not understand the significance of that act and were waiting to be told why it had hit their dear mistress to the quick. But Lady Gardener and even Mrs. Wizzle cried out in alarm. The meaning of that affront was explained by the queen herself. "He has ruled me guilty. Without a trial. I am branded the world over as an adulteress without a single bit of evidence." Her eyes blazed. "To be excluded from the Church as if I am too infamous even . . . even to be prayed for! How will I be buried then? When I seek and dream only of being placed for all time next to my daughter in England. He denies me even the hope of that."

At the thought of her daughter, Charlotte, who had fought her father and won the right to marry the man she wished, the queen reached for the comforting sight of her new daughter, the lovely English girl who had won her heart. Angelica too would be soon returning to England where her friend, the queen, would not be received. Hillary looked back at her with compassion and was too shocked and emotional to be able to say anything. And then, as if Princess Charlotte herself had spoken in her ear, Hillary walked toward the shaken lady and curtsied deeply to the floor.

Everyone cheered and then applauded. The queen reached down and not only was Hillary helped up from her curtsy but crushed in the lady's arms.

"You speak to me as my daughter would. Yes?" Hillary, all tears, could only nod. "She would say as you did, I am the *queen*. Act thusly. *I shall fight!*"

"We shall all fight, Your Majesty," Hillary whispered.

There was a general shouting. The queen hushed them. Controlled and herself again, she prepared as she had all her life to continue to its conclusion her final duel with her husband. "It is very clear then. I must return to England and take this challenge to him . . . to his very face. For I have the truth and I have all of you as my friends to support me."

That won universal cheers. All except from Viscount Wolverton. He was shaking his head at the idiocy of that decision, and then he met Hillary's eyes gazing challengingly at him from the queen's arms. Damn that woman, he thought, looking at the queen, realizing that the happy time between himself and the lady of his heart was over. It appeared they would be in the very thick of this battle between king and queen. He could only hope it would not become their battle as well. Hillary had turned her back on him and joined Lady Gardener.

Something cold went over his heart, and he remembered that Hillary was not averse to breaking their engagement and abandoning him. This

time, he swore, his face taking on the haughty
invincibility of generations of viscounts, he would
not permit it. No, by gad, not if he had to abduct her
from the court and take her back to England on his
own.

19

It was June 6, 1820 when the queen and the English part of her retinue arrived in Dover. Naturally Hillary was there, to keep up Her Majesty's spirits. The viscount had sailed ahead of the royal party on his own ship.

The last meeting between Hillary and Lord Wolverton had been difficult for both. Each was set on his course, and assumed the other was callously indifferent.

"I do not understand," the viscount had said. "Mrs. Wizzle and you can be accommodated on my own ship with all propriety and if you are concerned with the princess's . . . eh, queen's welfare, surely you could be of more use to her by returning ahead and discovering how things are, preparing the way for her, in effect."

"How in heaven's name can I discover anything? I

have no connections with society. Besides, the queen has enough supporters there waiting for her with privy information. She needs me by her for present support and constant comfort. Never has any one woman been so grossly and publicly maligned."

Lifting an eyebrow the viscount responded with irony. "Never has any lady ever looked less like a victim. In faith, she brings all on herself with her outlandish pranks. In my presence she has claimed to have nine children . . . yes, yes, I know, she means adopted, don't get your hackles up, but why give the illusion of immorality by such remarks? And she blatantly eyes every gentleman. She has done so to me. She is rash and reckless and this maneuver to sail back to England and confront the king is the most reckless of all! It is in essence taking on all of England, for he has the full power. It is demanding that she be tried, for I know and have told the prin—eh, queen, that the king would never try her in absentia. She is like a child warned not to put her finger in the fire and she plunges in her entire hand. Very well, let her be burned. She asked for it. She shall be tried and she shall lose."

Hillary had been chafing at the bit to oppose each one of his remarks. Now when he was finally silent, she took a breath and spoke calmly, for the last pronouncement did not require defense but faith. "She shall not lose. We welcome a trial to allow the truth finally to be told after years of a concentrated campaign to discredit her. The truth will out."

The viscount laughed openly at that. "You're still such a child. As is that woman. In her fifties, yet she has the headstrong attitude of a halfling. She has not learned in life that it is the *appearance* that matters, and she gives the appearance of being immoral. Look at her." He turned and pointed to the queen, who was playfully pulling at one of Bartolomeo's long mustaches ere sending him about his business. "That very looseness of manner is what has destroyed her. And listen to her voice." He put his hands over his ears. "It's almost as loud as her laughter. If she thinks she will win the good opinion of her judges in the House of Lords, I tell you—she shall not. She has never won over any of the gentry."

"She has the people," Hillary said. "And she has her friends, who will remain loyal to her with their last breath. As shall I."

They left it like that, with the engagement still on, but on shaky grounds, awaiting the outcome of the trial. In Hillary's heart, Lord Wolverton was on trial as well. The image of the hero who had rescued her was fading, pushed aside by the haughty English lord. Yet his eyes still had that special softness for her as he bid her good-bye. Pulling her to the balcony away from all her mothers, he kissed her thoroughly. "That has to last me until I see you again. A kiss to build my hopes on. And our future."

Hillary had kissed him back, but remained silent in reference to their future.

She missed him when he was gone. No one else stared at her throughout an evening to see her every thought. Yet she attempted to keep merry to hold up the queen's lowering spirits. There was no need for anyone to pretend laughter however at Lady Gardener's attempts to make Bartolomeo more palatable to the English. He was to come to defend himself, since his name had been brought into the matter. Her ladyship was insisting he trim his mustaches. "English people will find you a figure of fun—

they are of such length," she announced. The baron was hurt and outraged. They were his mark of manhood. He lovingly waxed them each morning. The queen was to decide.

At the last moment it was concluded that Bartolomeo was needed in Italy for the arrangements of Victorine's marriage. He would come only if essential. In the meantime he kept his mustaches.

Hillary missed sharing smiles with the viscount over Bartolomeo's idiosyncrasies and Lady Gardener's prudery; so she carefully saved up those stories to tell them when they next met.

But she did not regret not leaving with him on his ship. First, because it was a most salutary lesson that he could not have his own way at will. Second, which was a connection to the first, he ought to realize her *needs,* her *obligations* to the queen!

Every day Queen Caroline received another letter either from detractors who demeaned her character or supporters who were fribbles enough to advise that she not bring the battle between herself and the king to a head. The campaign of negativity would have overwhelmed the royal lady if Hillary had not been there to act as an antidote to its poison, which she did so effectively that Her Majesty was buoyed enough to proclaim, "I shall go to England if only one person supports me when I arrive!" And she further confided, "To tell the truth, there are moments when Gott himself says, 'That is the path,' and points—so how can one say no? I am not so alone since you have come to me, my Angelica. Someday, and I feel it will be soon, I shall see my daughter again, and I shall tell her about you. As we always told each other everything. We fought as a team. She won against her father, as you know. But she could not win against Gott. He is the greater king."

But it was discovered on landing at Dover, the English retinue aboard ship was not after all the queen's sole support. Nor were the white cliffs the only glorious sight awaiting them, rather there were mobs of people.

"Heavens," Mrs. Wizzle exclaimed, misinterpreting. "Did the king send them to harass us?"

Lady Gardener dismissed that possibility. "The king has never controlled the people, they have always been against him."

Her ladyship proved correct. The royal party was scarcely in its carriages when, from the shouts and the friendly waves and tossed flowers, it became clear, Queen Caroline indeed had popular support.

Her Majesty took up a bouquet and waved it, tossing back flowers to several children and winning more affection that way. There were prodigious cheers of support for her and against the king, exemplified by one man who jumped before her carriage and shouted, "Give it him, old gal!"

The queen nodded and threw him a kiss.

Lady Gardener had been urging her to sit down and merely wave, but that was not Queen Caroline's way. The people were throwing her love, and she must throw it back.

Society claimed she had made a spectacle of herself. The scandal spread that she had rushed down and kissed several good-looking men. But as much as society wished to alter the significance, the throngs of populace escorting their queen directly to her door in London had to be seen as troubling to the king's party.

The king ordered that she was not to have access to any of her erstwhile royal palaces, nor was her allowance continued. Seeing her so stripped of money and power, more aristocratic supporters made themselves scarce as well as their aid. Hillary offered Holly House for the queen's headquarters. But Lady Gardener was beforehand and had ordered the royal baggage to be brought to her London town house. That disappointed Hillary, but the queen assured her she should come to her home after they had won. Besides, it was agreed the queen had to be handy for the battle. Henry Brougham, the leading Whig in opposition to His Majesty's harshly conservative Tory government, was one of the first to come to the queen's aid. He had private information that the king would brook no delay. The more the people showed their support, the more eager was His Majesty immediately to press his case.

Indeed, they had scarcely settled into Lady Gardener's home near the fashionable Regent's Park, when Lord Brougham was back with the information that Lord Liverpool, the leader of the Tories, had prepared a Bill of Pains and Penalties to be heard in the House of Lords. It was whispered as well that the king had so many papers relating to the conduct of Queen Caroline abroad that they were laid in mountainous piles of green bags on the table. Another bit of news: the king's side was offering the lady the sum of fifty thousand pounds a year, her own private frigate to travel about, as well as honors due a queen of England abroad, if she would leave the country and never return.

Brougham urged her not to accept the terms, their very presentation indicating a weakness of the king's case despite the mounds of green bags. He himself would be her advocate before the House of Lords. He was relishing the opportunity.

The queen dismissed King George's offer without a blink. She would fight on.

Lord Brougham left in a happy mood. Lady Gardener was triumphant that the queen would not be bought off for even fifty thousand pieces of silver, but she warned, "We must be prepared for deviousness and blatant lies."

"Those have always been my husband's principal talents," the queen readily acknowledged, "I expect nothing less."

But Hillary expected something more from one of the king's friends. She had been home above a sennight and not heard from the viscount. Naturally from the moment she'd disembarked, her heart had told her he would be waiting for her on shore. That Lord Wolverton was not there was her first humiliation. That he did not subsequently pay a visit was offensive not only to her, who was ostensibly still his fiancée, but to the queen. Surely he owed Her Majesty that much courtesy after her months of open, liberal hospitality in Italy.

It was inexcusable, Lady Gardener decreed, and swore she would cut him if ever in his presence at one of the soirees. Only her ladyship still had entrée to the most social affairs. After her years of friendship many of the ton would not turn their backs on her as they did the queen. Lady Gardener planned to take Hillary along but that young lady refused to go if the queen was not welcome.

Her Majesty was grateful, although she made a halfhearted attempt to urge the young lady to leave her side and step out. But Hillary's loyalty became stronger the more others deserted. Lady Gardener had a duty to attend those affairs, for she was able to talk to the ton and gather clues as to which lord was leaning the queen's way. What she mostly reported was that while society disagreed with the king's bringing his queen to trial, they assumed from their own morals that the queen was guilty. Over one year previously a respected lord had visited the princess abroad and returned to spread reports that Bartolomeo was a giant of a man with equal "appetites." Society needed no more to set imaginations running. Basically all were looking forward to the trial. It would make such entertaining gossip, not to mention viewing, for those who could gain admittance. Summer was so dull a season, usually everyone adjourned to their country estates. But this time they were all huddled in the hot city waiting for the hotter trial to come.

Hillary found London stuffy beyond belief. There were no mountains there, thank heaven, but no breezes either. The back courtyard of the small town house was scarcely large enough for a turn. She was stifling. Mrs. Wizzle felt oppressed as well, so Hillary suggested they go for a carriage ride in Hyde Park. The queen sent her own coachman to protect them while she remained closeted with Brougham and Lady Gardener to plan strategy.

Miss Astaire and her companion were enjoying deep, refreshing breaths under the green trees when both were shocked to view Viscount Wolverton in a high-perch phaeton, trotting by. Hillary was unable to countenance his being in London and not having made a call. Mrs. Wizzle began to wave her lace handkerchief to get his attention, but was instantly stopped by Hillary's whispering, "*He* must make the first move." Her voice was stiff with injured pride.

"How can he," Mrs. Wizzle implored, "if he does not see us?"

Hillary's answer was made superfluous because the viscount did see them, aided by Mrs. Wizzle's not unobtrusive shaking of her parasol.

Quickly Lord Wolverton made an expert turn of his cattle, clearly demonstrating his standing as a champion whip, and stopped at their side.

With exuberance and gross audacity, he jumped down and was actually beginning to pull Hillary out of the carriage and into his arms before all. That familiarity Mrs. Wizzle would not allow. But his lordship would have disregarded that, if Hillary herself had not refused to descend. He was forced to stand at the side of her carriage, awkwardly attempting a conversation while looking up at her. He was quick to explain he'd just returned from a conference in Brighton and was shortly to make his visit to the queen.

"We have been in London nigh unto a fortnight," Hillary said coldly.

"I have just returned," he repeated emphatically.

"It was known to all the people that the queen had come. They did not find it too onerous to give up their daily duties to travel all the way to Dover to greet her. I admit I was disappointed not to see you there."

"Ah, your nose is out of joint. I am still to play the courtier to you, am I? Although you refused to come home with me. I must wait several months to be in your presence, but you could not wait a week. That says little for your fairness, but a great deal for your eagerness, so I shall not fault you."

Hillary flushed. He always managed to put her in the wrong. She naturally could not continue the

point, for as he had altered it, she would be showing
unseemly desire for his presence. Now he was
smoothly carrying on a discussion with Mrs. Wizzle.
To her complaints about the horrors of the sea voyage, he countered with an obvious gibe. "My ship
had a very smooth sail. We should have enjoyed it
prodigiously, all three of us, if one of us had not
been so stubborn and wishful of having her way
that she would choose the princess rather than her
husband-to-be."

His old sardonic, mocking self was apparently in
full flourish here in London. At their separation in
Italy he had seemed annoyed but still warmly loving. Had England hardened his heart and brought
back all his old cold ways? Stung and disappointed,
Hillary replied, "You have a problem, my lord, with
your titles. The queen is the queen. And you claim
yourself my husband-to-be, but do not act the part."

The old mocking glance was back. "You wish
more demonstrations? Mrs. Wizzle has already
scotched any welcome I wished to give. But if you
insist . . ."

He was laughing, and she wanted to laugh with
him. Her heart was beating quickly as the gray eyes
she missed so much were stroking her. But his attitude was wrong. She could not accept it. "I expect
we have much to discuss," Hillary said sadly. "I
have the distinct impression, my lord, you have not
benefited from your sea voyage, nor from your
return to England. I have the sensation I am facing a
stranger . . . and one I have very little wish to know
further."

The viscount attempted to persuade her differ-
ently, but Hillary remained guarded and distant.
But subsequently he was not backward in making

his promised visit to the queen. He called the very
next day. Lady Gardener was cool, Hillary still
guarded. Only Queen Caroline greeted him with open
affection, claiming how pleased she was to see a
friend. So many of hers had cut her dead. "But I am still
alive! And I shall be more so when this trial is over."

After much maneuvering, the viscount was at
last able to disengage himself from the queen and
have a private meeting with Hillary in the garden.
There was a small fountain there, which led him to
recollect the large one in Pliny's villa at Lake Como
and how they had both had quite a drenching.

"You deserve one now," Hillary said, still keeping
her distance.

"Why the blazes are you acting like this?" he said
loudly, taking her in his arms. "You need to be kissed
to remember who I am and what we are to each
other," he whispered, and kissed her again and again.
She responded at first, and then pulled away.

"You always assume that is the way to reach me.
You confuse me with Angelica, as I confused you
with my hero in Italy. Let us be frank. I have heard
rumors that your trip to Brighton was a conclave of
the king's forces. The very strategy being used
against us was planned there. You are back with
the king, are you not?"

"No."

Hillary felt a flash of hope shooting within her.
"You are not on his side?"

The viscount lifted his haughty head and felt he
must be honest with the lady—at least as much as
he needed to be. "I said I was not back with the
king. For I never left his side. I was at the conclave,
yes. You knew from the first that we were on opposite sides of this issue. I told you and the queen—"

"Liar!" Hillary ejaculated. "You told us both you had turned to our side!"

"I told you both I could see your side. And I can. But that does not mean I would forget in essence my very upbringing. One must support one's king. It is blatant treason not to. The personal issues are not relevant. The monarchy is."

"You are a traitor," the lady said in a small, choked voice. Her worst fears, her most constantly dismissed dreads were all true!

Lord Wolverton attempted to wipe away that expression, to argue her out of her opposition. "Confound it! Listen to the facts. There is more to this than you realize. You have just returned from Italy, where carbonari are running about causing dissension in the streets. Rebellion, radicalism . . . it must be suppressed. Henry Brougham has made this all a political issue. He wants Lord Liverpool's government to fall. That is why he urged the queen, if you will, to carry on with the fight. Because he wants it brought to the House of Commons, and then he can use it as a wedge to dismiss half the ministers. The queen has foolishly let herself be used by them. But egad, I will not join the Whigs against my own class! In your interest, my dear lady, and for the queen, who is more foolish than evil, I was the one who arranged to have those generous terms given her. Everything she wanted. She could go back to her Italy, with a frigate, with such a princely sum for her court and, *and,* mark you, with recognition of her as *queen* by the foreign governments. What else did she want all those years? She had no reason to be here. She is *not* English. Her brother, the duke of Brunswick, controls her own kingdom. She could live like a queen there on the sum I arranged. All she wished I gave her, and she turned it down flat. Without even a negotiation. I can only say that caused all those who wanted a bitter fight to triumph. And a fight it shall be."

Hillary shuddered at the extent of his perfidy. "Heavens, did you really expect her to slink back to Europe without her name having been cleared? Just for money! She asks not for luxury, but for truth! Because you have been dishonest with us, obviously you do not understand anyone else who would fight for truth."

"Come, come, my dear lady." The viscount laughed. "You who misrepresented yourself as Angelica, you who this moment, as my affianced, should be supporting me in all I wish for our future . . . *you* claim to be the prime supporter of honesty? Let us push aside these extraneous issues. Let us merely remember what we discovered—that there is a connection between us that can never be broken, though mountains may attempt to rise up and split us apart."

Hillary turned away from his deep, gray stare. "Stop that! I shall not be controlled in that way any longer. I trusted you with my life and love—" she began and had to catch her breath, feeling all her emotion overwhelming her, which give him the opportunity to interrupt, "You are my life and love."

"No," she continued, giving him a fiery look and holding up her hand to keep him away. "I was saying you may have been the rescuer of my life, but I trusted you with rather more than that. I trusted you *with my love*."

"You are correct to do so, for I have never loved a woman as I love you, in all your many guises. Nor shall I ever cease to love and protect you. That is mainly why I wished this case settled—to have you out of it. Don't you realize, my poor dear, you will be used in this case. Everyone who was with that woman will be used."

Hillary laughed. "That is what *you* do not understand. It is *my own honor* I am defending as well. For if it is agreed that Her Majesty ran a lewd court what does it say about me, a prominent member of it? Further, indeed, what does that say about you, who chose me?"

"I have no fear about my reputation. Nor about yours once you take on my name and my protection. My wife is above all gossip."

"Flummery! If the queen is not above gossip, how is it possible I shall be?"

"I shall arrange it," he insisted. "You need merely stay away from the queen and come to my estates with Mrs. Wizzle and your part in this will be forgotten."

Hillary's face was white with the outrage of that suggestion. "Never! I shall never leave my queen in time of her trouble. Do you think I am such a poor excuse for a human? Perhaps because you are! I stay true to those I love. It is a lesson you should learn in case you ever intend to ask another lady to marry you. For certainly you do not find me up to your specifications. Nor do I even recognize you as the man I once loved."

The viscount attempted to persuade her with words and with embraces, but Hillary had made her final statement. "We are obviously on two sides. We have been from the beginning. I thought we could come together, but the schism is too deep. I hope you find yourself a sweet, helpless Tory who shall approve all you do, for obviously you do not want me. And having had another look at you in your English guise, my lord, obviously I no longer want you."

"Pity," the viscount said, retrieving some of his hauteur, although his eyes were blazing. "You seem to be making a habit of breaking our engagement. I hope you do not live to regret it, for this time, I do not believe it will be worth my while to attempt to dissuade you from your decision."

"I shall not change. I shall never change sides. That is what loyalty is all about. We shall win, you know, because we have the right on our side."

"You shall lose, my dear lady. But beyond this petty royal mess, you have already lost. Do you really think in one's lifetime it is so easy to find the kind of love we have for each other? I can tell you it is not. If you insist on choosing the queen over me, so be it. I shall no longer pursue you. But the loss is deep, and it is yours as well as mine. But perhaps you didn't feel as strongly connected as I did. I thought our love could move a mountain and last for all time. I was mistaken. Only mine was that strong."

He bowed coldly and would have immediately left, but the two were gazing at each other in shock. As if a giant wall was rising up and they could do naught but watch it rise, higher and higher. Hillary turned away from that realization first, unable to allow him to see the welling up of her emotions, hiding them indeed from both him and herself.

Not till she heard the terrace door close did she persuade herself to look round and saw with both relief and despair that he was no longer there.

She could hear him making his farewells to the queen and could not return to the salon to be questioned. Rather for a while Hillary sat staring at the

fountain. Good God, she thought, her heart pounding. It was over.

She was well rid of him, if he was a turncoat. But
her heart beat heavily and before she knew it, there
was a flow of tears falling down her face.

"It's from the fountain," she said defensively,
squaring her shoulders. She was well rid of the
traitor. She and the queen would make every last
peer regret his cruel act and unjust words. Especially those of Lord Wolverton. That viscount of vanity!
That *knave of hearts!*

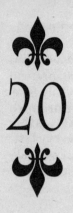

20

Almack's, the most exclusive club in London, where patronesses decreed who could and could not attend its balls, saw the return of society's favorite beau, Viscount Wolverton. The ladies, long denied his exhilarating presence, were agiggle over his entrance. But after half the evening they were prodigiously disappointed.

No longer did Wolf pick and choose the loveliest damsel and honor her with his attentions. Nor did he entertain the matrons with his witty asides on the current scandals. Nor did he retire with the gentlemen to the card room and win or lose with his usual bored, social ease. The gentleman rather strolled through the rooms as if looking for someone, his face a dark glower, and then, not finding whom he'd sought, conversed with an old friend for a moment or two, ignoring all the hopeful mothers of eligibles and the more blatant lures of the young ladies, and walked out.

On his way, Lady Prudence, the acknowledged diamond of the season, was bold enough to pretend nearly to walk into him, and then very prettily apologized. He made his bow, picked up her dropped handkerchief with a tolerant grin, and, making another bow, continued exiting.

"He noticed me!" Lady Prudence preened over the other ladies. "But wouldn't speak. His expression showed he'd lived through moments of blackest despair!"

Obviously Lady Prudence was a reader of gothic romances. Yet her interpretation of the viscount's rudeness did him no disservice, for the ladies were now doubly anxious to win him. The rumors were that his affianced provincial lady had been unmasked as an immoral member of the queen's wild court, and he had damned her to hell and broken off the connection. Lord Sherwood when subtly questioned by the fashionables claimed that as far as he knew the engagement was still on.

Actually Lord Sherwood was in a dashed pucker that his nephew would not take him into his confidence as to the exact state of the relationship. After all, he was the one who had arranged the entire matter. But Wolf would not discuss the lady.

"The choicest tidbits are of your finding the lady in a compromising situation and breaking off. Not that I believe that. Knew the young child. Always a sweet thing."

"Ha!"

"What does that 'Ha!' mean? That the on-dits are true?"

"Nothing is true in society. Everything is slightly

askew. Rather as if we were all living atop the tower of Pisa and must lean in the direction of its slant."

"Hmpf!" Lord Sherwood commented, and waited for a clearer interpretation, for it seemed from this evidence that the young lord's thoughts were in a muddle. Shocking change in the chap. Where were the lighthearted acts? The quips? The dancing or gambling till dawn? Sobered to the point where he made Sherwood feel like the youngster. They were driving in Hyde Park, back and forth, so the viscount could scan every carriage. He'd been doing that every day at the hour of the Grand Strut and always been disappointed. Today again, he'd not seen what he wished and was prepared to leave when his attention was caught by the sunset.

"Did you ever notice, Uncle, that the sky has golden glints only at dawn and sunset? One wakes up with the dawn and is foolish enough to think all day will be as resplendent and waits and waits for the gold again, but it only comes just before the final dark . . . to break your heart."

Lord Sherwood cast an indifferent glance at the slightly saffron sky to the east and shrugged. "Not much of a nature chap, meself." But next moment spotting an excessively lovely lady and her chaperon in the carriage to their left, Sherwood brightened considerably. Now there was a sight of nature he dashed well preferred to watch. And did so awhile, impressed by the young lady's style of driving a phaeton. He wanted to bring her to the viscount's attention, but Wolf was in such a state of the blue dismals, he'd probably make some acid comment and ruin the moment. So Lord Sherwood sat silently gazing at the yellow-haired charmer dressed in sunset tones. The lady flicked the whip, looped a rein, all with such dashing style, Sherwood could not resist shouting, "Well done!" To which the viscount turned in inquiry. But what astonished Sherwood was the ravaged look on the gentleman's face. If it weren't that he knew Wolf better, he would have believed the young pup had been given a fatal *coup d'amour*. Impossible fact! Impossible feat!

"What's well done?" the viscount pressed, at which Lord Sherwood indicated the lady's driving skill, hoping for some small interest. He was not disappointed. With a cry of triumph, Wolf immediately pointed his leaders and they were after the carriage on a trot.

Pleased, Lord Sherwood exclaimed, "You ain't dead yet, are you, old boy? Nor am I. Not if we can come to life at such a beauty."

He expected the viscount to pass the coach or at the most nod to the ladies, but what he did not expect was that he would risk the ladies' lives and limbs by cutting his coach directly in front of theirs and forming an obstruction in their paths. The young lady however was up to the occasion and smoothly reined in.

"Typical," her musical voice rang out.

The darkness from the viscount's face was gone. A new life was there as he laughed at her remark and brought his carriage to the side.

"Typical of what?" he said when they were close enough to converse. "Of me? Of the king's side? Of London traffic?"

"All three," the lady said coldly. "But particularly of you, my lord. Assuming that on every road you have the right of way."

Mrs. Wizzle interrupted with a civil greeting.

Only she of the mothers still had hope for the viscount. The viscount was all obligation for her graciousness and made the introduction to his uncle.

"Egad!" Lord Sherwood exclaimed. "Are you Miss Astaire? My dear little Hillary! Your father and I were best chums. I saw you at the funeral. Didn't intrude. Knew you before, though. Years ago, you were good enough to compliment me on my mustache. Thought it would make a jolly good strainer, if I recall," and he let out one of his exuberant laughs.

Hillary of course instantly recollected him and graciously extended her hand, saying with the loveliest smile, "But of course, Lord Sherwood. I could scarcely forget you. For months I bothered my father to buy me a mustache so I could look just like you. And I recollect you brought me a doll with china blue eyes. I called her Clarissa. She's still at Holly House."

The two were delighted to reminisce and Mrs. Wizzle was flustered by his gallantry to her as well. A merry time was had by the three, while the viscount contented himself with just gazing at Hillary. He needed that pause, he realized, just to feel himself come to life. For without the sight of her all these weeks, he'd felt a stultification that had made every moment an effort. It had become a gloomy world without the sun of his beautiful, golden Angelica, Wolf acknowledged. Continually he'd found himself at Lady Gardener's town house, only to stop at the steps, until one day he nerved himself to go up and leave his card. But that demeaning gesture had brought him naught. For the butler was so good as to inform him the ladies were not receiving, which he understood to mean, not receiving him.

His only hope then had been coming upon her at a social event. So he had doggedly attended every affair, looking for her, until that ploy was proved pointless when his friend, Lord Treat, mentioned none of the ladies of the queen's set were being given invitations. No hostess dared risk retaliation. For each day the bitterness of the king's camp grew more open. A case in point was Lady Blessington, a long-time supporter of the Prince Regent, known for her two-decade affair with Lord Avery; yet she went about claiming herself shocked by the queen's immorality. Point-blank the viscount had asked her the difference between a lord as a lover or an Italian baron, and she'd been vastly affronted. The double standard was so ingrained, none could see it there. Very much like a blotch on one's face one had long conditioned oneself to overlook. The king's blatant immoralities were blinked at, but the queen's supposed one affair was enough to justify cutting any young lady who knew her.

Lord Treat, to whom he'd confided his thoughts, looked at him in wonder and exclaimed, "By gad, Wolf! What gammon! That German lady is threatening the position of all us peers. Not done, old boy! Odd's blood, we must cut her down and all the radical rascals who support her! Not a domestic squabble this! It's our standing! It's our way of life. It's England!"

Exaggerated hyperbole but typical of most of society's reaction. Dash it, the viscount did not want the queen upsetting the applecart of his social ease himself! So high were the hackles on both sides, a battle was inevitable.

Yet if the battle was ahead, why had he allowed himself to lose the woman he loved in a preliminary skirmish? Her reaction to his simply announcing himself on the other side had caught him by surprise. She always did. From the beginning, unlike the ladies of his set, she had not bothered to defer to the general rules. She had her own standards, principally that she would never abandon the woman she felt was her mother! That he'd known all along. But he had not imagined, his pride would not allow him to assume, that in a choice between her love for him and for the queen, she would chose the queen without a qualm. It was one thing to give him the slip when she hardly knew him, but after they'd almost become one on the mountain, how could he possibly expect that royal lady still to have precedence? His sense of self had been dashed! For a few days the resentment peaked to the point that he saw himself as well rid of an ungrateful hoyden! He who had scorned love's effect all those years could scarce believe that he'd been so easily overcome by one beautiful face, and hotly denied it was a fatal wound, dismissing his condition as due to the enchantment of Italy, to the sunsets, the singing in the streets, the laughter, the bathing . . . and the blasted earthquake. But that conclusion would not fadge. For being in London's cool aristocratic social world did not alter his condition. He still ached for her.

Egad, it had been all holiday with him from the moment he'd met Angelica. And every day after. No sense in fooling himself any longer, he needed the reviving sight of her as one needed one's next breath. So he sought her here, there, everywhere, obsessed. And only now in her presence could he find any ease, as he stared his fill. She interrupted her conversation at one point and gave him a small suspicious stare, but he simply smiled at her from his heart. Astonished by that, she turned back in some confusion to Lord Sherwood.

Surely, surely, this feeling so strong in him could not have completely withered in her! No, he could sense her thinking about him. He wanted to lean over and pull her from her carriage into his own and ride off with her.

"I would not come," Hillary said matter-of-factly, as if he had spoken aloud. Triumphantly he cried out their connection still existed, till she dashed his hopes by replying, "Any linkage is fast fraying in the London climate where all is indifference and judgment and cold, cold hearts. Just as the queen and I and Lady Gardener are snubbed everywhere."

"You perhaps ought to know about snubbing. You would not even receive me when I called."

"I was not present. I do not snub or cast out old friends. Note, I am speaking to you. I still have hope for your redemption."

His lordship laughed at that. "You mean for me to admit I am on the wrong side?" he said, shaking his head in sorrow. "This is where I was born and have lived all my life. This is me. I cannot be other."

"Pity," she said, echoing him, and turned back to addressing Lord Sherwood.

He'd had his opportunity but not been able to reach her. She still saw them in a duel and would only accept his dishonoring himself by refusing combat. Which, by gad, he would not do. Yet the fact that she was speaking to him renewed hopes he would eventually win her.

Lord Treat was riding by. He stopped to be introduced. Trust that bounder, as nearsighted as he was, not to overlook a prime beauty. The viscount lazily made him known to the ladies with some secret amusement as to how this dyed-in-the-wool king's man would react to meeting representatives of the opposition. He'd expected some stiffening, but from his years of knowing the courtly manners of the lord, he was not prepared for the exclamation.

"Blast it, Wolf, how dare you introduce me to this . . . traitoress? As beautiful as you are, my lady, I cannot in all conscience bow to you. You are not worthy of any salute of honor. I send no greetings to your wild princess."

Hillary's face was white from the affront. Lord Sherwood was openmouthed, finally just able to utter some oaths, but unable to handle the situation. He had never been present when a gentleman insulted a lady. A duel was the only recourse. The viscount was grimly aware that was what he ought to do, but Lord Treat rather expected him to exhibit the same discourtesy, giving him a look as if to say, "Why are you not supporting me, old boy?"

"I expect my introduction was faulty," the viscount said coldly to his friend. "This is my fiancée."

Lord Treat flushed and mumbled something, but quickly made his exit without bowing to either lady.

Lord Sherwood was busy apologizing to the affronted women. The viscount was surprisingly furious with Hillary. "Do you see the position you've allowed that royal woman to put you in? Being pilloried by the best of society?"

Hillary laughed, but her eyes showed she was vastly disappointed in him. "If that is the best of society, one shudders to think of the worst! Or rather, it is just what I expected, actually. Do you know Lady Gardener was requested not to attend a certain hour of church at the abbey because her presence made the king's supporters uncomfortable? Society reflects its head, I suppose. You are all toadies to a giant toad. Well, for those who still have freedom to think on their own, we shall tell the truth when the trial begins and shame them all, shame those, I say, who have any shame left in them."

Eyeing him deliberately at that, she picked up her reins and would have left.

He reached over and stopped her, saying with all the dignity he could muster, "I shall speak to Lord Treat for his discourtesy to you, and I expect he shall send you a letter of apology. You have my own regrets for any rudeness you've been subjected to. But I cannot alter the thinking. They feel you are shaking the very foundations of our aristocracy. They see you as wild rebels threatening their estates and their wives and children. You must understand how deep the feelings are. I can see both sides. That is why I wished to avoid the confrontation. You are now in England, not the primitive, unrestricted society of Lake Como and the make-believe rules of the princess's court. Here there are certain standards, rules, things simply not done—"

"Done, but not admitted to," she put in.

"Very well, let us not quibble. Society is what it is. Since neither of us can change our side, let us go away from the fray. I long to take you away. Let us leave the queen and king to fight their own battle!"

His voice was earnest but he did not have much hope and he was correct.

For although her own heart was traitorously singing at the thought of the two of them running away from all that, she asked, "How can you leave?

I've been led to believe you have helped fuel the rumors against the queen. Is that the truth? Having done the damage, do you now expect to be rewarded for your falsity?"

She sighed deeply and looked away from his burning eyes. "You do not answer. I put another question to you, my lord. Do your reports extend to me? Were you more than a spy, but rather performing as directed by your royal master in *all things*?"

"Blast it." The viscount choked at that imputation. "You know my feelings for you were and always will be honest. I repeat. To the devil with both king and queen! Let us return to Italy. We can forget everything as long as we are together."

At the earnestness in his voice, Hillary allowed herself to smile. "You do not mean that. Nor could I ever do that. We are, it seems, irrevocably bound to our sides. The battle begins. I do not wish you well. This is not a sporting and honorable fight. Your side is using the lowest tricks. You besmirch yourself just to support them. But if you are more than that . . . and are rather the architect of their defense, you have stamped yourself irrevocably as a king's man. And that," she warned, having sensed that he expected to win her over once the case was concluded, "I shall never forgive . . . nor accept."

And with a flick of her whip, she sent the horses jolting forth.

Even after her carriage had disappeared into the darkening horizon, the viscount still remained motionless, as if he could not quite grasp with his mind what had happened, but his body did, and it stultified. After longing to see her, he'd wasted his moment on political issues, wasted his chance. Wasted. Lost.

Lord Sherwood was all agog and confusion. Long, deep silence continued until at last the viscount shook himself and spoke to his horses, and they moved on.

Lord Sherwood took that as an indication that he too could speak. "Egad, you really love her!"

"She is my heart," Wolf said softly, with such a regretful smile as one would speak of one already lost but never forgotten.

Sherwood shook his head. "Then fight for her, my boy. She is worth more than that fat idiot of a king and all his mistresses."

"She wants me to give up my honor. If I do that, I will have nothing left to offer her, for there would be naught left of myself."

Lord Sherwood thought about it for a moment and nodded. "It's England, old boy. Our very standards. Things will be all right and tight when the trial is over. Just wait it out. She'll forgive you for winning. Women do, you know. Trained to forgive. Wouldn't be a philandering husband around if they didn't."

But the viscount shook his head. "Not this woman," he said, riding on. The sun had set and there was darkness about him. "Egad!" he cried out from his heart.

"Quite right," Lord Sherwood said.

21

It was the day of the trial. The country was agog with excitement, taking it on rather as a sporting match, which in essence it was—a bruising battle between husband and wife, between Whigs and Tories, between lords and the people . . . and between Hillary Astaire and Lord Wolverton.

As had become the norm, outside Lady Gardener's home the crowds waited in growing numbers for their queen to appear. There was a song written by Thomas Macaulay that ended, "Thank Heaven, our queen is come," which they broke into every once in a while along with hearty cheers, especially when she appeared.

It had become the habit of the queen to appear on the hour. "So they should know, the good people, to plan their schedules. They must eat, yes? And they would not wish to miss me."

The love of the people was like a balm to her and all her supporters. Her Majesty's worst day was when the bill was placed against her in the House of Lords. It read: "An Act to deprive Her Majesty Caroline Amelia Elizabeth of the Title, Prerogatives, Rights, Privileges, and Exemptions of Queen Consort of this Realm and to dissolve the marriage between His Majesty and the said Caroline Amelia Elizabeth." Further on it mentioned the reason for this act or the charge against her: "most unbecoming and degrading intimacy with Pergami."

"They know it is not so," the queen had said, her face like a child, unable to believe that if something were not true, it would not be used against her. Lady Gardener had sniffed and claimed truth was never expected from certain people. Mrs. Wizzle had clucked her tongue. Hillary merely hugged the queen and told her what she really wished to hear. "*I* know. The *people* know it is not true."

"But I must tell the lords—it is they that shall judge me. I cannot wait for the trial. A pen! Paper! I shall write a letter to the king and tell him to stop this."

"I do not think he will listen," Mrs. Wizzle said in commiseration.

"True. He never listens. But that ought not stop me from speaking!"

Mrs. Gardener and Hillary agreed a letter from her would be the correct thing, Hillary because she always believed in whatever the queen said, and Lady Gardener because she thought the letter, which would doubtlessly be destroyed by the king, should also be sent to the press.

The next day there it was for all to read, in typical Queen Caroline style, from her heart and without thought, dashed off and yet effective for those who looked to believe and amusing to those who were too sophisticated ever to accept this open-hearted, enthusiastic lady's emotions. "If my life," she concluded, "would have satisfied Your Majesty, you should have had it on the sole condition of giving me a place in the same tomb with my child, but, since you would send me dishonored to the grave, I will resist the attempt with all the means that it shall please God to give me."

The king's forces had thought the letter ineffective and ignored its appeal. Lord Wolverton warned the two lords appearing for the Crown, Sir Robert Gifford and Sir John Copley, that this mention of her beloved Charlotte's death would be most effective.

"Nonsense," Sir John exclaimed, "that is a sham appeal to the emotion as false as the lady."

The viscount eyed the king's advocate with narrowed eyes. "I say, do you know your opponent at all? Not sham rhetoric, contrived as I gather you believe by Brougham and such. This is vintage Queen Caroline. Everything in her life relates to the death of her child. And Princess Charlotte, you recollect, was not only the favorite of the crowds, but even of the elite. She was the hope of our country, the heir apparent. Her death was a blow to us all. Women wept for months."

"A few tears . . . what matter? That is two years past."

Walter Scott was listening. A friend of the king's and a famed author, he felt as the topic now veered from politics to emotion, he was justified to judge, and he did so, saying emotions had to be taken at their flow or they ebbed. Now all concern must be about the charges. "The country will never bear the

queen coming . . . foul with the various kinds of
infamy she has been stained with, to force herself
into the throne."

"Indeed," Sir John agreed. "She is not fit. We have
green bag after green bag filled with testimony, witnesses more than can be housed, all testifying to
her baseness."

"All Italian menials, I expect," the viscount
replied in his bored, languid tones that he particularly affected amongst his set. The peers responded
well to that kind of ennui, but not to his points, and
were beginning to be suspicious of the viscount and
all his warnings. Nevertheless, on orders from King
George himself, the Crown's team were obliged to
be most polite to Lord Wolverton for the king
wished him content enough to testify—on his side.

It was that possibility that put Hillary in such a
pelter when the trial began. If the viscount dared to
be an active part of the charade against them, she
could never, ever forgive him. Not that there was
any hope of a reconciliation, but she still did not
wish to believe he was completely without honor
and truth. She would see.

Queen Caroline was most concerned about her
own appearance. "I must be there to face them all
down." Yet with that criteria it was curious that she
decided to wear a white veil. The intent was to
shield some of her emotions as she watched. "I will
not be gaped every moment!" But the final result
was typical of Caroline. A mishmash. Her black fig-
ured gauze dress, opulently trimmed with lace,
reminded all of her mourning and would have been
well if, as Lady Gardener said, it had less of a ball-
room look with all its lace. Then there was the
white veil. Not as diaphanous as veils usually were,

but of a thickness to appear like a shroud and show nothing of her face at all. It gave a comic appearance of a ghost coming back to haunt the proceedings. The ladies attempted to persuade her to leave off the veil or change it for one less obvious, but the queen was adamant. "I am a ghost and my child is a ghost, we shall soon be together in death. We stand here together behind this one veil. Behind which I am all queens . . . all ladies."

Hillary supported her to the extent that she, too, dressed with a veil, only hers was a wisp of gauze that came from a rather smart bonnet. Thus they entered the House of Lords with Queen Caroline leading, followed by Lady Gardener and Miss Hillary Astaire.

In a further indignity, Her Majesty was not greeted by the doorkeeper as was usual for people of the least title. And she was seated in a high chair that gave the illusion to all of a defendant in a dock. Lady Gardener was enraged, and further so, as no chairs were set for herself and Miss Astaire. "A queen must always be attended by her ladies-in-waiting," she told the harassed lord arranging all, and under strict orders to humiliate the queen. Yet he was a gentleman, and had known Lady Gardener for years. He relented and found low chairs for the two ladies. They sat at her feet. Their presence deflected from the image wanted. She looked like a queen with her ladies-in-waiting at her beck and call. Nor did Queen Caroline follow any of the other orders of the proceedings. Rather than silently sitting there and suffering each remark, she spoke back, as if judging each testimony. The Crown's counsel was infuriated, but Brougham merely laughed. "You would have her here to rub her face in it! Well, you must accept the consequences. A queen does not suffer in silence."

Nor was Brougham less amused at the outcome of the first days' trial. There was a parade of Italian servants. One testified that Queen Caroline had been seen kissing Pergami. It was assumed he meant by himself, but under cross-examination, it was brought out that he was a friend of a friend of the servant who had told him so. That dismissed his entire testimony. Another servant appeared who made Hillary gasp. It was Antonio, the husband of one of her own maids, Gina. Hillary looked about the courtroom to find the viscount. From the beginning she had avoided his eyes, not giving him the honor of returning his fixed glances. But now the outrage was clearly on her face. Not only did she recall his having used the newlyweds to keep tabs on her, but she had viewed with her own eyes his secret conversation with Antonio at the dock at Leghorn. He was his spy! Her eyes told his lordship what she thought of his perfidy louder than she could have shouted it. The viscount was shamed enough to turn his head away first.

Antonio testified at some length that he had seen with his own eyes Pergami coming out of the royal bedroom in the morning, damning evidence that heartened the Crown indeed. Brougham looked shaken, but the queen merely shouted out, "*Traditore!*"

That offended Antonio and he became more flowery in his descriptions. Lady Gardener in the intermission leaned over and discussed something with Brougham and when the cross-examination began it was soon unveiled that Antonio was a groom and not likely to be allowed in the lady's part of the palazzo. His response was that he had been repairing a balcony that led to the hall of the princess's entrance and thus had an unimpeachable vantage point. The queen shouted the answer before her counsel could reveal it. "There was no balcony there. Nor would you be repairing it next to my bedroom. No noise was ever permitted while I slept. Such menial operations would only happen when I was traveling."

The lords whispered amongst themselves. The argument weighed greatly with them. As masters they would hardly allow outside servants into their sleeping quarters at the early hour he had claimed, and certainly not for repairs. Pressed to be specific when these sightings had occurred, Antonio's story began to unravel. He had no definite memory as to the time. In fact his memory was so faulty he could not quite recall what he had testified an hour before. At last he resorted to one reply, again and again, regardless of the question asked, "*Non mi ricordo!*"

He did not remember. He did not remember by the day's end even his name. And by the week's end, "*Non mi ricordo!*" had become a catchword throughout the country. When further Italian servants were brought forth through the streets they were greeted by that cry and by rage from the English populace dubbing them paid informers. The Crown ordered guards for the witnesses but what was really needed was muzzles for them. For under Brougham's relentless examining, every one eventually used that damning phrase, "*Non mi ricordo.*" The Crown had given strict orders to the witnesses never to resort to that phrase, the mere sound of which invalidated everything else and had laughter ringing in the court. But Brougham prodded and pressed so that at length each one could not but resort to claiming they did not know, they did not remember. And that testimony went the way of the others.

The queen was triumphant, responding with thrown kisses to the crowds that escorted her back and forth to Westminister each day.

The beau monde who had believed that Queen Caroline had enjoyed herself with a six-foot, fiery Italian, judging from their own activities and indeed from the blatant immorality of the king himself, now began to look at each other in astonishment.

"Wonders will never cease," Walter Scott exclaimed to the viscount. "Upon my soul, the queen must be innocent after all."

There was an emergency meeting of the king's counsel and supporters. It was decided, as suspected from the beginning, that the case could not be won on servants' words alone. A gentleman was needed. The very gentleman they had sent to the then princess's household to obtain irrefutable evidence of her disgrace. Lord Wolverton.

"I told you all," the viscount said, his eyes narrowing at the position in which they would thrust him, "I would not testify. I spent some time in the queen's presence and cannot in certainty myself claim she is immoral. Wild to a fault and free with her kisses to all. But that in full view of her court and usually more often to her daughters, Victorine and Miss Hillary Astaire. But anything beyond that, anything venial, I could not say. Indeed, I strongly suspect not. She apparently has taken gentlemen in disgust since her experience with the king."

No matter how appealed to, the viscount remained unshakable. He would not perjure himself. "Put me on the stand and I could only say what I have said here to you all. Consider well whether that would help. Under Brougham's questioning it would be further revealed that I was sent deliberately by the king himself to find evidence against his wife. That *I* sent Antonio and paid for his fare. No, I shall not be of help. Give up the matter. Allow the lady to have her name unbesmirched and let us get on with our lives, egad!"

But on consultation with the king, the case would not be dropped. The next day it became evident that since the viscount would not help them they would use him as they wished. He had specifically requested that Miss Hillary Astaire's name not be mentioned in court. Now they brought into court a German equerry who claimed to have seen Queen Caroline, Miss Astaire, and Pergami in a coach. He had ridden by and seen Miss Astaire reclining in the arms of Pergami and the queen leaning over and kissing them both. Clearly a case of ménage à trois.

The courtroom was rocked and shocked by such indecency. The very thought of the beautiful young lady-in-waiting joining with the queen in sharing the Italian lover's embraces was too exciting not to be believed. The king's side had thrown a large cannonball into the proceedings and definitely scored a direct hit. The queen was shaken, crying out, "Every word lies!" Hillary gave one fleeting glance at the viscount, expecting to see triumph, and saw rather rage. Whether at herself or the story, she could not attest, but she would not honor him with a glance again. Her heart was beating at the depravity of the lies and at the realization that her name was now forever besmirched. She would never be free of the taint thrown over her. Her only future would be to retire in seclusion to Holly House for the rest of her life.

The Crown's side was wily enough to request a recess at that point, when the worse was being thought and before Brougham could question this testimony. The victory the queen thought had been in her grasp was now slipping away. Even the people's cheers for the queen that day were less hearty, and Hillary was met with a few jeers.

Broughman questioned the ladies and believed their denials. "It is one thing to twist the facts, but it is devilish to invent an out-and-out falsehood of such a nature that it has the capacity to linger in the least prurient minds! Damn devilish! We need Miss Astaire on the stand to refute. Since the queen herself cannot lower herself to testify, it is up to you, Miss Astaire, to save the day."

There was an outcry from the queen, who would not put her darling into such a situation where they could "foul her up," she claimed. But Hillary was adamant. "What can they do to me? It is false. I shall say so. All the paid witnesses in the world cannot make so what is not so."

Yet that night Hillary was frightened. Not of testifying, for after having hung over a mountain awaiting one's death, speaking to a group of people ought not alarm. But she feared the king's counsel would trip her up, and she might hurt the queen. But that Caroline assured her could not happen. "Gott will put the words in your mouth!" With that conviction Hillary awaited her moment with tolerable confidence. There was a delay and Hillary became impatient. She walked the halls and was interrupted by a messenger with the notice that the queen wished her presence in the anteroom.

Following in a rush, Hillary found herself locked in a room with Lord Wolverton.

"Deceit again!" she fumed. "Does your side do naught but lie and cheat to turn the truth?"

"I must see you before you testify," he said softly. "They plan, I have discovered, since they've not been effective against the queen, to use *you* as their object. It shall thus be proven that the queen's influence corrupts an innocent and turns her into a lady of no morals. Your morality shall be the issue, do you understand? *This must not be!* You shall never recover! You are not a queen or king who is forgiven all. As a young, unmarried lady, it shall be fatal to your chances of ever being received in polite society."

Hillary shocked the viscount by merely shrugging and answering with a smile, rather than cringing, "What would you have me do? Admit their lies are true? What can, in faith, anyone do who is lied about? One can merely deny. Heavens, how foul has your side become! I shudder even to be in the same room, in the same country with people who stoop so low. This is the side you so proudly represent and claim you must honor? In my heart I thought somehow you would not be with them once they went so low. What a widgeon I am assuming enough decency in you or honor . . . or even love, not to allow this travesty!"

The viscount's face was white. "What are you saying? This is exactly what I wished to prevent! You know, your heart knows, I love you. You are everything I want in this world, and I have waited for you for long enough. Whatever happens, after this trial, I shall take you away."

"You jest! There is no longer any possibility of

that! I might still have feelings for you in my heart, for love is not immediately wiped away, but I could scarce marry a gentleman who tossed my honor and decency to the wolves. You were the Wolf I loved. But not your pack. Ah, heavens, if only I had never met you!" Hillary felt her eyes filling, and she fought to regain control. Taking a deep breath, she staunchly finished, "This shall be the last time we shall meet or I talk to you with any memory of our past feelings. Henceforth you will become one with the team that destroys me. When I testify in there, every word, every innuendo will not just come from the Crown's counsel but from *your lips.* Judge then if I could ever after be in your presence—let alone your arms."

Shattered, the viscount sensed the finality of her words and feelings. It recalled to him the same sensation when he'd watched her go over the mountain's edge. Once more did he cry out and in desperation attempt to bring her back by taking her into his arms. But Hillary did not even pull away. She merely looked at him from such distance and with such disdain, he had to let her go himself.

"Blast you, what is it you want from me?"

"I want the gentleman I met in Italy back again. The gentleman who thought less of his life than of rescuing me. I want you to stop dueling with me and show your love. Love is outside the limits of society. True love demands the ultimate in sacrifice. As do I."

"Say it openly," he responded with a gasp. "What is it you want?"

Hillary said it openly. "Testify for the queen and against the king. Then, and only then, shall I know you are not with them, and that their words hitting out at me are not yours as well."

The viscount had a constitutional dislike of being forced to do anything. If he had decided on his own, he might have agreed—but to be given an ultimatum and be expected to drop his sword weakly and surrender, *no!* All that was the Wolf in Lord Wolverton rebelled and forced him to gasp out gruffly, "To hell I will!"

Hillary gave him one last look, and then shaking her head, walked away from him. She had no time to think of her loss, although her heart was pounding. She had to return to court and fight a battle with all the king's men. And that apparently now included the viscount.

22

Hillary's vow never to give Wolf the privilege of her attention was immediately tested as the trial resumed. Brougham was beginning to cross-examine the equerry who had made the scandalous statements concerning her when the delivery of a note disturbed her concentration. Upon observing the signature, she was set to make a show of tearing it up, until the two short lines registered: "You have nothing to fear. The equerry will clear you."

At that point Hillary abandoned her vow never to glance at his lordship and gave him her archest look. How dare he communicate with her in any way when she had made clear their relationship was at an end!

Yet as the cross-examining continued, Hillary had to turn once more to stare at the viscount in surprise. For the equerry was now admitting that the lady he had seen in Pergami's arms was *Victorine*. He always confused the two young ladies, since Queen Caroline called both "daughters" and was very affectionate to both. In this case as well, the queen was kissing the young lady, held by her father, for Miss Pergami seemed to be on the verge of a swoon.

"In other words," the queen's counsel summed it, "this was a perfectly respectable occurrence. A young lady was overcome by the heat or sickness and her father, Baron Pergami, supported her in his arms, while her good friend, our gracious queen, soothed her and kissed her? Could you not see the picture that way?"

The equerry thought a bit, and then conceded he could easily have seen the picture that way.

Apparently the Crown was not willing for that version to remain. In its rebuttal they suggested since he had such difficulty telling the two daughters apart, could not the lady in Pergami's arms just as easily have been Miss Astaire?

Hillary held her breath and once more cast a quick look at the viscount, whose expression was of complete confidence. It was apparently well placed for almost immediately the equerry claimed it could not have possibly been Miss Astaire, for on rethinking the matter, he recollected the Italian gentleman had also called her "daughter."

So much for what had seemed like a victory for the Crown—wiped out by their own witness. And as he was the only one above the level of menial to testify, his evidence ought be given double weight by the gentlemen of the House of Lords, which must inevitably lead to exoneration of both Hillary and the queen. Brougham was jubilant at this development, as was Lady Gardener.

"Thank goodness," Hillary whispered, beginning to feel an easing in her chest of the band of anguish that had sprung up at the equerry's initial testimony. Another look at the viscount revealed him sitting nonchalantly back in his chair with a pleased smile on his face. Meeting her glance, he held it with some determination. Yes, she understood. He had caused the equerry to switch his testimony—whether through financial pressure or some other means, he had obviously done it. And further he wished her to know he had done it.

Hillary was uncertain of her reaction. For to the viscount's credit, he had not only protected her but the queen by having the equerry change his testimony about both. It was not the dramatic renunciation she had been hoping for. Rather a subtle, secret maneuver that did not expose him, yet had achieved the ends he wished.

After being so prepared for battle, Hillary felt somewhat defeated at the easy way the entire affair had been handled. She could not but recollect the viscount's favorite maxim from his fox-hunting days, "Go light over heavy terrain." So they had all, through his manipulating ways, been lightly carried over all hurdles.

That philosophy might well have succeeded with such a helpless opponent as a poor fox, but King George was made of sterner stuff and vaster power. Further, once having put his entire government in jeopardy to win his revenge and rid himself of his queen, he apparently intended to use any means, the heavier the better to achieve that aim. The king's counsel, using the simple expedient of ignoring evidence not to their liking, such as her exoneration, proceeded to call Miss Astaire to the stand.

Brougham, the queen, and certainly Hillary, were astonished. If it was proven she was not in the carriage, why was she being called? With trepidation Hillary cast one more of her glances toward the viscount.

It was vastly disheartening to observe his lordship as flummoxed as she. That boded ill. All along she had thought him in charge as far as the workings of the king's side. But this move had clearly landed him a leveler, for he was up and grimly huddling with the advocates. As she made her way toward the witness chair, she noted with double dismay his walking back to his seat and this time the look he sent her way was of deep regret. The queen did not content herself with mere meaningful looks, shouting, "This child should not be dragged into this!" When that did not avail, Her Majesty reached out and hugged Hillary, exclaiming, "Courage, dear one—these oafs cannot touch you!"

Lady Gardener was nodding and pointing to her stiff upper lip, indicating how to conduct oneself. Thus buttressed, Hillary's confidence returned.

At first the questions meandered, establishing her relationship to the princess, her position in Princess Caroline's court, and such. Then Sir John Copley, who was questioning her for the Crown, a man with a silky voice and sleepy eyes, struck like a snake. "Were you not engaged to an English lord of some standing, when at the urging of Her Highness you callously ignored your commitment and pretended to be legally and ethically free?"

Hillary gasped, but kept her composure. "I do not know which part of your question to answer, my lord. On my arrival at court I was no longer engaged to anyone. I had written, before leaving

England, a full letter to the lord in question, explaining the dissolution. Surely it is the right of every English lady to change her mind?"

Hillary felt she'd acquitted herself tolerably well and was astonished to find rather that Sir John was smiling as if she had fallen clumsily into his trap. "It is the right of every English lady," he pressed, pausing dramatically and then swooping down, "*if* she does so on her *own* and not at the behest of a faraway German lady. What?"

Hillary remained silent.

"You have no answer for that, Miss Astaire, I observe."

"I was not aware it was a question, merely your own conclusion. I have already given my testimony and will repeat it if you insist. I made the decision before ever meeting the queen."

"That is a direct evasion, my lords! Were you not at that time in correspondence with a lady-in-waiting to Her Highness, Lady Gardener?"

"I had been in correspondence with Lady Gardener since I was a child. Her ladyship was my mother's closest companion and has been good enough to interest herself in my future since my mother's demise. Indeed, she has stood in place of my mother, until I was fortunate enough to meet the queen and now am prodigiously blessed with two mothers . . . if not three. . . ."

"Your maternal relationships are not the concern of this trial, Miss Astaire," Sir John sternly reprimanded. "To return to the point, did not Lady Gardener in her letters attempt to persuade you to the injudicious course of breaking your engagement? Were not her letters geared toward that very course? And was not Lady Gardener in full confidence with the then Princess Caroline? Did not, in short, these two ladies, as I am attempting to prove, force you to this injudicious course . . . one that a young, unworldly lady would not have attempted on her own?"

Hillary cast a glance at Brougham, who was unhelpfully looking grim. Lady Gardener looked grimmer. Hillary felt she was on her own. "I made and always make my own decisions."

"Come, come, Miss Astaire. We quibble here. Who influenced your decision?"

"My own will, my own inclinations . . . and . . ."

"And?" Sir John eagerly pressed.

"And God."

"By Jove, are you telling me that God told you to forget all decency and break your father's last commitment and callously break the heart of one of the finest gentleman of England?"

Hillary finally let her eyes rest for some time on that finest gentleman. He was white with astonishment and humiliation. That surely was of no help to her. She could only rely on the truth and she said it in an even tone, "He was a stranger to me at the time. I wished to go to the security of Lady Gardener's protection. I had never had a season. I was unprepared for immediate incarceration in the institution of marriage."

"Is that your view of marriage, dear lady? Our proud English matrons would question that. Perhaps some German influence has been brought to bear on your thinking? Twisted it into a decidedly anti-British way. Which is the point of our questioning. Before you arrived in Italy, were you not known for your very sedate and simple style of dressing? Yet, after meeting the then Princess Caroline, did you not change your style? Dress in excess? Forgetting all decency and modesty?"

"No."

"No?"

"That was my answer. You characterized my dress after arriving in Italy as different from the way I dressed in England. That would be inevitable. There was the difference in climate. Furthermore, there was the fact that I was no longer in such heavy mourning as earlier. But my dresses were always marked by decorum. As I hope I demonstrate to you all today."

There was a murmur of agreement from the lords, for the lady was simply dressed in a white muslin with a high-necked gauze insert of a peach shade that matched the peach ruffles on her straw bonnet. Her light golden curls showed in their glory on her forehead and in glossy ringlets at her neck. All in all, as many a quizzing glass had affirmed, she was a beauty of the first water—a diamond, actually. The lords were not averse to her being kept on the stand for some time, just for the privilege of listening to her melodious voice. It would have added zest to their enjoyment if they could conclude with the Crown's counsel that she had a tinge of immorality. But the English sense of fair play had to admit that a change of this young lady's wardrobe in a warm climate was not the proof needed to back this most serious charge against the queen. Yet Sir John was fixated on Hillary's appearance.

"You are decorously dressed here, indeed. A vast difference from reports we have of your shockingly low necklines in keeping with the mode of your royal mentor."

"If you mean me," the queen shouted, "my child

would never let me dress her in my style. She has her own. It is my bane that she does not like lace or *ruffles*!"

There was a murmur and some laughter. Whatever point the advocate was going for was defused by the queen's admission of Miss Astaire's refusal to dress in Her Majesty's ruffly style. The damaging relevance of that was that if the queen could not influence her in so small a matter as dress, how then could the entire tissue of testimony be true—that the queen had influenced her toward a life of immorality, reflecting her own?

Refusing to acknowledge that he had failed to establish that point, Sir John moved along as if he had succeeded. "Now let us proceed from your shocking dresses to your behavior, which has been characterized by some as beyond hurly-burly, stopping just short of actually tying your garter in public. On that point at least, can we have a clear answer? Let us no longer seek to evade the truth! My lords here have had enough of their time wasted. Without any bark on it, Miss Astaire, did you not surround yourself with admirers? Were you not known as a consummate flirt? Did you not have several Italian suitors?" Confine your answer to one word, if you please—no or *yes*!"

"Yes."

"Yes, you are a consummate flirt!" he summed, rejoicing in scoring that point.

"No, *no!* You are confusing me," Hillary cried, tiring at this odious gentleman's prodigious jabs and not certain which to fend off first. Her gloved hand pushed away a ringlet that had slipped from under her bonnet to her cheek. It bounced back. That drew the gentlemen's attention while she attempted to gain control. Looking at the anguished face of the queen sharply brought back her duty to defend the lady. Newly strengthened and ignoring her own emotions, Hillary lifted her head and replied with some degree of calmness. "At court there were Italian gentlemen and Englishmen as well. Some of them paid me the honor of giving me compliments and requesting a dance or a stroll. But I was always chaperoned, either by Mrs. Wizzle, Countess Oldi, or Victorine. And often all three."

Sir John stared her down with excessive dislike. No well-bred English maiden ought to be able to withstand his cross-examination without collapsing into tears and thus showing her guilt. This lady was too cool, too composed. Obviously an experienced miss. He must at all costs expose her, break her down. "Stop this flummery, young lady. You may be accustomed to playing a deep game, but my lords can dig deeper. You are unmasked at last. We have reliable reports that even while engaged to an English lord you permitted yourself to be proposed to by an Italian count! Do you at least admit to that?"

Hillary was flushing now, as he was becoming more and more offensive. "I was not engaged to anyone during my time in Lake Como. I have already explained that. Count Guido was one of my admirers and he requested my hand in marriage, but I refused him. I was also being courted by an Englishman. I refused him as well."

"In other words you refused all the gentlemen who offered you a decent proposal!"

At that Hillary looked in desperation at Brougham, who was impassive and silent. The queen shouted, "Stop, you oaf! Stop tormenting this childs. She does not have to marry!"

"Precisely," Sir John pressed, triumphant. "You did not think one had to marry, for you had seen before you evidence of a lady enjoying the joys of love without the sanction of that institution! You preferred a freer life! Were you not free with your favors? Did you not kiss and so forth all the gentlemen about and lead them to the point of despair?"

"No," Hillary said. The only gentleman she had kissed in that manner was Lord Wolverton. She turned then to face that very wolf in sheep's clothing. For her friendship with Count Guido, her change of dress—even her breaking of their engagement—these were his very claims against her. Unquestionably it was he who had given this ammunition to the king's counsel. Sir John was the puppet, but the voice, the charges, were his! In retaliation for his being spurned, his lordship was now publicly humiliating her. But in such an open, heartless way that she would never forgive him or forget the degradation of this moment!

Sensing her conclusions, the viscount was shaking his head, unable indeed to believe what was occurring before him, before all. His gray eyes were steely in shock and growing rage.

The king's counsel called Hillary's attention back to himself. "Are you reflecting on your past conquests, or those to come? To attention, my dear lady. We do not dally here! This is a matter of gravest importance and only the truth will serve. Did you not in fact share with the then Princess Caroline not only her immoral dress, values, behavior, but at last proceed even to lovers! In short, let us no longer quibble! I put it to you, Miss Astaire, that this same Baron Pergami, who has been mentioned here for lewd behavior with the defendant was as well your own admirer . . . *if not lover!*"

"In the name of God!" the viscount shouted, standing up. "Cease this inquisition. Not having facts, must you invent them? This lady, as I can personally attest, is the height of respectability and decency. This entire trial is a farce. By now it should be clear to all, the testimony against our queen has either been bought or commanded. That I can *corroborate* myself. Blast you all! You have made me do what I was loath to do . . . testify against my king. But, egad, gentleman, you have gone too far! You have gone your length. Does not the obvious decency and honor of the lady here shame you at long last?"

In the midst of his speech and the shocked silence afterward, Wolf had marched up to Hillary and firmly, unequivocally, with a look round as if daring anyone to stop him, handed her down from the stand. "She shall no longer expose herself to your lewd insinuations," he announced coldly. "If the truth about this entire case must be known, *I* shall give it. I shall testify. No one knows more about both sides, for I was sent by the king to find proof of the queen's immorality. Ordered to find it, if you get my drift. Further, I have letters that make the entire case crystal clear."

The uproar in the room almost but not quite drowned out the queen's blessing the viscount for speaking the truth at last! Sir John was demanding that the viscount's words be discounted, claiming he was under the influence of the queen's tool, Miss Astaire. "I do not call him to testify," Sir John insisted.

"But I do!" Brougham finally spoke. "We call on Viscount Wolverton as a witness for the *queen!*"

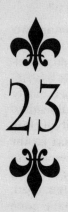

23

Throughout the House of Lords the hubbub and excitement reached a crescendo. In the midst of it, the Crown's counsel hurriedly conferred, resulting in a brief recess being requested. It was immediately granted, as there was no possibility of orderly proceedings continuing since the lords and the audience were shouting and cheering and would not be gaveled to attention.

The viscount would have stayed with Hillary then, but he was immediately surrounded by the king's men and all but bodily swept into the side chamber for consultation. Nevertheless he strained to remain one last moment to squeeze Hillary's hand in reassurance. That pressure was returned, along with a grateful smile from Miss Astaire, ere he was lost in the center of the king's men and marched out of the courtroom.

Fanning her red face, the queen could not quietly sit on her chair. She was in a fire of enthusiasm, waiting for the viscount to return and totally exonerate her and even prove the dastardly actions of the king.

There was a new flurry of interest in the crowd when Brougham was called out. Hurriedly he left, but not before throwing a confident nod to the queen.

Hillary was in a quake from her experience on the stand, unable to believe her ordeal was over. Mrs. Wizzle stepped up to embrace her, and Lady Gardener as well. The viscount had in essence exonerated them all. Hillary was once more awash in warm feelings for his lordship. Just as he had come to her rescue on the mountain, he had now literally stepped up and taken her by hand and removed her from her second moment of terror. It had become nigh unto an inquisition, as she'd been castigated, stripped bare before the leering lords and their quizzing glasses. Oh, how grateful had she been for his ending it! But as if that were not enough, he had gone on as she'd demanded and defended the queen, thus meeting her own criteria. Indeed, he had even gone beyond that by openly agreeing to testify *against* the king, Hillary recalled with a smile that almost couldn't be squelched. There could no longer be any question whose side he was on. At that conclusion, a warmth rushed throughout the lady. Her senses were in such a whirl, she needed immediately to find a seat.

Everyone could see Miss Astaire blushing. Most assumed she was still suffering from her testimony. To the contrary the lady was all aglow from the release of her affections for the viscount. So long determinedly dammed in, reined in, now they reigned supreme in her. The moment Wolf and she had touched hands, Hillary felt herself at home again. And safe.

Mrs. Wizzle was comforting her. Lady Gardener congratulating her. The queen embracing her.

Then their attention, nay, all attention, was caught by the joint return of the viscount, Brougham, and the king's counsel. It was quite unnecessary for attention to be called, it was already riveted on the next announcement, which after all those months of expectation, was anticlimactic.

"Upon consultation with the king's counsel, it has been decided that the issue shall not be pursued. Therefore the bill shall no longer be presented."

Next, in a twinkle of an eye, The House of Lords was declared in recess.

"What does this mean?" the queen demanded of a smiling Brougham.

"It means they yielded. The viscount would not be coerced out of testifying, although I gather there was much pressure applied. He held firm. Rather than allow his testimony to be heard, they dropped the entire presentment. In short, the king and his cohorts have failed of both objectives. Neither are you divorced, nor deposed."

"Regina still," the queen exclaimed triumphantly. "Regina still—in spite of him!"

Her supporters took on the cry, "Regina still!" and she was surrounded by crying, laughing, jubilant ladies and gentlemen. From a distance the doors were opened and the word was spread to the crowd waiting without. From the cheers rollicking back, it was evident the outcome was much approved. Urged to do so, the triumphant queen went out to meet her people. Lady Gardener and Mrs. Wizzle were swept along with her. Hillary sought to follow when she was pulled back and taken into a gentleman's arms.

"Regina still," Hillary whispered to Lord Wolverton, "because of you." He was holding her close, as if he would never again release her or risk her to the wolves of society, especially his own pack.

Lord Treat went by and stopped to make a show of directly cutting the viscount. Hillary turned in sympathy, but Lord Wolverton shrugged, indifferent to the price he must obviously pay for his act. "Confound them all! After the way they dared attack you in the face of your bravery, I dashed well do not wish to know them. *I* shall cut them all henceforth. How that blasted Copley could carry on in the face of your obvious decency and your being the epitome of truth up there appalls."

Naturally that evaluation of her performance and character could not help but please, nor could his stroking her face and whispering, "You are my truth and my love and my regina. And shall always be."

They held hands for a while just to get their bearings. But the emotion long denied them could no longer be suppressed, and Wolf took her into his arms at long last for a strong, hard, unreleasing embrace.

Decorum recalled them to their location and sent them rather quickly exiting the House of Lords.

The crowds outside, still shouting "God save the queen!" were closing in, almost oversetting her carriage as Queen Caroline rode forth through their midst, waving to all sides.

To keep Hillary safe, the viscount took her into his own closed carriage. But even in there, they could hardly talk over the din of hurrahs all about them. Yet words at this point were superfluous. They simply held on to each other, realizing that all impediments separating them had finally been swept away. They were free to claim each other. The dueling couple had surrendered their swords. The two opposite sides of the greatest rift in the kingdom had formed a lasting connection as their duel of hearts became a rule of hearts.

"But you lost so much," Hillary murmured, attempting to console.

Refusing to release her, Wolf assured her that whatever he'd lost could go to blazes! Even the world was well lost for the gain he'd achieved, or her glorious self.

With a great sense of contentment Hillary reveled in his words and then kisses. Gasping for breath, she cast a glance out of the carriage window and noted the crowds were now cheering their embraces as well. Flinching, she indicated their audience to his lordship, claiming playfully, "If we keep kissing in front of so many witnesses, someone is bound to testify to our immorality before some tribunal or other!"

"You are my wife," Wolf said with satisfaction, ignoring the crowds, "and there can never be anything immoral in our love . . . only in denying it."

Laughing, rejoicing, Hillary agreed to that.

Of a sudden, jointly inspired, the two turned and waved to the crowd, remaining directly before the window as they once more kissed to the cheers of their fellow Englishmen and the triumphal beating of their own hearts.

COMING SOON

Tame the Wildest Heart by **Parris Afton Bonds**

In her most passionate romance yet, Parris Afton Bonds tells the tale of two lonely hearts forever changed by an adventure in the Wild West. It was a match made in heaven . . . and hell. Mattie McAlister was looking for her half-Apache son and Gordon Halpern was looking for his missing wife. Neither realized that they would find the trail to New Mexico Territory was the way to each other's hearts.

First and Forever by **Zita Christian**

Katrina Swann was content with her peaceful, steady life in the close-knit immigrant community of Merriweather, Missouri. Then the reckless Justin Barrison swept her off her feet in a night of passion. Before she knew it she was following him to the Dakota Territory. Through trials and tribulations on the prairie, they learned the strength of love in the face of adversity.

Gambler's Gold by **Barbara Keller**

When Charlotte Bell headed out on a wagon train from Massachusetts to California, she had one goal in mind—finding her father, who had disappeared while prospecting for gold. The last thing she was looking for was love, but when fate turned against her, she turned to the dashing Reade Elliot to save her.

Queen by **Sharon Sala**

The Gambler's Daughters Trilogy continues with Diamond Houston's older sister, Queen, and the ready-made family she discovers, complete with laughter and tears. Queen Houston always had to act as a mother to her two younger sisters when they were growing up. After they part ways as young women, each to pursue her own dream, Queen reluctantly ends up in the mother role again—except this time there's a father involved.

A Winter Ballad by **Barbara Samuel**

When Anya of Winterbourne rescued a near-dead knight she found in the forest around her manor, she never thought he was the champion she'd been waiting for. "A truly lovely book. A warm, passionate tale of love and redemption, it lingers in the hearts of readers. . . . Barbara Samuel is one of the best, most original writers in romantic fiction today."—Anne Stuart

Shadow Prince by **Terri Lynn Wilhelm**

A plastic surgeon falls in love with a mysterious patient in this powerful retelling of *The Beauty and the Beast* fable. Ariel Denham, an ambitious plastic surgeon, resentfully puts her career on hold for a year in order to work at an exclusive, isolated clinic high in the Smoky Mountains. There she meets and falls in love with a mysterious man who stays in the shadows, a man she knows only as Jonah.

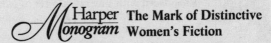 **Harper Monogram** **The Mark of Distinctive Women's Fiction**

LORD OF THE NIGHT
by Susan Wiggs
A Venetian lord dedicated to justice suspects a lucious beauty of being involved in a scandalous plot.

ORCHIDS IN MOONLIGHT
by Patricia Hagan
Caught in a web of intrigue in the dangerous West, a man and a woman fight to regain their overpowering dream of love.

A SEASON OF ANGELS
by Debbie Macomber
Three willing but wacky angels must teach their charges a lesson before granting a Christmas wish.
National Bestseller